Rosemary Allen has been writing on and off all her life. When her children left home, she took an English and media degree as a full-time mature student and then taught at the local College of Further Education. She has written around a dozen short stories, including *The Onion Man,* which was read on Radio 4. After she retired, she wrote her first novel, *Listening to Brahms*, about the ability of music to evoke memories of the past. She lives in Dorset, near her large, extended family.

The Baskett and Cockram families and all their descendants.

Rosemary Allen

SEARCHING FOR SAMUEL BASKETT

AUSTIN MACAULEY PUBLISHERS™

LONDON ∗ CAMBRIDGE ∗ NEW YORK ∗ SHARJAH

A CIP catalogue record for this title is available from the British Library.

ISBN 9781035801688 (Paperback)
ISBN 9781035801695 (ePub e-book)

www.austinmacauley.com

First Published 2023
Austin Macauley Publishers Ltd®
1 Canada Square
Canary Wharf
London
E14 5AA

Particular thanks to David and Sally Beaton for acting as my unofficial editors while I was writing the novel, and to my family and friends for all their encouragement. I should also like to thank Jan Spink and Derek Watson, who are direct descendants of Samuel Baskett, for allowing me to fictionalise the story of their family.

Table of Contents

Preface

Several years ago, I bought a 1766 edition of Bailey's dictionary. Inside was inscribed "Samuel Baskett, of Wareham Dorset, Surgeon, Apothecary and Man-Midwife". On another page, the names Mary Cockram, Lewis Cockram and Mary Baskett were written. And on the title page it said, "Charlotte Baskett's book". Intrigued, I decided to investigate. By trawling through the Dorset parish records, I pieced together family trees for the Baskett and Cockram families in Wareham and Swanage. So, all the main characters in the novel, and most of the minor ones, including the servants, are based on real people. They form the skeletal structure of the novel, and I have put flesh on the bones in the form of a fictional narrative. Several of them left wills, giving helpful information I was able to use in the story.

Prologue

At first, you think there is nothing in the attic, apart from dust and cobwebs. Then you see the chest, pushed into the far corner. It is made of dark brown leather, decorated with rows of brass studs, and secured by a large iron clasp. When you manage to open it, you see that it is crammed full of books, papers and many other objects. You decide to take them out of the chest one by one and realise you are able to piece together the story of a family.

On top is a small walnut cabinet. You take it out and open the drawers…

Part 1
Samuel Baskett

The butterfly suddenly flew off in the direction of the grave. Samuel watched to see if it would land on the coffin, but it continued to spiral up out of sight.

Last Sunday, in church, he had listened to his father preaching his sermon from the pulpit in the church. 'The body returns unto dust, and the spirit returns unto God who gave it,' he had said. 'In the next world, good men will achieve happiness and the wicked shall be punished.' How did his father know this was true?

'It is time to leave your sister, Jane, in God's care now.' His father turned away from the grave and led the way down the path, over the lane and up the drive to the rectory.

'May we look at the butterflies, please, papa?' Samuel wanted to see if he could find a butterfly like the one in the churchyard.

'Not now, Samuel. Go upstairs with your brothers. If your mother is awake, she will want to see you. Quietly, now.' Their father did not come upstairs with them but went straight into his study.

Before the funeral, Samuel had gone up to see his mother, but when he got to the door, he thought he could hear her crying, so he had tiptoed away again. Now she was sitting up in bed, looking very pale.

'We have seen the baby's soul go up to heaven, mama,' William said. 'God is looking after her now.'

Their mother smiled at him. 'Did you see it too, Thomas?'

'Yes, mama.'

'And I did, mama,' John said, who was only four, and tended to agree with anything his brothers said.

Once again, Samuel said nothing.

'Come, boys, your mama is tired. She needs to sleep.' Their nursemaid, Sarah, stood silhouetted in the doorway, little Robert in her arms, the sun from the window behind them shining on his fair curls. 'Come up to the nursery with me, John. It is time for your sleep.'

Because of the burial, there were no lessons that morning. So, Samuel decided to go downstairs to the kitchen instead, and see what their cook, Mary, was preparing for their dinner. She was cutting some mutton into pieces and Martha, the kitchen maid, was chopping vegetables; both their faces were flushed from the heat from the range.

'You arrived at the right time, master Samuel,' Mary said. 'Go and find Henry in the garden and ask him to pick some peas and bring them in to me, as soon as possible. And bring me some parsley and thyme, please.'

In the garden, he found Henry, the gardener, in the vegetable patch.

'What are you doing, Henry?'

'I be putting out they cauliflower plants, so you can have them for your dinner in the winter, master Samuel.'

'Mary wants some peas for our dinner today. And I am to bring her some parsley and thyme to put in with the mutton.'

'And how is your poor mama today, master Samuel?'

'She is tired and sleeping now. We watched papa putting the baby's coffin in the ground.'

''Tis a bad business. You boys would like a sister to play with, I should think.'

'William said the butterfly we saw today was the baby's soul. Do you think it was, Henry?'

'I don't know about that, master Samuel. You run along now, and take they herbs back to Mary in the kitchen.'

One of Samuel's favourite places was the rectory kitchen. He could sit at the table with one of his books, while Mary and Martha were busy peeling, chopping and stirring. They left him to read in peace. His favourite book, that summer, was *A Description of a Great Variety of Animals and Vegetables.* He had already read the first part about animals with four legs. Part two was about birds, and he had reached page thirteen, which described the Little Owl and the Little Horn-Owl. And there was more to come – fishes, insects, then plants, fruits and flowers. Today, George, who had driven the boys' grandfather from Shapwick that morning, was also sitting at the table. Whatever he was saying, made Martha blush and laugh.

'Now then, George, you leave Martha alone,' Mary said. But Samuel could see that she was also blushing – or perhaps it was just the heat from the range. Henry came into the kitchen with the peas, and Samuel continued reading to the sound of Martha shelling them – the pop, as she opened the pod, followed by the sound of the peas falling into a basin.

Upstairs, in the nursery, his brothers would be running about, making a noise; his little brother, Robert, would be strapped into his wooden baby walker and would be bumping into things; his brother, John, would be on the floor with his wooden puzzle. Perhaps, Sarah would be reading aloud from *A Pretty Little Pocket Book*: 'Great A and B and C and tumbledown D, the Cat's a Blind Buff and she cannot see,' she would be saying. Last year, Samuel had loved this book, but now he felt he was far too grown-up. It was much more peaceful here.

Their grandfather stayed to have dinner with them. As well as the mutton and peas, there were turnips and carrots and little onions, and afterwards a rice pudding. Sarah took some dinner up to the nursery for John and Robert. William, Samuel and Thomas were allowed to sit at the table, as long as they were quiet while their father and grandfather talked. Sarah had told the boys that morning, that their mother would stay upstairs until she was stronger. Samuel missed her. She always made the dinner table a happy place to be, and their father was always much more cheerful when she was around.

After their dinner, Samuel went out into the garden again. It was very hot and he lay down on the grass under one of the apple trees. The sun was shining through the leaves and he could hear the buzzing of a bee, as it flew over his head towards the lavender bushes. He watched a beetle, glossy and black, as it made its way busily through the blades of grass. He could hear the swish of a scythe from the other side of the garden and smell the freshly cut grass.

'Can we go and see the kittens again, Samuel?' Thomas had arrived so quietly, that his voice made Samuel jump.

There were five kittens in the stable. When they were born, a week ago, their eyes were tightly shut and their fur had not yet grown properly. Now their fur had grown longer and they were starting to escape from their basket and run around the stable, so that Tabitha had to keep carrying them back in her mouth. Tabitha was white, with marmalade and black patches and Samuel wondered why only one of the kittens was the same colour. One of the others was black all over, two were marmalade with little white paws, and the last one was black and white.

Samuel and Thomas bent down to stroke the kittens and Samuel picked up the black and white one, which started to scramble up on to his shoulder. It had white whiskers and eyebrows, white paws and a white bib. Its fur was as soft as down, its claws as sharp as needles.

'Will papa let us keep them all, do you think, Samuel?' Thomas asked. 'We could have one each. I should like the one that looks like Tabitha.'

'We will have to ask him.' But Samuel remembered that, last year, all of Tabitha's kittens had disappeared after a few days. His father had told Henry to drown them all. But these kittens were still here, so perhaps they would be able to keep them this time.

They went to find Henry. He was still cutting the grass under the apple trees. He paused and leant on his scythe when he saw the boys.

'Why are Tabitha's kittens different colours, Henry?'

'Well now, master Samuel, I should think 'tis because of Mrs Tucker's big black tom.'

'Why would that be, Henry?'

'You'd be better asking your papa that sort of question.' Henry turned away from the boys and started to cut down a patch of nettles.

When they went back into the house, the study door was open. Their father was sitting at his desk, spectacles in hand, peering at a book in front of him. He had taken his wig off and was wearing his embroidered cap, which Samuel knew meant he had finished working for the day.

'Can we look at the butterflies now, please, papa? I want to find the orange butterfly we saw in the churchyard.'

His father glanced at his gold pocket watch; he beckoned the boys over to the small cabinet, which stood on the chest behind his desk and opened one of the drawers. And there it was. The label beneath the butterfly said it was a "Small Tortoiseshell". Beside it was a "Large Tortoiseshell", the one underneath that looked as if it had eyes on its wings, was a "Peacock" and beside it was a "Red Admiral".

In the next drawer, were rows of blue butterflies. Most of them had white edges to their wings – the Common Blue, the silvery-blue Chalkhill Blue and the Adonis Blue – but next to each of them was a dull brown butterfly.

'Why are they different colours, papa?' Thomas asked.

'The darker ones are female,' his father said. 'And they are all speckled brown under their wings. God made them all different colours, to make the world as beautiful as possible.'

'And what about Tabitha's kittens?' Samuel said. 'Henry said it was because of Mrs Tucker's big black tom.'

'You will understand when you are older, my son.' His father turned away and opened another drawer lower down in the cabinet. 'That is a thrush's egg and that is a blackbird's. And this one is a wren. You see it is much smaller than the others.'

Samuel had seen the collection many times, but never tired of looking at them. Some of the eggs were light blue, some brown, some white and many of them were speckled with different colours.

'I should like to collect things, papa. I think I shall collect beetles. I could put them in the drawers with the butterflies and the birds' eggs.'

'An excellent idea, Samuel,' his father said. Samuel thought it was not a good time to ask about keeping the kittens. He also wanted to ask why there was such a variety of creatures and plants in the world, and why God had allowed his baby sister to die. He decided that he would ask his mother, when she had recovered and was not so upset about losing another little girl. Her answers to his questions usually made more sense to Samuel than his father's.

It was soon time to go up to the nursery for their supper before going to bed. Their little brother, Robert, was banging his rattle on the arms of his highchair and was starting to cry. Sarah gave him his teething stick to chew.

'He is not a happy little boy. His gums are sore,' she said. 'His new teeth will come through soon and he will feel much better.' She picked him up and took him through to the bedroom. Samuel could hear her singing quietly and he remembered how, when he was a much smaller boy, she had sung nursery rhymes to him when he could not sleep. The sound of her voice now, brought back the most comforting of feelings.

The older boys started to eat their bread and milk, which Mary had brought up from the kitchen. It was still light outside and would be until long after they had gone to bed. Samuel could hear a dog bark in the distance and a bird singing in the tree, outside the window.

'Time for bed, John. And you, Thomas,' Sarah said, coming back into the room.

Samuel went over to the window seat and looked out. He could see Henry wheeling a barrow over towards the compost heap, and wished he were still down in the garden. He opened his book and turned the pages to look at all the pictures of birds, fishes and insects, including butterflies. William came and sat next to him. Samuel peered over to see what he was reading. *An Account of the Conversion, holy and exemplary Lives and joyful Deaths of Several Young Children* – not the sort of book he, Samuel, would enjoy reading. But then William never wanted to do anything their father might frown upon. He had told Samuel that he wanted to preach in the church when he grew up, just like his father and grandfather. But Samuel already knew he would rather save babies from dying, instead of allowing them to have "joyful" deaths.

When she was well, his mother would always come into the nursery to say their prayers with them, before they went to sleep. She would ask God to bless everyone in the family and all the servants in the rectory, then all the little girls who had already gone up to heaven – two more called Jane and one called Elizabeth, after their grandmother. Today, Sarah said the prayers instead, but it was not the same. Samuel had a slight feeling of unease; of a lack of the warm security his mother gave him. He lay in his bed, in the room he shared with William and Thomas, thinking about all the questions which puzzled and worried him, until he fell asleep.

So, now you are looking at five little boys tucked up asleep in their beds, in a Dorset rectory. You are getting to know Samuel Baskett, and his four young brothers and want to know what will become of them. You pick out another object at random from the chest in the attic – this time a fossil...

Chapter 2
The Ammonite

Thursday, 15 May 1755 – Sherborne School, Dorset

The ammonite's ribbed spiral shell is embedded in a piece of shale rock, which fits comfortably into the palm of your hand. In the eighteenth century, it was believed that fossils were anything dug out of the earth – including stones, metals, salts and other minerals – and which had been deposited in the earth by some unknown means. But you know that the ammonite is the fossil of a form of life which became extinct millions of years ago; it was a relative of the present-day octopus, squid and cuttlefish. What can you see now?

At first, you have difficulty picking out Samuel Baskett from the dozens of boys walking out of the chapel and into the school. But then, surely, that must be him? Older, of course. He must be fifteen by now, but something about the shape of his mouth and the dark chestnut colour of his hair hasn't changed. Since you met Samuel and his brothers seven years ago, yet another little girl called Jane was born. She also died within a few days.

It is just after Whitsun; the summer holidays will begin tomorrow. Today, some of the boys at the top of the school, including Samuel's brother, William, will be performing a play written in Latin – Andria *by Terence. Although the play is a comedy, the performance is not to be taken lightly; being spoken entirely in Latin, it is not meant to be for entertainment, but a serious event, aimed at improving young minds. In the audience will be the headmaster, Joseph Hill, together with John Toogood, one of the governors of the school, and some visiting families of the boys, come to fetch the boarders home.*

Samuel put his hand into his pocket and fingered the outline of the spiral shell embedded in the fossil's surface. He had picked it up earlier in the year, while walking on the beach with his brother William and their friends, Lewis and

John Cockram, who lived in Swanage. Since then, it had become a sort of talisman for Samuel, representing the secret life he lived when he was alone. He was still far more interested in learning about the stars above him and the creatures and plants all around him, than what his father thought important and what he was taught at school.

He was relieved that after breakfast they would be having their last lessons before coming back to school after the Whitsun holiday. His father had agreed that William and he could stay with the Cockram family, at Newton Manor, in Swanage for a few days, returning to Owermoigne in time to go to the Sunday services. Samuel enjoyed the liveliness and bustle at Newton, in contrast to the more solemn atmosphere at home. The library there was Samuel's idea of heaven.

He could not wait to look through Mr Cockram's microscope, at the slides of insects and plants, and to see again the stars in the night sky through his telescope. And above all, he was looking forward to his discussions with Lewis, who was the only person, Samuel felt, he could tell about what he wanted to do with the rest of his life. Lewis, who was two years older than Samuel, knew that he would inherit Newton Manor from his father and would have to devote his life to running the estate. But Samuel knew he wanted to save lives.

Samuel found his mind wandering during the morning, even having to be nudged by John Cockram, Lewis's brother, to answer "Sum", when his name was called by the Master. The older boys were occupied in the last debate of the half, so there was an occasional uproar as someone failed to respond to a question. John Cockram was called on to recite a speech by Tacitus. Samuel hoped he would not be called next, as he found the long passages in Latin not only difficult to remember, but also extremely boring.

At least if the lesson had been arithmetic, he would have found it more engaging, although the lessons were always very basic and did nothing to stretch his mind. The younger boys, including his brother, Thomas, were occupied in their daily Latin linguistic practice. With the combined noise of the three classes as background to his thoughts, Samuel gazed out of the window and began to think about his visit to Newton Manor and to make a mental list of all the topics he wanted to talk about.

He got the fossil out of his pocket, and wondered once again how the shape of what looked rather like one of the snails in the garden, had become embedded into the stone. Lewis might have a theory. When he was last at Newton Manor,

Mr Cockram had told him that he knew of a book called *Systema Naturae* by someone called Linnaeus, who was from Sweden. He wondered whether Mr Cockram had a copy of the book yet. It was in Latin, but that would not present too much difficulty. Samuel found it immensely satisfying to be told that Linnaeus had arranged all plants and animals in order, according to their basic characteristics. He wondered how his fossil would fit into this idea.

At last, the bell rang for dinner and there was a great deal of noise, as all the boys pushed back their chairs and filed out of the school room. It would not be long now before their visitors started to arrive. Samuel was looking forward to seeing his mother again. She always had a kindly word to say, not only to him and his brothers, but to his friends too. His father would spend most of his time speaking to Mr Hill, the headmaster, Mr Toogood, the governor and Mr Sampson, the vicar from the Abbey. He wondered if his parents would bring John and Robert with them this time. John would be coming to the school next year, but perhaps Robert was still too young and would stay behind with Sarah.

Immediately, after they had finished eating their dinner, the boys who were to perform in the play went to change into their costumes. Samuel had no idea what to expect.

'You will see that John Templeman is playing the leading part, as usual,' Lewis said over his shoulder as he left the dining hall.

'Who are you playing, Lewis?'

'You will have to wait and see, Samuel, but you will have difficulty knowing which I am. That is all I shall say.'

Samuel secretly thought John Templeman rather arrogant. He was one of William's friends and seemed to take himself far too seriously. His four older brothers had all been to the school before him and they had all taken leading parts in the school plays.

He went outside with the other boys to wait for the carriages. One of the first to arrive was that of Mr and Mrs Cockram.

'How are you, my boy?' Mr Cockram jumped down and strode over to greet his son, John.

'Very well, thank you, Father.'

'And Samuel! Good to see you again. I hear you are to join us for a few days.'

'Yes, sir. I am greatly looking forward to looking at the stars again through your telescope. And I wonder, sir, if you have a copy of Mr Linnaeus's book yet.'

'Indeed, I have, Samuel. I shall show it to you tomorrow.'

'I am very much looking forward to seeing Lewis in this play,' Mrs Cockram said, climbing down from the carriage. 'He wrote to say I shall think him very strange.' She embraced John and shook Samuel by the hand.

'We do not know what part he plays, mama,' John said. 'Samuel's brother, William, is in the play also, but we do not know who he plays either.'

Another, rather larger and grander carriage drew up near them. Samuel recognised John Templeman's brother, Richard, climbing down, followed by a lady, Samuel assumed was his mother. A fashionably dressed gentleman joined them from the other side of the carriage.

'How very good to see you, Mr Cockram and Mrs Cockram. Have you met my daughter, Mary?' He gestured towards a young girl, about Samuel's own age, standing slightly apart from the group. She wore a pale blue dress made of the airiest of fabrics, reminding Samuel of the blue butterflies in his father's cabinet. The brim of her hat hid her face, as she looked shyly down to the ground. But as she looked up towards Mrs Cockram, the most radiant of smiles spread across her face. And from that moment, Samuel found it impossible to take his eyes away from her.

'Samuel!' his father's voice broke the spell and he turned to greet his parents and his brother, John. The visitors were now making their way inside for the start of the play, and Samuel found himself trying to sit where he could see Mary Templeman, without obviously staring at her. He realised his heart was beating faster than normal. He had never felt like this before. The only young girl of his own age he knew, was the new maid at the rectory and she certainly did not have this effect on him.

Once everyone was seated, two boys came and drew back the curtains in front of the stage and the scenery was revealed. There were three houses, each with an altar in front of it and each had a notice above the door. The one on the right read, "Simo's House", the one on the left "Glycerium's House", and the one in the middle, "Chremes' House". A boy dressed in a Greek tunic entered. 'A street in Athens,' he proclaimed. Looking somewhat embarrassed, he turned and walked off the stage again.

After a pause and an expectant buzz from the audience, John Templeman, dressed in Greek robes, entered and strutted up to Simo's house. He was followed by two other boys in tunics, carrying some vegetables and another carrying a ladle, presumably meant to be his servants. Once the characters started to speak, in Latin of course, Samuel's mind began to wander and he allowed himself to look along the row in front of him, to where Mary Templeman sat between her parents. Her fair hair was escaping from beneath her bonnet, with a strand curling over her cheek. Samuel wondered what it would be like to touch her smooth, pale skin.

He found it difficult to understand the plot of the play, which seemed to involve mistaken identities, characters wanting to marry the wrong person, and somewhere along the line, a baby. The main source of entertainment, though, was seeing his fellow pupils dressed up. Samuel was waiting to see Lewis and did not immediately recognise him when he finally appeared in the third scene. He was wearing a long, straggling grey wig and cap and caused considerable merriment among the boys in the audience when he started to speak in a high, querulous voice.

He was playing Lesbia, an elderly nurse, the only female character actually to appear in the play. By that time, the play had descended into farce. Only Mr Hill and Mr Toogood appeared not to find any of it amusing. Samuel noticed that even his father managed a smile when William entered, playing Chremes, bent double and leaning on a stick.

Eventually, everyone seemed happy. A slave, who had been put in shackles, was released, Chremes and another old man embraced, then they both embraced Chremes' son, Pamphilus, who was then presented with the baby, which he carried into the house of Glycerium, who was apparently the baby's mother. Everyone clapped, the performers bowed and the play was over.

Now, Samuel decided, he must find a way of speaking with, or at least being near, Mary Templeman. Once again, he fingered the outline of the spiral shell on the fossil, his talisman.

Tea was to be served to the guests before they departed for the holidays. The boys whose parents were there could also take tea, so Samuel followed his family into the refectory. Looking around he caught a glimpse of blue and there was Mary Templeman, standing some distance away next to her brother, Richard. As their parents came up to them, Mary turned and looked straight towards Samuel. Seeing he was gazing at her, she immediately looked down, but he found it impossible to move, so that when she again looked up towards him, she blushed and held his gaze – for how long, Samuel could not tell. The spell – and Samuel could only describe to himself, what was happening as a spell – was only broken when he felt a hand on his shoulder.

'Samuel,' John Cockram was saying, 'my parents wish to leave, and your travelling chest is already on our carriage. We need to find William.'

'Yes, yes, of course. I shall say goodbye to my parents and join you outside.'

Samuel turned again towards Mary Templeman and saw that his brother, William, was in conversation with Richard Templeman. A perfect excuse to get nearer to her.

Her eyes were blue. Her mouth turned up slightly. Her nose was straight. Her waist was slender. And now he must leave without being able to say a word to her.

'Mr Cockram is ready to leave, William.'

'I am ready, Samuel.' William took Mr Templeman's outstretched hand. 'Goodbye, sir. I shall look forward to visiting you in Dorchester.'

Mr Templeman turned to Samuel. 'You would be welcome to accompany your brother to take tea with us next week.'

'I should like that, sir, thank you.'

Climbing up into the coach, Samuel could scarcely stop smiling. Life seemed good. Tomorrow he would look at Mr Cockram's copy of Linnaeus's book and next week he would once again see Mary Templeman.

So now you watch Samuel, his brother and his friends drive away on this warm May afternoon, on their way to Newton Manor, near Swanage in Dorset. What, you might think, will Samuel be able to say to Mary Templeman about his feelings for her? The answer, of course, is precisely nothing. In any case, at fifteen, he scarcely knows what these feelings imply. You once again delve into the chest and bring out a small, worn leather case...

Chapter 3
The Fleam

You remove the top, and take out what looks at first like a large penknife. From the brass case, you pull out one of the two steel blades. Attached to it at right angles there is what looks like the end of a small dagger. This implement is a Fleam, a bloodletting device used to make an incision in a large vein.

In the three years since you last saw Samuel, the direction of his life has changed beyond recognition. He has never wavered from his intention to save lives, not souls. His brother, William, is already up at Oxford, expressing his intention to follow his father and grandfather into the church; his younger brothers, Thomas and John, have shown no signs of deviating from this path. So, when Samuel said he wanted to become a surgeon, his father was not pleased. And when Samuel expressed his doubts about the existence of God, he didn't go so far as disowning his son, but made it quite clear he would not help him to secure a place to study.

As usual, Samuel turned to his friend, Lewis Cockram, for advice. And as usual, Lewis solved the problem. A Scottish surgeon, William Hunter, had set up a pioneering anatomy school in London in 1846, where he was joined two years later by his younger brother, John. Samuel would live with other students in the school and attend anatomy lectures.

So now you can see Samuel and several of his fellow pupils, in the midst of a crowd of onlookers, including three physicians and four surgeons. They are watching what you soon realise is an event, which today would result in violent protests and demonstrations by animal rights campaigners.

Samuel stood, mesmerised, as John Hunter tied a yelping dog to his dissecting table. The aim was to prove William Hunter's theory, that fats were absorbed only in the intestines and not by the veins, adding to the knowledge of the workings of the human body. But Samuel found it almost impossible to watch as John Hunter slit open the dog's belly and began pouring warm milk through a funnel into the gap. Hunter turned and triumphantly addressed his audience. Having only recently arrived at the school, Samuel found it difficult at times to understand John's lilting Scottish accent.

'You will observe, gentlemen, that the lacteals are now turning white as they convey fat from the gut, while the veins remain filled with blood – and only blood.'

As he watched the mongrel writhing on the bench, he thought of the Cockrams' brown and white spaniel, Brune, and how distraught Lewis's nine-year old sister, Mary, would be if her beloved dog were to be treated in this way. But this dog had been picked up off the street as a half-starved stray, and after Hunter had repeated his experiment several times with the same result, the poor creature died. John Hunter turned to his students.

'I thank you, gentlemen, for your attention. As you know, we have procured the corpse of an unfortunate young woman who died suddenly just before giving birth. When you have dined, you will return to watch, while I dissect her corpse. Never before have we been able to study a nine-month-old foetus.'

Samuel had many times seen corpses being delivered to the back entrance of the school, under the cover of darkness. It was an open secret that they had been obtained by grave robbers or directly from the hangings at Tyburn. The body of this young woman had arrived wrapped in a sack the previous night.

Samuel had already formed a friendship with a young American from Philadelphia, the son of a physician, William Shippen. They had arrived at the school at the same time. Billey was four years older than Samuel and had already studied anatomy in Philadelphia with his father. After the final lecture of the day, they often stayed up discussing anatomical points and life in general. They were both in awe of the Hunter brothers and John in particular, who proved to be a charismatic and inspiring teacher.

'Have you ever seen the corpse of an unborn child, Billey?'

'No, Samuel. But my father has been present at many births and believes he has saved the lives of many women and children.'

'I have four brothers, and I should have had four sisters, but they all died as tiny babies. And my father just says it is the will of God. But would God, if he exists, let that happen? I do not think so.'

'Which is why we are here, Samuel, is it not? We both want to save lives.'

'Did you know, Billey, that before Mr John Hunter started operating here in England, every surgeon would amputate diseased and injured arms and legs without thinking that there might be an alternative way?'

'It is no different in America. But when I have finished my studies here, it is my intention to return home to work again with my father and to implement Mr Hunter's methods.'

At three o'clock, after they had dined, the two young men once again went to the dissecting room and joined their fellow students around the table, on which lay the corpse of a young woman. John Hunter stood ready, dissecting knife in his hand. His brother, William, stepped forward.

'Gentlemen, allow me to introduce you to Mr Jan van Rymsdyk, who will be drawing the dissection at every stage. It is our intention to publish ten plates, which will be engraved by my colleague from Scotland, Mr Robert Strange.'

As John Hunter stepped forward to make the first incision, Samuel felt a shudder run through his body. Although he had arrived scarcely a month before, he had already started to dissect his own corpse. Not for the first time, he wondered whether he would ever get accustomed to the smell of putrefying flesh in the dissecting room and the first sight of the internal organs inside a corpse. He would soon have to be present at operations on living people and later perform them himself.

After making the first cut into the abdomen, John Hunter peeled back the skin to reveal the bulge of the womb.

'As you know, gentlemen, the foetus can only obtain nutrients and oxygen through the placenta. I shall now inject the veins and arteries with coloured wax. My aim is to demonstrate to you that the mother and the foetus have separate blood systems. Now observe as I cut through the wall of the womb, that the fully developed child is already in the inverted position and ready to be born.'

The baby was curled up as if it were asleep. Samuel could not believe it would not soon yawn, stretch its fingers and toes, sigh and open its eyes. His lost sisters would have looked just as perfect.

Sitting close by, Jan van Rymsdyk was drawing each stage of the dissection using red chalk. At the end of the session, Samuel and Billey went over to him.

'Your drawings are very beautiful, Mr van Rymsdyk,' Billey said. 'When they are engraved and published, I shall take copies back to America for my father.'

'You are very kind, sir. But it is the baby who is beautiful. I merely copy what I see. I have had the privilege of working with Mr John and Mr William many times.'

'Indeed,' John Hunter said, joining the group. 'Mr van Rymsdyk's drawings of less developed foetuses will be included when the engravings are published.' He turned to Samuel and Billey. 'You will both be welcome to come to my rooms later this evening.'

'Samuel,' Billey said, as they sat at supper, 'tomorrow I hope to attend a musical evening at the home of Lieutenant Robert Home. You will be very welcome to accompany me. His daughter, Anne, is considered a talented poet. And her friend, Miss Alice Lee, will be there also, Samuel. She is the niece of an acquaintance of my father, Mr Ludwell.'

Samuel laughed. 'My dear Billey, you are blushing. Am I correct in thinking that you have affectionate feelings towards Miss Lee?'

'The moment I saw her, Samuel, I knew she was the only woman I wanted to marry.'

'And does Miss Lee know of your intentions?'

'I have not yet had the courage to speak more than a few words to her. But her eyes, when she looked at me have told me she might welcome my attentions. Have you ever experienced feelings like that, Samuel?'

'I have never told anyone before. She is the sister of one of my brother's friends from school. But she comes from a wealthy family and I doubt very much if we will be allowed to marry. I fell in love with her the moment I saw her. Her name is Mary Templeman and she has the fairest hair, the bluest eyes and the most beautiful smile of anyone I have ever seen. I have met her only twice since that day. The first time was when I visited her family with my brother.'

'Were you able to speak with her?'

'I sat beside her at tea and we spoke of my interest in the natural world and the heavens. I told her that the previous week I had stayed with other friends from school and had looked at the stars through their father's telescope and at a butterfly's wing through a microscope. Mary told me she had never looked through a microscope and I foolishly said that one day I would buy her one, so she could look at a butterfly's wing whenever she wanted.'

'And the next time?'

'It was just before I came to London. When we first met, we were only fifteen. And would you believe it, Billey, we discovered we had been thinking

31

of each other ever since. So now, yes, we have spoken of our feelings. She said she would wait for me. We promised each other we would tell no one. When I return to Dorset, I intend to set up as a surgeon. I shall then be in a position to ask her father for her hand.'

The evening gatherings in John Hunter's rooms were always very convivial occasions. When Samuel and Billey made their way upstairs later that evening, a great shout of laughter greeted them as they opened the door.

'Come in, come in!' John Hunter turned to one of the other students. 'A drink for these gentlemen, Mr Baillie.'

The room was warm, the air smoky and the atmosphere relaxed and welcoming. Arranged on numerous shelves around the room were the carefully labelled jars containing specimens preserved in alcohol – a baby crocodile emerging from its egg, a deformed human foetus, the brain of a cat, a human tooth transplanted into the head of a rooster. Every student was eager to be invited to these gatherings, not only for the company but also to hear John Hunter's reminiscences about his experiences since he had arrived to join his brother in London. At last, John rose and began pacing the room, a beer tankard in his hand, his unruly, coppery hair uncovered by a wig.

'I hope I have already convinced you that it is your duty to question the methods of most of the physicians and surgeons of today. Let me give you an example. When I was working in St George's Hospital, I came to believe that bloodletting – performed with the fleam you all now possess – should be used with caution. Undoubtedly, it is still necessary on some occasions, but I have seen many patients die when too much blood has been taken from them.'

John paused as he filled his tankard again and took a long draught before continuing. 'I was often present at operations to amputate the limbs of the unfortunate patients brought into the hospital in great pain. I recall observing an elderly man with a large swelling behind his knee.' He paused again. 'What causes this, gentlemen?'

'It is an aneurism, sir,' Billey said.

'And what causes it, Mr Shippen?'

'An artery, or a vein becomes swollen and without treatment will burst and cause death. I have seen this happening to several of my father's patients.'

'Mr Shippen is correct. But I came to be convinced that their limbs could be saved by tying the artery above the swelling and allowing the blood to find an alternative route. I have already performed this operation on a dog, which made a full recovery. I have yet to attempt it on a living patient, but fully intend to, when the opportunity arises. But I must stress again, gentlemen, that without an accurate knowledge of the workings of all parts of the human body, these new ideas are not possible.'

Billey Shippen got to his feet. 'Sir, I was particularly interested today in the dissection of the pregnant young woman. My father has delivered many babies in America but many have died. He is most interested in the work of Mr William Smellie here in London.'

'Before he set up this school, my brother, William, lodged with Mr Smellie and attended his lectures on midwifery. Before you return to America, I would advise you to attend his lectures yourself and learn in particular about his use of forceps. He has saved the lives of numerous babies in this way.'

As he sat before the fire, drinking his beer, Samuel wondered whether the lives of his sisters might have been saved by the simple use of forceps. And another thought came to him.

'Sir, I also was most interested to watch your dissection this afternoon. I wonder whether the same method could be used when the mother is still alive, if only to save the life of the baby.'

'This was tried in Ireland a few years ago. But unfortunately, both mother and child died following the operation. The loss of blood was almost certainly the cause of the mother's death. But in an emergency, it might well be tried – at least to save the baby.'

As they left the room later that evening, Billey paused at the door.

'Samuel and I will be attending a musical evening at the home of Lieutenant Robert Home tomorrow evening, sir. We would be most honoured if you would join us. Mr Ludwell, an acquaintance of my father, has invited us – I believe you already know him.'

'Indeed, I do. I shall see you tomorrow then. Goodnight, gentlemen.'

As he prepared for bed, Samuel reflected on the day. By the time he went to sleep, he had decided in his mind how he would live the rest of his life. Back in Dorset he would set up as a surgeon, apothecary and man-midwife, and convince his father that he had chosen the right path. He would marry Mary Templeman with the blessing of her father and they would be blessed with the birth of many healthy, happy children.

You now see Samuel sleeping peacefully, while outside, London life continues into the night. At the back of the school, there is a knock at the door and another corpse is delivered fresh from St Paul's churchyard nearby. In the street outside, a drunken sailor searches out one of the numerous prostitutes and later falls down to sleep among the rotting vegetables from the market, next to a gin-sodden mother and her unfortunate child.

The next object you bring out of the chest, is a pyramid shaped wooden case with a small brass handle on top...

Chapter 4
The Microscope

Tuesday, 23 October 1764 – Dorchester

Inside the case is a small, brass microscope, with rack and pinion focusing, made in the early eighteenth century, by Edward Culpeper. At the bottom of the case is a small drawer containing four objective lenses and seven microscope sliders, made of bone, holding labelled specimens between pieces of mica. You place one of the sliders on the stage of the microscope and look through the eye piece; you see the iridescent blue of a butterfly wing; another slider contains the cross-section of a bean seed.

When Samuel had been at the anatomy school for two years, John Hunter had enlisted as an army surgeon, and Samuel decided to join him as his assistant on the hospital ship, Betty. Britain had been at war with France for five years and victory was in sight; the aim now was to capture the French island of Belle-Ile.

Just before he left for Portsmouth to join the ship, Samuel received news that his mother had died. He had always been closer to her than to his rather aloof father, and she had been supportive when he decided to train as a surgeon. Returning to Owermoigne for her funeral, he realised he had nothing in common with his father or brothers, other than Thomas, who was living in London. William was already a curate and John had followed him to Oxford.

Now, Samuel is back in Dorset, working in Blandford Forum, as assistant to an apothecary; he is about to fulfil his ambition of setting up as surgeon, apothecary and man-midwife. Lewis Cockram has been staying with Samuel in his lodgings, and they are now sitting in the stagecoach on their way to Dorchester; it is Mary Templeman's twenty-fourth birthday and Samuel is holding a special gift for her on his lap.

'Courage, my dear Samuel! Her father will surely give his blessing when he hears of your prospects.'

'It is not only her father but also her brothers. Whenever I meet them, they make me feel so small and insignificant.'

'That is nonsense, Samuel. Have they fought for their country? No, they have been living a peaceful life of luxury here, in Dorset – as indeed have I. Have they endured seasickness and braved the French cannons as you have? No, they have not.'

The carriage gave a sudden lurch and Samuel clutched the box containing the precious microscope.

'We shall see. But did I tell you, Lewis, that I had two pieces of good news last week? I received a letter from my friend, Billey Shippen. As you know, he married his sweetheart, Alice Lee, and they returned to Philadelphia two years ago. Now they have a daughter and have named her after Alice's friend, Anne Home.'

'And the other news?'

'Anne Home has become engaged to John Hunter. I played a part in their meeting about six years ago. Billey and I persuaded him to come with us to a musical evening at the house of Robert Home, Anne's father.'

'Were they attracted to each other then?'

'I know he was to her – he talked about her a great deal after that evening, but she scarcely noticed him. Then two months ago, Lieutenant Home asked John Hunter to come to his house. Anne was unwell. Among other things, she was suffering from wind in her stomach.'

Lewis laughed. 'What did he prescribe?'

'He gave her a course of worming medicines and purgatives and persuaded her to take cold baths. She not only recovered, but also fell in love with him. They make a strange pair – John is fourteen years older than Anne, and is not at all cultured. She writes poetry and is a talented pianist and singer.'

They arrived at Puddletown and two of their fellow passengers alighted from the coach. Lewis looked at his pocket watch. 'We shall be arriving at Dorchester in good time. What a difference the turnpike road makes.'

'What time are we expected?'

'At about two o'clock. We are to dine at three.'

Samuel jumped up to help an elderly lady climb on to the coach. Lewis took some of her parcels and handed them to her again as she sat down on the seat opposite.

'Thank you. You are most kind. I am on the way to visit my niece in Dorchester. She and her husband have invited me to stay for as long as I care to.'

'We are also on our way to Dorchester. We are to visit Mr Templeman and his family,' Lewis said.

'Oh, my dears, I know of Mr Templeman. He drew up my brother's will last year. He is very well thought of in the town.'

She told them that her name was Mrs Pearce, that her husband had died fifteen years previously, that it was their great sorrow they did not have children, but that her niece, Jane, was like a daughter, as her mother, Mrs Pearce's sister, had died when Jane was born. Samuel began to wonder if she would talk all the way to Dorchester, but eventually her head nodded forward and she began to snore gently.

'Now, Lewis, tell me about life at Newton Manor. How is your father?'

'He is still missing my mother, even though it is seven years now since she died. But he tries to keep cheerful. I have taken on most of the running of the estate now.'

'Then I should think it is about time you found yourself a wife. Have you anyone in mind?'

Lewis hesitated. 'Do you remember visiting us just before you went to London?'

'Of course. Mr Best and his family dined with us.'

'And you remember his daughter, Ann?'

'I remember walking in the garden and I remember you both disappearing for some time after we had all returned to the house.'

Lewis smiled. 'The family are still frequent visitors. Miss Best and I have spent a great deal of time together recently.'

'She has dark hair and pretty apple cheeks. Am I not right?'

'Indeed, you are. I have become very fond of her – as has my sister. Mary is fifteen now and lacks any feminine company since her governess, Miss Clark, married Mr Cox from Langton in February.'

'She must miss her. Mary was very fond of Miss Clark, was she not?'

'She was very much part of the family and we all miss her. But at the present time, my brother, John, is the one giving us much cause for concern. He has fallen in love with Hannah Kent, the daughter of a baker in Corfe Castle, and intends to marry her before Christmas. Her father thinks they are being too hasty and that John will not be a reliable husband for his daughter. I think he may well be right.'

Their elderly companion suddenly awoke with a start. 'I believe I may have slept a little. Are we soon to arrive in Dorchester? I do hope my niece knows when the coach is due. I shall not know what to do if there is not someone to meet me.'

'We shall wait with you if she is not there. Do not fear, Mrs Pearce, we shall not desert you!'

They shortly drove into the yard of the King's Arms in Dorchester. Lewis and Samuel jumped down from the coach to help Mrs Pearce with her parcels. She was immediately greeted by her niece and her husband.

'Jane, these gentlemen are on their way to visit Mr Templeman. They have been most kind to me during the journey.'

'My aunt worries a great deal when she travels alone. I believe she thinks there will be a highwayman hiding in the shadows at every turn, waiting to rob her of all her possessions! I thank you, sirs, for looking after her.'

'It was a pleasure, madam.'

Mr Templeman's groom, James, had brought the carriage to meet them, so they were soon arriving at the home of the Templeman family on outskirts of the town. When they were shown into the drawing room, Samuel at first thought that Mary was not there. A bewildering number of people were gathered in the room. Mr Templeman came across to greet them.

'You will know nearly everyone, I am sure. My son, William, and his wife will be here shortly to complete our party.'

John Templeman joined them. 'My dear Lewis, it is good to see you once again. I hope your father is well. Samuel, I hear you are now a medical man. My brother, Peter, has a medical practice in the town. He will join us tomorrow. And I should like you to meet a good friend of my father, Dr Cuming. He has been a physician here for many years now.'

As they crossed the room, Samuel at last saw Mary. Once again, she was wearing a pale blue dress and her fair hair was topped by a knot of blue ribbon. She was sitting beside her sister, Susannah, who lacked her sister's grace and prettiness; Samuel suspected her main aim was to protect her younger sister from unsuitable young men. Dr Cuming was sitting in a corner of the room in animated conversation with a good-looking, middle-aged woman, whom he introduced as his very good friend, Miss Polly Oldfield.

'Mr Templeman tells me you were a pupil of Mr John Hunter in London. I shall be interested to speak with you about his methods, which I believe have caused a great deal of controversy. And now you are setting up on your own in Wareham, I hear.'

'Yes, indeed, sir. My intention has always been to return to Dorset.'

Before they could say any more, William Templeman and his wife arrived and the ensuing bustle gave Samuel an opportunity to sit down next to Mary. With her sister present, he was able only to greet them both in the most formal way, but seeing the look in her eyes and the blush on her cheeks he was in no doubt that her feelings towards him had not altered during the years they had been apart.

Samuel hoped he would be seated near Mary at dinner, but she was on the opposite side of the table, flanked by her two brothers, Nathaniel and William. Had they been placed there specifically to guard their sister because they knew of her feelings? What chance had he now of being accepted into this intimidating family as a future brother-in-law? Lewis had urged him to be courageous. He felt far from courageous now. He realised that Mrs William Templeman, seated on his right, was addressing him.

'I believe you were at school with my brother-in-law, John?'

'Yes, madam, indeed I was. But he is three years older than I am. My friend, Lewis Cockram, who is seated beside him on the other side of the table, is the same age.'

'William is pleased that John has also decided to become a lawyer. My husband is the oldest of the brothers, of course.' She paused only to take a spoonful of her soup. 'You will know that he was mayor of Dorchester eight years ago, just before my first daughter Ann was born. She is named after me and our second daughter is called Elizabeth, after my mother-in-law. We also have little Lucy who is just four years old. We have not so far been blessed with a son. We shall, of course, call him William.'

As he was obviously not expected to reply, but just smile and nod, Samuel was able to snatch a few glances in Mary's direction. She suddenly looked up and smiled at him. Her brother, Nathaniel, followed her eyes across the table and looked at Samuel, a slight frown on his face. Was this a warning? Suddenly, Mrs William Templeman dropped her spoon with a clatter into her soup bowl.

'Has no one noticed that we are thirteen at table?'

Everyone stopped talking and looked at her.

'My dear,' her husband said quietly, from across the table. 'You know that is nonsense.'

'No, Mr Templeman, you do not know that. We should have insisted that your brother, Peter, come today. We should not have accepted his excuses.'

'He is a busy doctor, my dear. He has to think of his patients.'

Perhaps, Samuel thought, he would have an ally in Peter Templeman. Perhaps the whole family would not be against him. But first, he must speak to Mary and give her the microscope, now safely tucked away in his travelling case. Only when she had accepted his proposal of marriage could he approach her father. He would surely have an opportunity tomorrow, before he and Lewis returned home.

They were soon served the next course – roasted turkey and woodcock, followed by hot buttered apple pie. Everyone continued their interrupted conversations and began to eat, although Mrs William Templeman sat silently beside him and ate little. Miss Polly Oldfield turned her attention to Samuel.

'I hope you do not believe the nonsense about the number at table, Mr Baskett.'

'No, madam. I like to think of myself as a reasonable man, relying only on logical beliefs.'

'Quite right, my dear fellow,' Dr Cuming said. 'My friend, Miss Oldfield, is fortunately a most sensible woman. I would not be as fond of her as I am, if she were not.'

Miss Oldfield patted Dr Cuming affectionately on the arm. 'I am very lucky, Mr Baskett, to have someone who looks after me so well.'

Samuel wondered why they were not married. They made a handsome couple and seemed completely at ease with each other. He hoped that if he were lucky enough to have Mary as his wife, they would be as happy in each other's company when they reached that age.

After they had finished the meal, Mary's brother, William, rose to his feet. 'As you all know, today is my sister, Mary's, birthday. I am sure you will join me in wishing her happiness in the years to come.'

There was a general murmur of approval, while Mary smiled and blushed. When the ladies had left the table to go into the drawing room, Dr Cuming turned to Samuel.

'Now, Mr Baskett, I am eager to hear your opinion of Mr John Hunter's theories of how surgery should be conducted.'

'I admire him greatly, sir, and I learned so much from him. He believes the most important thing is to save lives and to do that one must have a detailed knowledge of anatomy. Many surgeons still amputate limbs without a second thought. John Hunter has taught me how to mend those limbs. He believes in the power of nature to heal.'

'And I believe you accompanied him when he enlisted as an army surgeon. It must have been a very distressing time.'

'I could never have imagined the horrors I was to see. I still dream about the frantic shouts and screams of the men. And we also had to act as physicians, when many of the soldiers became infected by typhus, malaria, smallpox and other fevers.'

Samuel realised that Richard Templeman, whom he remembered from his school days as being rather pompous, had been listening to what he was saying. 'My brother, Peter, will be most interested to hear of your experiences when he arrives tomorrow.'

By this time, everyone around the table was listening. For the first time, Samuel thought that perhaps Mary's family would not dismiss him as an unsuitable husband after all.

'While I was in London, I went with my friend Billey Shippen to Mr Smellie's lectures on midwifery. I hope to save the lives of mothers and babies by what I learned then.'

'Where are you intending to practise? Lewis tells me you are working in Blandford with an apothecary at present.'

'I have found premises in the middle of Wareham. After Christmas, I shall move in and set myself up as surgeon, apothecary and man-midwife. I just hope the people of the town welcome me!'

To Samuel's surprise, Nathaniel Templeman stood up and raised his glass. 'I think we should drink to Samuel and wish him success in the future!'

Mary's father put down his empty glass. 'Gentlemen, we shall now join the ladies. I believe my daughters intend to entertain us shortly.'

Samuel dared to be more hopeful than he had been for a considerable time, as he walked from the dining room into the parlour, where the ladies were finishing their tea. Lewis came up beside him.

'I do believe, Samuel, that you are to be approved,' he said quietly. 'The Templeman family is not as threatening as you once supposed. Even Nathaniel, whom I always thought was disapproving of everything, seems to be on your side. You know he is now curate at Holy Trinity here in Dorchester. You should ask him to perform your marriage ceremony.'

'I know you are teasing me, Lewis, but my fears are very real. My whole future happiness is at stake.'

Susannah was already seated at the spinet and Mary stood beside her. She looked directly at Samuel as her sister started to play. When she began to sing, her voice was soft and sweet.

"How gentle was my Damon's air,
Like sunny beams his golden hair;
His voice was like the nightingales:
More sweet his breath than flow'ry vales.
On ev'ry hill, in ev'ry grove
Along the margin of each stream
Dear conscious scenes of former love:
I mourn and Damon is my theme.
Each flow'r in pity droops its head,
All nature does my loss deplore,
All, all reproach the fairest swain
Yet Damon still I seek in vain".

Samuel was in no doubt; Mary was singing the song just for him. He was her "Damon"; he had gone away but was now returned to claim her as his own. As the song came to an end, he saw that Lewis was looking at him with a slight smile on his face. He could imagine what his friend would say if he told him of his thoughts. 'My dear Samuel, do not be so fanciful. As usual, you are being far too timorous. Be bold!'

As Mary prepared to sit down, her father leaned forward in his chair. 'Sing the new song by Mr Arne, my dear. Susannah, I believe you have the music?'

Samuel could not keep his eyes from Mary's face, as she once again started to sing.

"Blow, blow, thou winter wind
Thou art not so unkind
As man's ingratitude;
Thy tooth is not so keen,
Because thou art not seen,
Although thy breath be rude.
Heigh-ho! Sing Heigh-ho! Unto the green holly:
Most friendship is feigning, most loving mere folly:
Then heigh-ho, the holly!
This life is most jolly".

And he was still looking at Mary, while two card tables were brought out for a game of whist. He saw, to his delight, that Mary declined an invitation to play with Dr Cuming and Miss Oldfield, who were then joined by Mary's brother, William, and his wife. Samuel also refused an invitation; he and his family never played cards, so he had little knowledge of any games. Lewis and John Templeman sat down at a table together and continued to chat loudly until Susannah and her mother joined them. Apparently, the only talk allowed was about the game, which was obviously considered a serious business.

'Nathaniel, Richard and I will leave you, my dear,' Mr Templeman said to his wife. 'We shall be playing billiards until supper.'

Samuel could scarcely believe that nobody seemed to notice that he and Mary were free to sit together, tucked away in a corner of the room. Lewis's words echoed in his head. 'Courage, my dear Samuel!' He turned to Mary.

'Do you believe that loving is mere folly, as it says in the song?'

'No, dear Samuel. I think love is the most important thing in life.' She looked at him, smiling. 'I have been thinking of you all the time you have been away. You are my Damon, Samuel.'

Samuel glanced at the card players, all now engrossed in their games, and took Mary's hand in his.

'I have a present to give you tomorrow, for your birthday. It is something I promised you before I went to London.'

'How mysterious, Samuel.'

'But this evening I must ask you something – something I have been thinking about ever since I returned from London. Mary, would you consider becoming my wife? You would make me the most happy man in the world. But I would quite understand if feel you must refuse me until I have proved I can be successful as a surgeon. I have found the perfect place to live and set myself up in Wareham and…'

'Stop, Samuel! My answer is yes, of course, yes!'

'But your father…'

'I think you will find my father already knows of my feelings for you. I found it impossible to hide them from him. Why do you think he asked you and Lewis to join us today?'

Mary had stopped whispering and raised her voice. Samuel became aware that Lewis was looking in their direction and that Susannah, then John Templeman and his mother were following his eyes. He immediately withdrew his hand from Mary's.

'I shall speak to your father tomorrow morning. Then I shall return to Blandford and start planning a home for you in Wareham.'

The room was cosy; the lamps had been brought in and the fire was burning brightly. Samuel and Mary sat in comfortable silence together, listening to the remarks of the card players. Later, when the tables were put away, it was time for supper. On their way to the dining room, Samuel could see that Susannah and Mary were in deep conversation. Susannah was frowning slightly and shaking her head at what Mary was saying. If her brothers had been won over to his cause, it appeared her sister had not.

'Mr Templeman, we must return home,' William's wife said. 'It is late and I cannot bear to sit thirteen at table again. Please ask for our wraps.'

'My dear Ann, my mother will be most displeased if we go.'

'Indeed, she will,' his father said, joining them. 'I have good news for you. Peter has arrived. He joined us for our game of billiards, so we will be fourteen.'

Mary walked beside Samuel as they approached the supper table. 'My brother's wife always makes difficulties. I am sure they will leave immediately after the meal is finished.' She sat down next to Samuel and started to help herself to the remains of the turkey from dinner. 'She is quite sure the reason she has not had a son is that each of her babies was born when the moon was full. Or perhaps when there was no moon. I cannot remember. It makes no matter.'

Samuel laughed and looked at Mary affectionately. 'I am pleased you do not believe in such foolish superstitions. You will make a splendid surgeon's wife!'

After supper, the guests not staying the night began to depart; Samuel and Lewis were not leaving until the following morning.

'You will see that Dr Cuming is making a great show of attending carefully to Miss Oldfield's wraps, telling her how cold it is outside,' Mary said. 'He will see her safely home, carrying a lantern, as it is so dark outside without a moon. It is a cause of great amusement to my family. We wonder why they do not marry, but they seem very content to remain as they are.'

Shortly afterwards, Mary and her mother retired to their rooms; the gentlemen remained in the drawing room for a further drink.

A momentous day in Samuel Baskett's life is drawing to a close. Will he take the opportunity of speaking with Mr Templeman this evening, or will he wait until tomorrow morning? And will he get the permission he so longs for to marry the love of his life?

You delve into the chest again and bring out a small, oval case…

Chapter 5
The Apothecary Scales

Friday, 16 October 1767 – North Street, Wareham

The case is metal and has been japanned to simulate tortoiseshell. Inside, is a pair of hand-held apothecary scales, used for weighing medicines and chemicals. When you lift the scales out, you can see the brass pans are fastened to cords attached to a steel beam. The set of brass weights are measured in scruples; each scruple is equal to just over a gram.

Mr Templeman has agreed to Samuel and Mary's betrothal, but he insisted that, before they married, Samuel would have to have set up a successful practice in Wareham. Just before Christmas, Samuel took Mary to Owermoigne on the first of several visits to the rectory. To his delight, it was obvious that his father welcomed her as the daughter he never had, and she in turn became very fond of him. Eventually, he and Samuel tacitly agreed to forget their differences and often discussed Samuel's progress in establishing himself as a surgeon.

The house Samuel took in Wareham fronted on to North Street and he immediately converted one of the front rooms into his apothecary shop and another, smaller room into his surgery. He consulted Mary about the decorations and furnishing for the rest of the house; she expressed her preference for light, airy rooms and decided on white wallpaper with small blue sprigs for the bedchamber and yellow damask paper for the dining room and parlour. Everything else she left to her "dearest Damon".

Samuel and Mary have been married for six months now. This morning you see Samuel moving briskly about his shop, tidying away jars and bottles, which he puts on the shelves behind him. He is wearing a white shirt and blue waistcoat; his hair is somewhat dishevelled, but is still a dark chestnut in colour.

Samuel put on his spectacles to peer down at a receipt book, then reached up to a shelf behind him, and took down a blue and white jar on which was written "PULV. TURPETHI". He carefully weighed out some of the contents and then added equal measures of some more pulverised herbs. He looked up as the shop door opened.

'Good day to you, Mrs Hutchins.'

'Good day, Mr Baskett. I am here as my husband is suffering greatly from the gout this morning and is in need of more of the medicine you gave him last month.'

'I am making up some more at this very moment, madam.'

Samuel took some of the mixture he had just prepared, wrapped it up carefully in a fold of paper and handed it to Mrs Hutchins.

'Perhaps you will remind Mr Hutchins to take a dose in three or four spoonsful of white wine before his breakfast.'

'Indeed, I shall, Mr Baskett.' As she was about to leave the shop, Mrs Hutchins turned back again. 'It would please me greatly if you and your charming wife would come to take tea with us very soon – shall we say on Tuesday next?'

'That is most kind of you. My wife is feeling a little unwell this morning, so I will not disturb her now, but I am sure she will be delighted to visit you both.'

'It will do Mr Hutchins so much good to take a rest from his writing. I scarcely see him until dinner time on most days, and then he disappears into his study again. On Saturday, he writes his sermon and on Sunday, he is occupied with taking the church services. I sometimes regret having saved so many of his papers from the great fire.'

'No, no. You did the world a great service, madam. We all greatly look forward to learning all about the history of our county of Dorset when the book is published.'

'I shall convey your kind words to my husband. Perhaps you will be good enough to add the expense of the medicine to my husband's account?'

'Of course. Good day to you, madam.'

Samuel started to measure out more ingredients in order to add to the stock of medicines in his shop. He was interrupted by their maid, Betty Brown, who was returning from her visit to the shops. She had kept house for Samuel since he moved in over three years ago and stayed on ever since. She was a jolly, plump, very capable girl, the daughter of a butcher in the town.

'Ah, Betty, I should be most grateful if you could go up to my wife and ask her whether she feels a little better.'

Betty put down her basket. 'I have collected a letter for her, so will take it to her now. I think you and I both know why she is feeling bad, sir.'

Samuel smiled. 'And it is for the happiest of reasons.'

'And there is a letter for you also, sir.' Betty took it out of her basket and handed it to him. At that moment, the door at the back of the shop opened.

'How are you, dearest Mary?' Samuel put down the jar he was holding and went over to embrace her. Betty handed Mary her letter, picked up her basket and left them together, smiling to herself.

'I feel very well and ready to help you in any way you wish.'

'Mrs Hutchins came for some more medicine for Mr Hutchins' gout, so we need to add one shilling and sixpence to his account.'

Mary sat down at the desk and took out a ledger from a drawer. Samuel was delighted at how easily she had learned his system of accounts, and how much she enjoyed keeping them neatly up to date.

The shop door opened again and a distraught-looking man burst in.

'Mr Baskett, sir,' he managed to say. 'Can you come quick. Mrs Cribb is in labour and is in great pain.'

'How long have the pains been going on, Mr Cribb?'

'She started yesterday evening, sir, but the baby is nowhere near being born.'

'I shall come at once. I hope to be back before dinner, my dear.' Samuel picked up his bag, gave Mary a quick kiss on her cheek and followed Mr Cribb out of the shop.

Samuel considered his work as a man-midwife to be one of his greatest achievements since coming to Wareham. At first, he had been met with suspicion; it was not a man's place to be present at a birth and even now, many women refused to be attended by anyone other than another woman. But gradually the news spread in the town that Mr Baskett was to be trusted. Today, as he hurried through the streets with Mr Cribb, he once again remembered his little sisters, who had not survived their birth.

An elderly lady, looking very anxious, was with Mrs Cribb, who was indeed in great pain and distress. Once Samuel had examined her, he realised he needed to use his forceps to grip the baby's head, which was already visible.

'Your baby will be born very soon, Mr Cribb. You will help me by fetching some hot water and towels.'

Mr Cribb was obviously still very agitated and Samuel thought his job would be easier if he were out of the room. He managed to calm Mrs Cribb down somewhat and grip the baby's head with his forceps, so that when the next contraction came, he was able to deliver the baby safely just before its father returned.

'You have a lovely baby boy, Mr Cribb.'

'We are calling him William. I have been so anxious, Mr Baskett.'

'Look after them well. Your wife is exhausted.'

'My mother will be here to help us for a while.'

As he walked back through the streets, Samuel felt that life was good. It was a sunny autumn day, the love of his life was waiting for him at home and he hoped he would soon become a father himself. And he was succeeding in his ambition to save lives. Mrs Cribb and her baby would most likely not have lived without his skill. What more could he want?

Mary was still in the shop when he got home. He took his watch from his pocket and opened the case. Nearly dinner time.

'Mrs Cribb has a healthy baby boy. Can you make a note in the midwifery account book to charge them ten shillings and sixpence? And make a note it was a laborious birth with forceps.'

Samuel charged his patients according to their means. Sometimes he would charge nothing. Mr Cribb was a shoemaker and had a modest, but steady income. Last year Mr William Cole paid him double that amount, when his wife gave birth to their daughter, Molly.

'Martha Harris came in with her little boy whilst you were away, Samuel,' Mary said. 'He is not yet a year old and looked very sickly and pale. He was coughing and his eyes were very drowsy. She asked for some syrup of poppies, as she had heard it would soothe his cough. I told her to go home and put him to bed and try to keep him cool and that you would call in to see him. I hope I did the right thing, Samuel?'

'You were absolutely right, my own Mary. I very much fear her little boy has the beginnings of either the measles or smallpox. It is difficult to tell at first. I believe John and Martha Harris have already lost one little boy before I came here. I shall call in directly after we have dined.'

Five years ago, Lewis Cockram had written to him from Swanage to tell him how, in the space of a few months, over forty people had died from smallpox in the town, among them many babies and small children, so he was well aware how swiftly an epidemic could spread. Soon after he came to Wareham, Samuel had decided to put in place a programme of inoculation against the disease. While he was living with John Hunter, he had learnt how to take a swab from a smallpox pustule. It would then be inserted into a small scratch on the arm of his patients, resulting in a mild form of smallpox. The procedure had first been undertaken in Turkey and brought to England over forty years ago.

As Samuel anticipated, many people had been reluctant to subject themselves to such a risky procedure, not least because he charged two guineas for each person. The breakthrough had come the previous year when a wealthy merchant in the town had come forward with his wife, children and servants to be inoculated and later let it be known that none of them had become seriously ill as a result. Today, Samuel looked in his ledger to see whether John Harris and his family were on his list. He could not find them.

When they sat down to their dinner, Samuel was surprised that Betty had made them a curry – something that Mary normally refused to eat.

'This is unexpected, my love, but very good.'

Mary laughed. 'I suddenly knew this morning that I had to have something spicy to eat today, so I sent Betty out to buy the ingredients. And afterwards we are having one of Betty's almond cheesecakes. I know it is one of your favourites, Samuel.'

'I think this confirms what your sickness in the mornings was already telling us.' Samuel looked affectionately at Mary, who blushed. 'I would guess we can expect our little son or daughter to be born sometime in May next year. I could not be more delighted.'

It was still light when Samuel set off to visit John and Martha Harris's little boy. When he returned, Mary was sitting by the fire in the lamplight, sewing.

'I very much fear little Thomas has the measles – his tongue is coated white, so I do not think it is smallpox.'

'That is a mercy, Samuel.'

'But the measles can be just as dangerous. He has a high fever, but as you know, I am always reluctant to bleed young children. I have advised his mother to bathe his legs and feet with lukewarm water, and to keep him in a darkened room, as there is a danger of blindness if he is in a bright light.'

'Can you treat him – at least so he is more comfortable?'

'I have given him some syrup of poppies to help with his cough and his breathing. He already has a few spots on his face, so I have given his mother an ointment of flowers of sulphur to relieve the itching when the rash appears on the rest of his body. There is nothing more I can do.'

'We will just have to hope we can protect our baby from these dreadful diseases.' Mary paused thoughtfully. 'Now, I shall ring for Betty to bring in the tea and we will not speak any more of these sad things.'

When Betty had brought in the tea, they sat in a comfortable silence for a while.

'I forgot to tell you, Samuel,' Mary said, getting up and going to her desk. 'The letter I received this morning was from Susannah. She writes that Ann – our brother William's wife – is to have another baby in March. She says she hopes this time to have a boy. Of course, it will depend on the moon, will it not? Samuel, if we have a boy, perhaps we could call our baby William?'

Samuel laughed. 'It will probably not please her. She will think she has reserved the name for herself. Our little boy will be named after your father. And my mother's father was also called William, so she does not have exclusive rights to it.'

'Susannah also writes that William is about to become Bailiff of Dorchester once again in a few days.'

'Is there any office in Dorchester that William has not held?'

'He has not yet been the Member of Parliament, but no doubt Ann would consider that a great honour too! But I have left the best news until last.'

'What is that, my love?' Samuel never tired of looking at Mary's smile when she was truly happy.

'You remember my dearest friend, Edith Stickland?'

'Of course.'

'Her sister, Lucia, has become betrothed to my brother, John, so she will be in our family soon. Susannah does not know when they will marry, but I do not suppose it will be before our baby is born. I shall write to Susannah tomorrow and tell her our news. I am so happy that I want to share it with the people I love the most.'

Mary sat down by the fire again and resumed sewing. She had almost finished the patchwork quilt she had started to make over two years ago – after Samuel had asked her to marry him and her father had agreed to their betrothal. She bent down and took out a square of blue silk fabric from a small basket by her feet. She began to sew it on beside a square of red silk. When she had begun the quilt, she had told Samuel that the regularity of the design particularly pleased her. Now, as he watched her, absorbed in her work, Samuel remembered that she had also told him she was sewing her love for him into every piece.

'I forgot to tell you, Mary,' Samuel said. 'Mrs Hutchins has invited us to take tea at the rectory next Tuesday.'

'I shall like that. It is always interesting to find out how much more Mr Hutchins has written of his history of Dorset.'

Samuel picked up a letter from the table beside him. 'And the letter I had today is from Peter Beckford, who is a friend of Lewis. I met him at Newton Manor a few years ago.'

'I do not think I know him.'

'No, he has been travelling around Europe for some time. But now he has done a remarkable thing. Last year, while he was in Italy, he met a most talented young musician named Muzio Clementi. He decided to bring him to his house here in Dorset and pay for his musical education, until he reaches the age of twenty-one.'

'How old is he now?'

Samuel looked through the letter. 'Peter writes that he is scarcely fifteen but has already composed an oratorio and a mass and plays the keyboard with remarkable skill.'

'Was his family happy that their son was taken away so young?'

'Peter does not say in his letter. But I believe I have heard it has become fashionable for Italian musicians to be brought to England by rich landowners after their Grand Tour of Europe. We shall have an opportunity to ask him next month, as he has invited us to a soirée at Steepleton, when the young man will be playing the harpsichord. He says he has also invited Lewis.'

'I shall greatly look forward to hearing him – and to seeing Lewis again. Has he told you when he plans to marry Ann Best? They have been betrothed for two years now, have they not?'

'We must ask him when we see him. Ann might also be at Steepleton.'

'I hope she will be. I have grown very fond of her.' Mary got up and put her letter back on her desk. 'Now I shall ask Betty to take in the supper.'

When they went into the dining room, Samuel was not surprised to see various pickles set out on the table and smiled to himself as Mary helped herself eagerly to a great quantity with her cold meat. Samuel and Mary had already established a comfortable way to occupy their evenings. Samuel would settle down to read a newspaper or magazine. He would read out passages he thought might be of interest, while Mary was occupied with her sewing. So, after they had finished their meal, they returned to the parlour.

'There seems to be considerable unrest in America among farmers in Boston,' Samuel said, turning the pages of his newspaper. 'They are objecting to the taxes being imposed on some goods imported into the country. I will write to Billey Shippen and ask him for his opinion. I miss his company, but am very pleased he is carrying on his work in the hospital in Philadelphia. His little son, Tommy, is two years old now and little Nancy four.'

'It would be good to meet them all, but it is so far to travel.'

'It also says in the newspaper that Benjamin Franklin is back in London. He has come to look into why the postal service takes so long to reach America from here. I met him briefly when I was in London, as he is a friend of Billey's father in Philadelphia. We went to his lodgings to hear him playing the violin, but afterwards, he spoke of his interest in the theories relating to electrical fluid. He told us that before he left America, he had flown a kite into a storm to prove lightning is electricity. And now Joseph Priestley, here in England, is performing similar experiments and has written a book. I hope to buy it when I am next at the booksellers.'

'And now here you are, back in Dorset, away from the excitement of meeting new people in London.'

Samuel smiled affectionately at Mary and put down his newspaper. 'I am just where I want to be, my own girl. And now it is getting late and time for bed, I think.'

Mary got up, folded the quilt and laid it on a small table by her side. 'This will soon be ready for our bed, my own Damon. I shall then start to make a coverlet for our baby's cradle.'

Samuel put out the lamp and lit a candle. He took Mary's hand and led her up the stairs to their bed chamber.

You leave Samuel, asleep with Mary in his arms, full of hope for the future and looking forward to becoming a father. He is using the knowledge he gained while he was living with John Hunter, to become a respected surgeon, apothecary and man-midwife. He is eager to learn more of the momentous discoveries of his time – discoveries we now all take for granted.

You decide to bring out the next object from the chest. It is something soft, wrapped in blue fabric, which looks like a piece of one of Mary's dresses…

Chapter 6
The Pin Cushion

Saturday, 21 May 1768 – North Street, Wareham

You carefully unfold the fabric. Inside, is a small, circular pincushion made of cream silk satin, quilted with silk thread, dividing it into a grid of small diamond shapes. There is a frill of satin around the edge. It is stuck with handmade pins, showing the date "1768" and the inscription: "Welcome dear Babe".

What of Samuel's life since you last met him? Little Thomas Harris died of the measles, but William Cribb continued to thrive after his difficult birth. Samuel was unable to save the sickly baby daughter of his friends, William and Jane Clavill. She was born in February and died a month later. She was their ninth child; all but two daughters died before their third birthdays. Samuel has delivered ten more babies, and eight of them have survived. And it is gradually becoming known that Mr Baskett is more skilful at pulling out teeth than the local barber.

The Reverend John Hutchins still suffers from gout and has still not completed his History of Dorset. Lewis Cockram and Ann Best have at last named a date for their marriage, which is now less than a month away. And William and Ann Templeman have had a fifth daughter, whom they have called Frances.

Samuel and Mary's baby is three days old. They have named him William, as they had planned. His birth was not easy; Mary was in labour for over twenty-four hours and Samuel had to free the umbilical cord from around his baby's neck. To Samuel's delight, Sarah, his nursemaid throughout his childhood at the rectory, has agreed to come and take care of William. Mary is still weak and pale, but is sitting up in bed, with her baby beside her. His cradle is covered with a quilted cream satin coverlet, matching the pincushion. On the bed is the quilt

Mary was stitching when you last saw her. Now, Samuel is sitting beside her, holding her hand.

'I do believe,' Mary said, smiling and looking down at her son, 'that his hair will be chestnut, just like yours, my love.'

Baby William started to stir, opened his eyes and let out a lusty cry. 'And let us hope he keeps his mother's big blue eyes,' Samuel said.

'I think he is a hungry little boy,' Sarah said, coming into the bedchamber. Her hair now had a greyish tinge and her face had a few wrinkles, but her presence still spread an air of order and calm. She bent down to pick up the baby and Samuel was reminded of seeing her pick up his little brother, Robert, in the nursery at the rectory.

Samuel got up. 'I must go downstairs to the shop, dearest. I shall ask Betty to bring you some posset; it will help you to get strong again. Then you must rest.'

'I shall change little William's clout, then he can have his feed, sir,' Sarah said. She sat down with the baby on her lap.

There were some in the town who thought that Samuel's opinions on the care of a baby after its birth were dangerous. He advised new mothers not to wrap their infants tightly in swaddling, but to let them exercise their limbs. He also disapproved of using the services of a wet nurse and thought a mother should suckle her own child, whatever her status in society. He was delighted that Mary had already started to feed their baby herself.

Downstairs in the apothecary shop, Samuel sat at the desk to write in his account book. His hand was not as small and neat as Mary's and he was looking forward to when she could again make the entries. Mrs Hutchins had come in yesterday to pay her account and to collect some more medicine for her husband's gout. Today, Mr Baker came in for some laxative mixture and Mrs King wanted some ointment for her little boy, who had scalded his hand. Everyone who came to the shop was delighted to hear the news of little William's birth.

Later in the morning, the door of the shop opened and Mrs Jane Goodwin came in. She and her husband, Joseph, had married shortly after Samuel came to live in Wareham, and a year later, he delivered their first daughter; in November last year, a second little girl was born. Mary and Jane had soon become friends, visiting each other frequently.

'Mary has been resting and is still weak. But I know she will be pleased to see you.'

'Do not worry, Samuel. I shall not tire her, but I should so much like to meet baby William.'

'And how is little Jane?' Samuel said. 'I hope she is growing stronger.'

'I do not think she will ever be as lively as her sister. But she is sitting up now and taking her food better than before.'

Samuel opened the door behind the counter. 'Betty!' he called out. 'Will you take Mrs Goodwin up to see Mrs Baskett?'

Betty appeared, holding a posset pot in her hand.

'Certainly, sir.'

Almost immediately, a labourer from one of the farms outside the town came into the shop and stood awkwardly beside the counter.

'I have come 'bout the bullock, sir.'

'Ah, yes. Tell Mr Collins to give the powder to the animal in a quart of ale. I have written this down for him.'

'Thank you, sir. I do forget these things. And Mr Collins do say, he want some more ointment for his sheep what have the scab.'

Being in a small country town meant that Samuel was often asked by the local farmers to help them, if the traditional remedies for their animals were ineffective. Mr Collins had come in the day before, worried that one of his bullocks had "the yellows", as he called it. Samuel had promised to make up some powder for him, from a receipt he had copied down during his time in Blandford Forum before coming to Wareham.

Shortly after the farmer's man left, Jane Goodwin came back downstairs.

'William is certainly a healthy little boy, Samuel. He has just fallen asleep after his feed. Mary looks very tired, so I have left her to rest. I shall call in again next week, when she is feeling stronger.'

'Give my greetings to Joseph. Tell him he is welcome to call in at any time.'

'I shall, Samuel. Good day to you.'

Samuel opened the door for her and stood looking up and down the street outside. It was a warm, late spring day. He was greeted by several people as they passed. Mrs Hutchins stopped to say that her husband was busy, as usual, writing his sermon for the next day and that she was on her way to buy some fabric for a new summer gown.

A carriage drew up outside the shop. At first, Samuel could not see who was inside. The groom jumped down to open the door, and out stepped Mary's sister, Susannah, followed by her brother, John.

'My dear Samuel,' he said. 'I have come to Wareham on business today, and so I have brought Susannah with me. She would not rest until she had been able to visit Mary and your little son. And now I must continue on my way, but I shall call back for Susannah in about an hour.'

Once she was inside the shop, Susannah turned to Samuel, an earnest look on her face.

'I have a message from Ann, William's wife. She is most anxious to know whether you have given up your notion of not employing a wet nurse.'

'Mary will tell you she is very happy to feed her baby herself. She…'

'And my brother, Peter, agrees,' Susannah went on. 'And he thinks the baby will only be safe from the cold, if he is wrapped in swaddling and says that this is only way his limbs will grow straight and strong.'

'You all know my opinions differ from the traditional ones, so you will scarcely be surprised I have not given up my "notions" as you call my beliefs.' Samuel was finding it difficult not to show his displeasure. 'And now, we must not quarrel. It is a very happy time for us.'

'I am merely passing messages to you.' Susannah looked indignant. 'I do not always agree with my family.'

'I am pleased to hear it.'

'And I am sure Ann thinks your baby is a boy because of the phase of the moon, although she has not said so yet!'

'Mary is still weak and needs to rest,' Samuel said, leading the way upstairs. 'But I know she will be very pleased to see you.'

Mary was awake when they entered the bedchamber. Her face lit up when she saw her sister, who sat down on a chair beside the bed.

When Samuel went downstairs again, a young girl was waiting for him in the shop, looking very distressed. He recognised Jenny, one of the daughters of Henry and Nanny Bestland, who attended the Old Meeting House in the town.

'Ma sent me, Mr Baskett, sir. We do need your help.'

'Tell me, Jenny, what is the trouble?'

''Tis my sister, sir. Molly. She have got another fit.'

'Has she had many before?'

'Yes, sir.'

'And she has recovered quickly?'

'Yes, sir. Gramm'er, she do put a culver on her stomach.'

Samuel had been told about the belief that, by plucking the breast feathers from a live pigeon and placing it on to the stomach of the child with the fit, the convulsions are transferred to the bird.

'And sometimes, she do take her shoes off and make her breathe the inside,' Jenny added.

Samuel had not heard of that before, but he knew he could not always prevent people believing in the old remedies. 'But this time it has not worked?'

'No, sir. Ma did want you to come back with me. Please, sir.'

'Wait here, Jenny.' Samuel ran upstairs. Mary and Susannah were talking quietly together, with the baby asleep beside them. 'I am going out for a little while, my love,' he said, giving Mary a kiss on her cheek. 'I know you are in safe hands. I shall be back soon, in time for dinner.'

Downstairs, Samuel reached for a bottle behind the counter and poured some of the contents into a small bottle. 'I shall give your mother some medicine which will stop your sister having more fits.'

By the time Samuel arrived at the home of the Bestland family, Molly, who he guessed was about four years old, had recovered from her fit and was lying on the bed she shared with her sister. Samuel knew that none of the treatment given to children who had fits was likely to be effective. But he also knew that many children stopped having fits as they grew older and that the condition was rarely fatal.

Mrs Bestland approached the bed to lay a coverlet over her daughter, who was now sleeping. 'Mr Squibb, at the Old Meeting House, he do say our Molly be possessed by the devil, Mr Baskett. He did pray for her after her last fit, but now she have had another. What do you think, sir?'

'I do not think that is right, Mrs Bestland. I believe something in Molly's brain causes her seizures, and that she may stop having them when she is older. The best thing you can do is to look after her, as you are doing now, and not to worry. I have brought some medicine which may help her. You should give her about forty drops of it to her in a measure of whatever liquor she likes, twice a day. It is a mixture of oils – rosemary, juniper and aniseed.'

When he returned to the shop, Samuel thought he had been away only about half an hour. What he heard as he opened the door would stay with him for the rest of his life. Mary's scream echoed through the house, as Susannah came rushing down the stairs towards him.

'Samuel, oh Samuel, come quickly. We do not know what to do. There is blood everywhere.'

Upstairs, Mary lay on the bed, exhausted and feverish. When Samuel examined her, to his horror, he realised that part of her placenta had been retained after the birth and was now coming away. He knew that the accepted ways of stopping immoderate flux – giving her laudanum, bathing her in warm water – would be useless. His only hope was that once the placenta was removed, the bleeding would cease.

'Oh, my love, what have I done?'

The following hours turned into a horrific nightmare. Samuel could do nothing more. Mary continued to bleed. She gradually got weaker until she lost consciousness.

At twenty minutes before midnight, her baby beside her, she died in Samuel's arms.

Samuel was distraught. He continued to blame himself for Mary's death. He wondered if he would have done anything differently, if he had not been so emotionally involved, if he had been delivering a stranger's baby. Samuel wrote to John Hunter, asking if he could have done anything to save Mary. John replied immediately, that he must not blame himself. It could have happened to anyone. His task now was to care for his son.

Mary's death caused a rift between Samuel and the Templeman family that never mended. Although it had nothing to do with his "notions", they implied that without them, Mary would still be alive. Her brother even told him it was a punishment by God. So, Samuel insisted, against her family's wishes, that Mary should be buried at Shapwick, where his father was vicar in addition to being rector of Owermoigne and that his father should take the service.

And what of little William Baskett? His nursemaid, Sarah, took charge straight away, arranging to take him to the rectory at Owermoigne the next day, where she knew of a reliable wet nurse, who could feed him. While spending most of his time in Wareham, Samuel frequently went to the rectory, getting to know his son and finding comfort in being with his family. William was finally baptised by his grandfather in September that year.

You might think this is the end of the story, but you can see there are many more objects in the chest. You decide to bring out the next one to see where it takes you...

Part 2
Mary Cockram

Chapter 1
The Bird Cage

Friday, 16 May 1755 – Newton Manor, Swanage, Dorset

At the bottom of the chest is a little wire bird cage; there is a wooden drawer underneath and a metal handle, with a hook attached, on the top. Its bars are bent; its door and perch have fallen to the floor.

Now, you can see a young girl, aged about five, sitting by an open window, a brown and white spaniel lying at her feet. The bird cage, with a canary inside, is hanging beside her. This must be Lewis Cockram's sister, Mary; she has the same dark curls and the same brown eyes. As you watch, she opens the door of the cage and the little bird hops on to her hand. The door of the drawing room bursts open and a boy, about two years older than Mary, rushes in.

'Mama says we can all have our dinner out in the garden!' William danced around Mary in his excitement.

'Stop, William. Charlie is frightened.' Mary opened the door of the cage and the bird hopped back in.

'And cook is making a special pie for us. And we are to have some chicken and some ham and a cake.'

Mary knew that it would soon be time for their lessons. She had already learnt her alphabet and her numbers and Grace was teaching her to read from the books in the nursery. William had told her that he would soon be having his lessons from Mr Harding, who was already teaching her brother, Thomas. Her mother had given her a doll on her birthday, but she had already tired of playing with it; what she really wanted to do was go outside to play with William. Boys seemed to have far more fun than girls.

'Come, William,' she said. 'We can go into the garden before our lessons, and you can push me on the swing. Here, Brune.'

The dog leapt to his feet, wagging his tail enthusiastically, and followed Mary and William down to the bottom of the garden, where a swing hung from the branch of an oak tree. Mary sat on the seat, and William started to push her.

'Higher, William. Higher.'

Mary was fearless. As a baby, she was sitting up and walking very early, and Grace often had to stop her climbing out of her highchair and tumbling to the floor.

Yesterday, her father and mother had gone to fetch her older brothers, Lewis and John, from school for the holidays. They had also brought back William and Samuel Baskett to Newton Manor. Mary remembered that last time Samuel came, they had all gone for a walk on the beach. Samuel had helped her to find some shells to start a collection, which she had arranged on a shelf in the nursery. Samuel had been excited when he also found a fossil, which he had told her was called an ammonite.

This morning, Lewis and John had gone riding with William Baskett. Thomas and William already had their own ponies and she could not wait to join them. Her father had promised that when she was six, he would buy her a pony of her own. She was pleased that Samuel had said he would stay behind to talk to her father and she looked forward to listening to what they were saying.

All too soon, Grace hurried down the garden, calling them inside for their lessons. Upstairs in the nursery, Mary sat looking out of the window; all she could think about was going outside again. Yesterday, Grace had been quite cross. 'I have more trouble with you, Mary, than with any of your brothers,' she had said. Mary did not want to displease Grace, for she was very fond of her, but the book she had been reading to them was tedious. It was called *A Pretty Little Pocket Book*. It showed pictures of boys, but not girls, playing games – baseball and cricket – and also told children how to behave and not to go birds-nesting.

"Here are two naughty Boys,
Hard-hearted in Jest,
Deprive a poor Bird,
Of her young and her Nest".

As Grace was reading, Mary could see her mother talking to their gardener, George, below the window. And there was Samuel, walking quickly across the lawn. She knew he was planning to look at a special book her father had bought.

Now Grace was reading a rhyme from another book.

"Mistress Mary, quite contrary,
How does your garden grow?
With Silver Bells, And Cockle Shells,
And so, my garden grows".

Mary thought the rhyme was rather silly, as only plants could grow in a garden. She had her own little piece of ground in the vegetable patch. George had helped her to plant some beans and lettuce. She had told him she also wanted some flowers, so he had given her some sunflower and poppy seeds. She went every day to see how they were growing, to water them and to take out the weeds.

At last lessons were over and Mary could go downstairs. As she passed the study, she saw that her father and Samuel were looking at a book lying on the desk. William went past her and out into the garden, but Mary stopped by the door. One of the things she liked best, apart from looking after her canary and her dog, was to listen to the conversations of her family.

'Did you know, Samuel,' her father was saying, 'that Linnaeus studied medicine and that his father was a clergyman, like your own father?'

'No, sir, I did not. I very much hope to study medicine, but fear my father will not be pleased at my decision.'

'You must do what you feel is best for you, Samuel. I did not have a choice. I knew I would inherit Newton Manor, just as Lewis knows he will after I am gone. And do you know, the best thing I did in my life was to marry Sarah Pushman. You must always do what your heart tells you.'

Samuel and her father continued to look at the book and Mary could not resist joining them.

'Come and look, Mary,' her father said.

Drawings of leaves of different shapes covered one of the pages.

'I have seen leaves like those in the garden, papa.'

'That one is from an oak tree,' her father said, 'and that is a primrose. What others can you see?'

'That is a strawberry, papa. And I think this one is a daisy.'

Samuel pointed to the opposite page. 'The man who wrote this book arranged all living things into groups. See, there are some small leaves on either side of a stalk, but these little ones are in a circle.'

'Like a clover leaf.'

'Yes.' Her father turned to another page. 'And here are drawings of different kinds of flowers. Some have five petals and some six. And here are a lot of little flowers growing together on top of the same stalk.'

'Are there pictures in the book of the shells Samuel helped me collect?'

'There certainly are,' her father said, shutting the book. 'We can find them later, as it is nearly time for dinner.'

Samuel turned to Mary. 'After we have eaten, you could see how many different flowers and leaves you can find.'

'And you could help me, Samuel.'

A table and chairs were set out in the shade of one of the apple trees in the orchard. Grace was helping Jenny, the parlour maid, to bring their food out from the kitchen – ham, chicken, pickled salmon and cook's special hare pie. Mary managed to sit next to Samuel; she wanted to talk to him about what else she could collect. Her spaniel, Brune, lay quietly at her feet. As usual, when all the family were gathered together, there was a great deal of noise and chatter, especially among her brothers and their friends.

'You would not have recognised Lewis in the play yesterday, Thomas,' Samuel said. 'He was wearing a long grey wig to make him look like an old woman, and spoke in a high, trembling voice. And my father and mother scarcely recognised William. He was playing an old man, bent double and leaning on a stick.'

'I was a nurse, so I had to look after a baby,' Lewis said. 'They gave me a piece of wood wrapped in a blanket to hold. And, of course, John Templeman played the most important part. His parents and his brother, Richard, came to watch. And he has a very pretty sister, has he not, Samuel?'

Mary saw Samuel's cheeks turn pink. 'It was a very enjoyable day,' was all he managed to say.

Her father turned to Samuel's brother, William. 'You will be leaving school this year, will you not?'

'Yes, sir. I shall be studying at university, to follow my father and grandfather into the church.'

The conversation now began to be tedious. Mary quietly put her hand under the table and gave Brune a piece of chicken. She looked up into the apple tree; a blackbird was singing his heart out on a branch. Not for the first time, she wondered whether it was right to keep Charlie, her canary, in his tiny cage.

Perhaps she should let him fly free. George collected seed for her to give Charlie; she had put a cuttlefish in his cage and sometimes she gave him a piece of apple. Would he come back to her if he were not able to find his own food?

Grace came down the garden carrying a seed cake and an apple pie. When she had put them on the table, she went to speak to Mary's mother. 'Cook is preparing some pineapples, madam. I shall bring them when they are ready.'

'That is splendid, Grace,' her mother said, smiling.

Mary had been into the glasshouse with George and seen the pineapples growing in pots. He had told her they had to be kept inside to keep warm. They could only be grown outside in hot countries.

'Have you seen our glasshouse, Samuel?'

'No, Mary. Perhaps you could take me to see it tomorrow, before William and I have to go home.'

Grace brought out the pineapple slices arranged in a bowl. 'Samuel,' Mary said, 'do you think my canary, Charlie, would like a piece? I know Brune would not like it.'

'You could put some in Charlie's cage to find out.'

When they had finished eating, Mary took Samuel's hand. 'Now you can help me look for leaves and flowers.'

'You should be careful, Samuel,' Lewis called after them. 'She will try to make you her slave if you let her.'

Samuel laughed. 'I can see you have a collector in the family. I shall enjoy showing Mary how to press the leaves and flowers when we have picked enough.'

'Why will we do that?'

'If you put some paper round them and then put them between the pages of a book, they will dry out. Then you can stick them into your own journal.'

'I could draw them too.'

'That is a good idea.' Samuel reached up to take a leaf from the oak tree and gave it to Mary. 'And look. Here is an acorn. It has been here since the autumn when it fell from the tree. If you plant it into the ground, it might grow into another tree.'

Mary put the acorn into her pocket. Perhaps she could put it into her own garden. 'What is that big tree?'

'That is an elm. See, the leaves have little teeth.' Samuel picked one up from the ground.

'It is like George's saw. He uses it if he wants to cut off a branch from a tree. What are those little white flowers, Samuel?'

'Wood anemones. You could pick the flowers and the leaves. And there are some primroses.'

Mary soon had more leaves and flowers than her pocket could hold. 'Come, Samuel, you must show me what to do now.'

On the way back to the house, they met Mary's mother coming down the garden.

'Look, mama, Samuel has been helping me to start my collection of leaves and flowers.'

'That is very kind of you, Samuel. Mr Cockram is waiting for you in his study.'

'Mama, may I go too? Papa said there were drawings of my shells in his book.'

'You may go until Grace fetches you,' her mother said. 'It will soon be your bedtime.'

'And Samuel is to tell me how to press my collection.'

'Put the flowers in water, Mary, then you can do that in the morning.'

'Before I take Samuel to the greenhouse. Please, mama, may I stay up until it gets dark. I should like to look through papa's telescope with Samuel.'

'That will not be possible, Mary. It will not be dark until very late this evening. And you have taken up enough of Samuel's time already.'

Mary decided she would stay awake until it was dark. If she crept downstairs, she was sure her father would let her stay to look at the stars.

When Mary followed Samuel into the study, her father already had the book open at the page showing shells – some like a fan, some spiral shaped, some joined together by a hinge.

'I remember looking at my father's collection of butterflies when I was about your age, Mary,' Samuel said. 'He also has a collection of birds' eggs. I decided to make my own collection of beetles but did not like having to kill them. I think you are better with your shells and leaves and flowers.'

'Papa, may I stay up to look at the sky through your telescope this evening? Mama says it will be too late.'

'Indeed, it will, Mary. We can look through it together in the winter, when it will be dark before your bedtime.'

Later, as she lay in bed, Mary wondered what her father and Samuel would see through the telescope. Would there be a moon? How many stars would they see? Would there be a comet tonight?

You have now met Mary Cockram for the first time. After trying to stay awake, she can no longer keep her eyes open; she is now sleeping peacefully in the nursery at Newton Manor. Her father and Samuel have taken the telescope outside. The moon has not yet risen; the sky is black and the stars are clearly visible. Mr Cockram is pointing out the constellations to Samuel – Corvus, Centaurus and Ursa Major. Astronomers at that time already thought it highly probable that each star was a sun, with a system of worlds moving around it; they called the stars which could not be seen with the naked eye "telescopic stars".

You are beginning to get fond of Mary, and wonder whether you will see her again soon. You delve once more into the chest and bring out what you think at first, is a cricket ball…

Chapter 2
The Pocket Globe

Friday, 1 September 1758 – Newton Manor, Swanage, Dorset

You are holding a spherical fish-skin case in your hand. When you open it, you see it contains a terrestrial, or earth globe, which fits easily into your hand. Turning it round, you see that Europe, Africa and America are quite accurately depicted, but the shape of Australia, or New Holland, is still approximate and Tasmania, or Van Diemen's Land, is attached to the mainland in the south. A map of the heavens is painted on the inside of the case.

What has been happening at Newton Manor since you last met Mary? Nearly a year ago, her mother died suddenly of a fever. Her father was devastated and for a while refused to leave the house; her brother, Lewis, took over the running the estate. Grace is now housekeeper and Mary has a governess, Miss Clark. John left school and has decided to work in the family quarry business with his uncle, Thomas Pushman. Her brother, Thomas, is now at school, but William still has lessons from his tutor, Mr Harding,

You find Mary in the garden of Newton Manor. Although she is not quite nine, she is already a talented artist, and is keeping a journal, which she is illustrating with sketches of the plants, birds and butterflies she sees in the garden. Today, her lessons are over for the day; she is in her vegetable patch, drawing a pumpkin. Her spaniel, Brune, is lying down beside her.

'Here she is!' Lewis's voice made Mary start. Looking up, she saw her brother and Samuel Baskett coming down the path from the house. 'Samuel has come to see us before he goes off to London.'

'May I see?' Samuel said, peering over Mary's shoulder at her drawing.

'I grew it from a seed,' Mary said, scrambling to her feet. 'I wanted to draw it before I gave it to cook. She is to make a pie with it for our dinner. And look,

Samuel, I planted the acorn you picked up when you helped me start my collection of leaves and flowers. I think it is too big now for my garden.'

'Perhaps George could dig it up for you and plant it in another part of the garden.'

'I shall ask him when I have finished my drawing. He will be coming to cut the pumpkin shortly to take it to the kitchen for cook. Why are you going to London, Samuel?'

'I am to learn how to become a surgeon.'

'But you will come back again soon?' Mary knew she would miss Samuel a great deal; she always looked forward to his visits.

'I hope to come back to Dorset and help cure people.'

'Could you have saved mama?' Mary was afraid Samuel would see she was about to cry.

'I do not know, Mary. I was so very sorry to hear she had died.'

'I should like to learn how to cure people when I grow up.'

'I do not think that would be possible. No girls are allowed to train as physicians or surgeons and I know your father would not allow you to work as a nurse.'

'Mr Best and his family will be dining with us today,' Lewis said. Mary knew he was trying to change the subject. She managed to smile, for she was especially fond of Ann Best, who was the same age as Lewis.

Samuel and Lewis left Mary to finish her sketch and went to sit on the seat at the bottom of the garden. Mary could see they were talking very seriously about something; she wanted to know what they were saying. She finished her drawing by adding the stem at the top of the pumpkin, then went to find George, to tell him it was ready to cut and ask him to move her oak tree. She went inside to put her diary safely upstairs in the school room, before going outside again to join Samuel and Lewis.

'Does she feel the same, Samuel?' Lewis was saying. They stopped talking when they saw her approaching.

'What were you talking about, Lewis?'

'Nothing for your ears, little sister,' Lewis said.

'I was asking Lewis about the farm,' Samuel said, but Mary could tell by the expression on his face that was not true. 'I have decided to call your brother Farmer Williams in future.'

'And what do you think I should call you, Samuel?' Lewis said.

'I hope I shall not deserve to be called a quack!'

Mary was puzzled. 'Will you be keeping ducks, Samuel?'

Her brother and his friend both laughed. 'A quack is someone who pretends he knows how to cure people, but Samuel really will learn how to cure people.'

Brune went up to Samuel and lay down at his feet. Samuel fondled the dog's ears and he wagged his tail. 'Tell me, Mary, why is he called Brune?'

'That is what we always call our dogs. I remember we had an old dog also called Brune, but he died.'

'My father had an uncle called Brune,' Lewis said. 'Then there was a cousin, who died about thirty years ago. He was also called Brune. There is a story in the family, that he left careful instructions in his will about his funeral. The church bell should begin tolling at eight o'clock in the morning and continue until three o'clock in the afternoon and his coffin should be buried close by his mother's grave. Then he wanted eight of his tenants to be the pallbearers, all wearing silk hat bands and special mourning gloves.'

Mary thought he sounded a very strange man. 'I did not know that, Lewis.'

'There is more. He never married and lived alone with his housekeeper, Sarah Smith. He left money to her and also to his brothers and sisters and their children and to the poor of this town and Corfe Castle. Then there were his friends – Samuel and Thomas Serrell, Richard Brine, Jonathan Cole, Henry Vye. The story goes that they would all go drinking together and that was probably what caused his death.'

'I would have liked to have met him,' Samuel said, laughing. 'Although I do not think he would have included me as one of his drinking friends!'

'Unlike my brother, John,' Lewis said grimly. 'We have heard that he spends most of his evenings drinking in The Bankes Arms, in Corfe Castle.'

Mary could hear chatter and laughter coming from the direction of the house. Mr Best and his family had arrived. She ran up the garden to greet them, followed by Brune, and more slowly by Lewis and Samuel. She knew she would be expected to spend time with Elizabeth Best, who was twelve and always wanted to tell her what to do and where to go, which was very tedious. She could see Elizabeth standing beside her brother, Richard, who was about the same age as Samuel, and was not in the least interested in speaking to her. Ann greeted her affectionately and asked her about her garden, her collections and what she had been learning with Miss Clark.

'Papa has given me his pocket globe, so Miss Clark and I have been looking at it in my lessons. I can find out where all the countries in the world are. I should like one day to travel to some of them, but papa says I am much too young.'

Ann smiled. 'It might be possible one day.'

Mary's father came out of the house to greet the visitors. 'It is a most pleasant day. It would give me great pleasure to show you around our garden.'

'I want to show Ann my garden, papa.'

'We shall come to it later, Mary,' her father said, somewhat impatiently. He turned to his guests. 'Our gardener, George, is very proud of the peaches we grow. I shall ask him to pick some for our dinner today. I think you will find they have a splendid flavour.' They all walked down the path to the walled garden, where the fruit was ripening on the trees.

Elizabeth Best was walking beside her. 'Do you like my new gown, Mary?' she said. 'Mama says it is the latest fashion. And I am to have a new cape and bonnet for the winter.' Mary did not know what to say; she had no interest in what she was wearing. She sometimes wished she could dress like her brothers; her skirts got in the way when she tried to run and they caught on brambles in the wood.

As usual, Mary began to find Elizabeth's company tedious. She did not want to talk about anything other than her appearance and had no interest in her lessons, apart from sewing and embroidery. Mary enjoyed the mathematical problems Miss Clark gave her to solve and the books she recommended. Last year, they read *Tales of Mother Goose*, but now she was older, she found the stories rather foolish. Miss Clark had just begun to read *Robinson Crusoe* to her, but she knew Elizabeth would not be interested in a story of a man living alone on an island.

By now, they had arrived at the vegetable garden. Mary took Ann's hand. 'Come and see my garden. We are to have my pumpkin for dinner today and yesterday, I pulled up some carrots and picked some beans to give to cook.'

'You should not do everything Mary tells you to do,' Lewis said. 'I have already told Samuel she would make everyone her slave if she could.'

Ann laughed and followed Mary to her corner of the vegetable garden.

'I have sown some spinach. It will be ready to eat in the winter. And George has given me some little cabbage plants.'

'You are becoming an expert gardener, Mary.'

'When I am older, I should like to have a big garden of my own.'

73

'Perhaps when you marry, that will be possible.'

'Why is it only possible if I marry? And Samuel says I would not be able to be a surgeon because I am a girl. I wish I had been born as a boy.'

Mary felt close to tears. She turned away and bent down to pull out a weed from among her young spinach seedlings. Ann knelt down beside her and put her arm round Mary's shoulders.

'My dear Mary, do not be distressed. I am sure you are still missing your mother. But you should think of all the things you enjoy doing. You have your garden and your collections and your drawings. And you are lucky to have Miss Clark as your governess. She seems to know a great deal about many subjects. All you can do now is take an interest in everything and learn as much as possible.'

'I thought I should like to go to school, like my brothers, but Lewis says he has learnt more since he left than he did while he was there. And my father is showing me the stars through his telescope and lets me use his microscope too.'

'Then you are very lucky, Mary. Come, let us join the others. I think it is nearly dinner time. We shall soon be eating your pumpkin pie.'

Lewis was waiting for them by the house. 'Ann, I want to show you something in the orchard.'

'May I come with you?' Mary wondered what there was to see in the orchard.

'No, Mary. You should go inside to prepare for dinner. And Samuel wants to know about your collections.'

Ann smiled at Lewis and took his arm. They walked slowly down to the bottom of the garden, their heads close together, and disappeared among the trees in the orchard. When Mary went inside, Samuel was nowhere to be seen. In the drawing room, she found herself standing alone, while her father, her brother William and their guests were all talking around her. She was relieved when she saw Samuel come into the room shortly before their dinner was ready to be served, and pleased that Miss Clark was also to eat with them. On most days, she and Miss Clark would have their dinner in the schoolroom with William and his tutor.

Mary noticed that Lewis and Ann had still not returned from the orchard. They came back just before they all sat down at the table in the dining room; Ann's cheeks were pink and Lewis's hair looked as if it had been blown about in the wind. He went up to his father, and Mary heard him apologise for their lateness. When they took their seats, she was disappointed that Samuel was at the other end of the table, next to Ann's sister, Sarah. Mary herself was sitting between her brother, William, and Miss Clark, with Elizabeth Best opposite. Lewis took his place beside Samuel, who said something to him, which made Lewis laugh.

'Elizabeth is speaking to you, Mary,' Miss Clark said.

Elizabeth was leaning forward from across the table and frowning at Mary. 'I asked you whether I could go upstairs to look at your gowns when we have finished dinner.'

'I have nothing that would interest you, Elizabeth. My gowns are not of the latest fashion.' Mary wanted to show Samuel her collections, but perhaps she could do that when the Best family had gone home.

Elizabeth was pushing the pumpkin pie around her plate.

'Do you not like the pie, Elizabeth? It is made from the pumpkin I grew in my garden.'

Elizabeth looked puzzled. 'Why do you have a garden of your own?'

'I like to watch the plants grow from their seeds,' Mary replied.

'I would find that most tedious,' Elizabeth said, turning away and smoothing down her hair.

Mary knew there was nothing more to say. The conversation appeared to be much more interesting at the other end of the table. She could hear Samuel telling Mr Best that he was to stay with someone called John Hunter, while he was in London and go to his lectures. She concentrated on eating her dinner and trying to hear what else Samuel was saying, but there was too much noise, especially when Richard Best, who had a very loud voice, joined in the conversation.

She knew that Miss Clark would later tell her not to be disagreeable to their guests and that she would have to take Elizabeth upstairs after dinner. Perhaps her pocket globe or her shells would be of more interest to her. She doubted it.

After dinner, her father took Mr Best into the library, while Lewis, Samuel and Richard Best went into the garden once more.

'Now, Elizabeth,' Ann said. 'I think we should go up to the school room with Mary and look at her collections.'

'And her gowns and bonnets,' Elizabeth said.

'If that is what you wish. Come, Mary, show us the way.'

Upstairs, Mary opened her cabinet. On the shelves inside, she had neatly arranged her collections of shells, stones, birds' eggs and feathers of different sizes and colours.

'And see, I found the skull of a rabbit in the wood last week. And when we walked on the beach in the summer, I picked up a cuttlefish bone. My father told me it is a shell from inside the fish, which is very strange. And here is a robin's nest which dropped to the ground in the garden. I had been watching the robins flying backwards and forwards with worms in their mouths and could hear the baby birds cheeping when they arrived at the nest.'

'Why have you kept these old snail shells?' Elizabeth picked one up, looked inside it and put it down again in another place.

Mary quickly put it back where it belonged. 'I noticed they all have different patterns and colours, which I find most interesting.'

'Where is your canary?' Elizabeth said, picking up its empty cage.

'Charlie died last year. I felt sad, but he was about ten, so he was older than me, and papa said they do not usually live longer.'

Mary was relieved when Sarah Best came upstairs to say they were about to leave, before Elizabeth had a further opportunity to ask to see her gowns and bonnets; but she was sorry that Ann would be going home.

'I shall come and visit you again soon,' Ann said as she climbed into their carriage. 'You can show me the drawings you have made.'

'I should like that.'

Shortly afterwards, Miss Clark came out to tell her it was nearly her bedtime.

'But I wanted to show Samuel my collections.'

'Samuel will be staying with us for another day, so you will be able to do that tomorrow.'

'Will you read some more of *Robinson Crusoe*, please? I want to know if he is alone on the island and if he gets rescued.'

'I shall read the next chapter, then it will be time to have your supper and go to sleep. Now say goodnight to your papa, then come upstairs.'

Later, as Mary lies in bed, she can hear Lewis and Samuel in the garden below her window; she cannot hear what they are talking about, but their voices are lulling her to sleep, as the light begins to fade.

You have learned more about Mary Cockram – that she is becoming a very determined young girl, with an orderly mind, eager to find out as much as possible about the world around her. You decide to pick out the next object from the chest. Nestling near the bottom is a small leather-bound book, which you guess could be Mary's journal…

Chapter 3
The Journal

Monday, 31 May 1762 – Newton Manor, Swanage, Dorset

You open the book carefully; its pages are fragile after all these years. The first entry is dated June 1761; the final entry is for the thirtieth of May, 1762. You notice how Mary's writing has changed over the year and how her drawings have become more detailed. You decide there will be time later to read the complete diary. There are a few blank pages at the end of the book and you are curious to know why Mary stopped writing so abruptly.

Life in Swanage has not been affected by the crowning of a new King George two years ago; but since last year, over thirty people, including many babies and young children, have died of smallpox in the town and a dozen more will die by midsummer. At Newton Manor, Lewis has become secretly engaged to Ann Best.

Mary's brother, John, is still a cause of concern for the family; he continues to drink heavily, and is rumoured to be consorting with various young girls in Corfe Castle. William is still at school and Thomas is at home, helping Lewis and his father to run the estate. Mary is now twelve; she looks after the chickens on the farm and has learned how to milk the cows. It is now early morning and you find her in the farmyard.

'Come here, chick-chicks!' The chickens came running across the yard, as Mary scattered grain for them. She wanted to make sure her favourite, a speckled Sussex hen, rather smaller than the others, got its share of the food. After emptying her basket, she went into the barn to collect the eggs to take back to the kitchen. There were nine in the nest box, some still warm. Cook would be pleased. It was nearly time for her lessons, but first she wanted to say good morning to her special cows, Lottie and Daisy. They had just been milked and were out in the meadow again with the other cows, munching the grass; as Mary leaned on the gate, they ambled over to greet her.

As he had promised, Mary's father had bought her a chestnut pony, small and sturdy, with a long white blaze. He was in the far corner of the field and when he saw Mary, he trotted over to her. She stroked his nose and he nuzzled up to her. She gave him the piece of carrot she took out of her pocket. 'What a good boy you are, Hodge. I shall see you later for our ride.'

She returned to the garden. Her spaniel, Brune, was now ten years old and getting less sprightly; he was lying asleep under the apple tree and got up slowly, wagging his tail in greeting. When she had taken the eggs to the kitchen, she went up to the schoolroom, for the first lesson of the day and soon became absorbed in solving some more mathematical problems.

Last month, Miss Clarke had started to teach her algebra and she was also continuing with her French lessons. But the best time was when she was allowed to look at her father's copy of *Systema Naturae* by Carl Linnaeus, which she had first seen when Samuel Baskett was visiting them seven years ago. She had begun to base her own drawings on those of Linnaeus and to find some of the plants in the garden and fields at Newton Manor. The book was written in Latin; Lewis had at first helped her to read it, but now she was beginning to understand it by herself. Miss Clarke had suggested they could begin to learn Latin together, something that usually only boys did. A friend of Mr Cockram, Mr Cox from Langton, had agreed to drive over once a week to teach them both. Today was to be his first visit.

Later in the morning, her father and a tall gentleman came into the room.

'Miss Clarke, may I introduce you to my good friend, Mr Cox? As you know, he is an expert in the Latin language.'

'It will be a great pleasure to instruct you and your pupil, madam,' Mr Cox said, bowing to them both. 'I believe you have a copy of the book by Carl Linnaeus. I shall be most interested to see it and to help you translate it. But first, I must teach you how the language is constructed.'

Mary got up from her desk, took the book from the shelf and laid it on the table. 'I can already read some of it.'

'I shall leave you with Mr Cox and return later,' her father said.

'I have brought a Latin Primer with me for you to examine.' Mr Cox sat down at the table opposite Mary and Miss Clarke. 'I shall leave it with you to look at during the week, before my next visit.'

By the end of the lesson, Mr Cox had explained some of the rules set out in the book. Mary thought she would enjoy learning Latin. It seemed a very orderly language. At the end of the lesson, they looked at Carl Linnaeus's book together and Mary managed to translate some of the descriptions. Miss Clarke was obviously enjoying Mr Cox's company, for they were talking and laughing together; Mary had never seen her so lively.

When the lesson was over, they went downstairs. In the hall, Mary's father was standing with Lewis, who was reading a letter.

'I have received a letter from Samuel. He writes that life on Belle-Isle is much more peaceful now the fighting has stopped.'

'When will he come back to Dorset, Lewis?' Mary was eager to know when she would see Samuel again.

'He says here that he will return to London this summer. But John Hunter hopes to go to Portugal with the troops to defend the country from the Spanish.'

'I am pleased Samuel will not be putting himself in danger again,' Mr Cockram said. He turned to Mr Cox. 'Lewis's friend, Samuel Baskett, has trained to be a surgeon with John Hunter in London. When Mr Hunter enlisted as a ship's surgeon, he decided to accompany him. But it has always been his intention to return to Dorset and set up a practice.'

Lewis continued to read the letter. 'He says here that they have been studying the lizards on the island and have discovered something very curious about the creatures. If you catch one by its tail, it can escape by detaching it and leaving it in your hand. The tail then continues to move by itself if it is touched.'

'I saw a lizard in our garden the other day,' Mary said. 'Do you think the same thing would happen here?'

'I do not know, Mary. But Samuel also says that the most astonishing thing is that the lizards grew new tails and sometimes they even generated two tails where the first one had broken off.'

Mary thought she would try to find a lizard again and then pick it up by its tail to see what happened. She could make a drawing of it in her diary to show Samuel when he next visited them.

Soon afterwards, Mr Cox took his leave, saying he would return at the same time next week to continue their lessons. Miss Clarke accompanied him to his carriage and Mary noticed that she stood watching it until it had disappeared from sight.

Mary went to check on her garden. This year, she had decided to plant herbs in addition to the vegetables. Before she died, her mother had kept a receipt book and noted down the various medicinal uses of herbs – thyme to heal wounds, lemon balm to aid digestion, sage to help cure headaches. Mary had planted the seeds in neat rows and she was pleased to see they were growing well. Her oak tree was already almost twice her height, although George had told her it would be some years before it started to produce acorns. She thought Samuel would be pleased to see it was flourishing in its new position on the edge of the orchard. She decided to sit on the seat that had been placed underneath it. Brune came up to her and put his head on her lap. She fondled his ears and he wagged his tail. It was not yet dinner time, but she felt surprisingly weary. She thought she would close her eyes and rest for a while.

'Wake up, Mary! It is time for dinner,' Miss Clarke was gently shaking her arm.

'Have I been asleep? What is the time?'

'It is nearly four o'clock. You looked flushed, my dear Mary. Do you feel unwell?'

Miss Clarke bent down and put her hand on Mary's forehead.

'You have a fever, Mary. Go upstairs to bed and I shall ask Grace to bring you some broth.'

Brune followed her upstairs and lay down on the end of her bed. She was relieved to be able to rest; her head was beginning to ache and her throat felt sore. Would Samuel have been able to make her better? She wished he was not in France, for he would surely know what to do. She was dozing when Grace came upstairs; she managed to take a few sips of broth, but then gave the bowl back to Grace.

Later, Miss Clarke came into the room. She sponged Mary's head with a flannel. 'Your father has sent for Mr Williams, Mary. He will give you something to cool your blood.'

'I do not want Mr Williams to use leeches. They did not help mama in the least before she died.' Mary thought perhaps she had the smallpox; she had heard her father talking with Lewis about the number of people in the town who had the illness and she knew many of them had died.

Miss Clarke smoothed down her bed linen. 'Mr Williams will decide what to do. In the meantime, my dear Mary, get some rest.'

Mary found it was difficult to lie still. She was hot, sweating and thirsty. As she dozed, she was aware of Lewis, then her father, then Mr Williams arriving at her bedside. They were speaking about her as if she could not hear them.

'There are no specific symptoms of the smallpox yet,' Mr Williams was saying. 'You should let me know if any lesions appear on her hands or face. There is a possibility that it could only be cowpox. Does she milk your cows at any time?'

'She enjoys helping on the farm and does sometimes milk her special cows,' Lewis was saying.

Then her father's voice. 'She is normally such a lively girl. All the family is so very fond of her.'

When she awoke later, it was getting dark. Miss Clarke was sitting quietly near her bed. She let out a cry. She thought she could see leeches moving on her pillow.

'No leeches. Take the leeches away.'

'There are no leeches, Mary.' Miss Clarke rose from her chair and approached the bed and put her hand on Mary's forehead once more. 'You are delirious, Mary. They will disappear when the fever leaves you.'

Later, when she opened her eyes again, it must have been in the middle of the night, for she could hear an owl was hooting outside and see moonlight shining in through the window. Miss Clarke had left the room and Grace was there instead.

'Where is Brune, Grace?'

'He is lying beside you, Mary.'

Mary put her hand down and the dog licked it.

Grace rose from her chair and put a cup to Mary's lips.

'Mr Williams has given you some syrup of poppies to ease your sore throat.'

She was comforted to know that Brune was by her side and that Grace was caring for her, as she had done when she was a baby. She finally fell into a deep, peaceful sleep.

So now you know why Mary stopped writing her diary. If you search the chest, will you find another volume? You hope so. You also hope that Mary has cowpox, which is a relatively mild disease and which will later play an important part in eradicating smallpox.

The next object you take out of the chest, is small square wooden box, which at first looks unpromising…

Chapter 4
The Orrery

Saturday, 22 December 1764 – Newton Manor, Swanage, Dorset

But when you open it, you see it contains what you realise is a small circular orrery – a mechanical model of the solar system. Larger versions would have included all the known planets, but this one just shows the Sun, the Earth, the Moon, together with Mercury and Venus. The centre of the base is a sunburst of gold, surrounded by sky blue. Attached to the side, is a small handle, which, when turned, shows the annual rotation of the bodies around the sun; the Earth can be turned on its axis directly. Above, raised on small wooden columns, is an outer ring, showing both the old and the new calendars, the signs of the Zodiac and the points of the compass.

Mr Williams was correct when he surmised that Mary's illness was cowpox. A small number of lesions, which became raised and crusted, appeared on her hands, but none on her face. Her fever left her after three days, and she was soon able to get up and sit in the early summer sun, her spaniel, Brune, constantly by her side. While she was ill, Miss Clarke continued her Latin lessons with Mr Cox, and later that year they announced their engagement.

This year, Mary's world has been turned upside down. Miss Clarke married Mr Cox in February, and went to live in Langton. Then, in June, her beloved dog, Brune, died at the age of twelve, leaving her bereft. Soon afterwards, Samuel returned to England and went to work for an apothecary in Blandford. In October, Lewis returned from visiting him in his lodgings, and announced that Samuel had become engaged to Mary Templeman from Dorchester.

Mary was devastated. She had secretly been hoping, that he would ask her to marry him when she was old enough. She is determined not to tell anyone, but to devote her life to study. In the absence of a governess, she is spending most of her time in the library at Newton Manor, reading as much as she possibly can.

It is now three days before Christmas. Tomorrow, Mary's brother, John, will marry Hannah Kent, the daughter of a baker, in Corfe Castle. Both families are against the marriage; Hannah's father, because he knows of John's reputation for drinking; Mr Cockram, because he thinks his son will be marrying beneath him.

Mary is now fifteen, and today you find her in the library.

It was a cold, clear, winter's day. A bright fire was burning in the hearth. Mary was sitting alone, looking through the frost-covered window; outside, George was sweeping up the last fallen leaves from the grass, his footsteps and his wheelbarrow leaving green tracks on the white lawn. A volume from Mr Cockram's library lay open on the table in front of her, together with the orrery her father had given her for her birthday in September. The diagram of the constellations in the book was complicated, but Mary managed to find Mercury and Venus, together with the Earth and Moon. She slowly turned the handle on the orrery and the planets began to revolve around the sun.

She could hear her father and Lewis approaching the library door. 'There is a letter in the latest *Gentleman's Magazine* about a new seed furrow plough,' her father was saying. 'I should like you to read it, as I believe it may improve upon Mr Tull's seed drill.'

'I shall give it some consideration, Father,' Lewis said as they came into the room.

Mary knew she would never be involved in running the estate, but thought Lewis should take advantage of all the modern methods available.

'Ah, Mary.' Her father came over and stood behind her, as she watched the planets revolving.

'I find it difficult to understand the diagrams in this book, papa.'

'I believe we have a pamphlet which explains the principles in simpler terms.' Mr Cockram went over to the bookshelves. 'Yes, it is written by Mr James Ferguson. It also explains how to predict solar eclipses. You will recall there was an eclipse in April this year, but it was not easily seen in this part of the country.'

'Thank you, papa. May I look through the telescope this evening, if it is fine enough?'

'We shall see, Mary. Now, I have some news for you. Mr and Mrs Cox are arriving soon and will stay until tomorrow. I believe Miss Clarke – no, Mrs Cox, of course – has a surprise for you, a present for Christmas.'

Mary forgot about trying to be a serious young lady and leapt up from her chair in delight.

'She can look through the telescope with me this evening.'

Lewis laughed. 'You do not change, Mary. Perhaps Mrs Cox will want to spend her time differently.'

'And what is my present?'

'If we told you, it would not be a surprise!'

After her father and Lewis had left the room, Mary soon became absorbed in studying the pamphlet about the constellations.

Sometime later, she heard a carriage arriving outside. Going to the window, she could see Mrs Cox climbing down, carrying a wicker basket. Her studies forgotten, she ran into the hall to greet her old governess and her husband.

'My dear Mary,' Mrs Cox said, 'how lovely to see you. I trust you are well, and looking forward to Christmas.'

'Our cousins from Whitecliff Farm are to come for dinner, and cook is busy preparing the goose and has already made the puddings.'

'My dear Mrs Cox. Welcome!' Mr Cockram came out his study, carrying his copy of the *Gentleman's Magazine*. He turned to greet his old friend, Mr Cox. 'I believe you will be interested in some of the articles in this edition, my dear fellow. In a letter that purports to be by a father to his daughter, it sets out the correct rules for writing and speaking. I would appreciate your opinion. For instance, here it distinguishes between the use of the past tense and the participle.'

'Mary, you have not asked me what is in the basket.' Mrs Cox bent down to open the lid. 'Come, I believe you will be pleased with our gift.'

Mary knelt down beside her. As Mrs Cox lifted the lid, a small, brown and white furry head looked out. Mary was, for once, speechless.

'Take him out,' Mrs Cox said, smiling. 'I know how sad you were when Brune died and we thought you would like one of his cousins.'

When Mary lifted out the little puppy, he nuzzled up against her shoulder and licked her face.

'And he's really mine?'

'Of course. He loves you already.'

Mary felt tears come into her eyes. She kissed the top of the little dog's head. He had the special, tender smell only puppies have.

'I shall call him Brune, just like all our other dogs.' Her brother came downstairs at that moment, smiling at Mary's delight. 'Look, Lewis! You and papa knew all about him, did you not?'

'Mrs Cox thought it best to ask us, before giving him to you, and of course we agreed.'

'It is the best present I have ever had. I shall look after him and train him myself. He will need a drink after his journey, will you not, Brune? And I shall find you a new blanket to put in your bed.'

Carrying her puppy, Mary went into the kitchen to find cook. To her surprise, a bowl of water and one for his food, were already side by side on the floor, together with the dog basket and a new blanket. Grace greeted her, smiling. Mary stood in the doorway.

'I do believe everyone knew about my present before me!'

'We had to get everything ready for him. And cook has prepared some special food.'

Mary could no longer stop her tears running down her cheeks, until Brune's ears became quite damp. She felt truly happy for the first time since the beginning of the year. Suddenly there was hope; life was, after all, worth living.

She put the puppy down by his bowls. Everyone in the kitchen watched as he lapped at the water, gobbled up his chicken meal, sniffed around a little, climbed into his basket and promptly fell asleep.

As Mary left her new puppy sleeping and came out of the kitchen, she could hear voices in the hall. She realised it was her brother, John, and his betrothed, Hannah Kent.

'We have come to persuade you to attend our wedding tomorrow, Father.'

'It would give us both great happiness, sir,' Hannah said. 'My father and mother, they will be at the church at noon and have said you will be welcome afterwards to take dinner with us.'

'I rarely go out these days,' her father said. Mary knew this was not true. Only last week, he a took the carriage to visit Mr and Mrs Cox at Langton. At that moment her brother, Thomas, joined them. Mary knew he had been in the barn helping to milk the cows.

'Thomas,' John said. 'Will you and Lewis not come to our marriage tomorrow? And Mary and William will be most welcome too.'

'It is too cold to travel so far,' her father said. 'I believe there may be snow tonight, so it would not be possible for the carriage to reach Corfe Castle.'

'If the weather permits, John, I shall be at your wedding tomorrow,' Lewis said.

'May I go with Lewis, papa?'

'You know my opinion, John,' Mr Cockram said. 'If your brothers and sister wish to attend, I will not stop them, but I shall not be there myself.'

He turned abruptly and went into his study.

Mary could not understand why her father disapproved of her brother's marriage. She herself was quite fond of Hannah. She had only met her a few times, but she always seemed a very jolly girl. Now, she went over to Mary and gave her an enthusiastic hug.

'We shall be having such a merry time, Mary. I dare say we shall have dancing.'

Mary noticed, not for the first time, that Hannah spoke in the same way as their gardener, George. And she had a particularly loud voice. Perhaps that was the reason her father disapproved of the marriage.

'Will you take tea with us before you leave?' Lewis led the way into the morning room and rang the bell. 'I am sure you will wish to be back in Corfe before dark.' Mary realised John and Hannah would not be asked to stay for dinner.

When Grace had brought in the tea and some cakes, Mr and Mrs Cox came in and greeted the couple in a cordial way, but Mr Cockram did not join them.

'My mother, she have made my bridal gown,' Hannah said, helping herself to a cake. 'You will see tomorrow, Mary. And we have been baking the cakes and puddings and making the goose ready for cooking. And my mother, she do says if we have a fall of snow tomorrow, we shall have good fortune.'

Everyone seemed relieved when Grace came in carrying Mary's little spaniel.

'Brune has woken up, Mary, and says he would like to see you!' The puppy struggled to get down and went over and rested his head on Mary's feet. 'He knows you already. He will be a good friend.'

'Oh, what a darling! May I pick him up?' cried Hannah.

'I believe he is happy here,' Mary said.

'We must leave now, Hannah.' John had spoken very little since his father had refused his invitation. He now rose and gave Hannah his arm. 'We will collect your wrap and say goodbye to my father.'

'If you say so, John.' Hannah looked disappointed, but no one said anything to persuade them to stay.

Once John and Hannah had left, the house seemed very quiet and peaceful. Mr Cockram joined them in the morning room and sat by Mr Cox, discussing the letter in the *Gentleman's Magazine*, as if they had not been interrupted. Mrs Cox sat with Mary and asked her how her studies were progressing.

'I have been trying to understand how the solar system is arranged and intend to look through papa's telescope at the sky this evening to try to find Venus. I hope you will join me, Mrs Cox.'

'Of course I will, Mary. I have missed our lessons together. Mr Cox hopes you are continuing to study the Latin language.'

'I am now able to read Mr Linnaeus's book without much difficulty. And I want to show you my journal. I have continued drawing the flowers and leaves and birds I see in the garden and I have been keeping a diary of the weather each day this year.'

'I am very proud of you, Mary. You are becoming a fine young woman. And one day, you will find a young man who will fall in love with you.'

Mary found herself blushing. She knew she had already found the one man she wanted to marry, but also knew he was to marry someone else.

'Samuel is not the only young man you will meet, you know, Mary.'

'How did you know? I have tried to keep my feelings secret from everyone.'

'I believe I know you better than anyone, Mary. Your secret is safe with me. You will one day look back at your young self and not believe you are the same person. I, too, once had strong feelings for a man who married someone else. That must also be our secret. But now, I am very happy. Mr Cox is a good, kind man.'

'I have decided not to marry anyone else. I shall remain here and keep house for papa. And I shall continue studying and perhaps, one day, I can travel to the countries we used to read about together.'

'Now, Mary, I should like to see your journal.' Mary was grateful Mrs Cox had changed the subject. She had been trying not to dwell on Samuel's impending marriage.

It was beginning to get dark already; the sky was overcast and Mary noticed a few flakes of snow floating past the window. Although she had asked her father's permission to attend John's wedding, she was already beginning to feel anxious about the journey and to dread the wedding celebrations. Perhaps it would not be possible to travel tomorrow. Perhaps the snow would block the road between Swanage and Corfe Castle. Last year they had been snowed in after Christmas, unable to leave Newton Manor for nearly a month. It made Mary feel very protected and secure, as if the snow were wrapping her in a warm blanket.

After dinner, there was a break in the clouds and Mary went outside, carrying her new puppy. The moon was new that night; cook had told her it was unlucky to look at a new moon for the first time through glass. But soon the stars were obscured by the rapidly thickening clouds, so her father did not bring out his telescope.

The family and their guests settled down to a quiet, domestic evening. Mary's father and Mr Cox, together with Lewis, continued to discuss articles and letters in the *Gentleman's Magazine*. Mary was intrigued by a drawing of a large fish, over four feet in length, with three rows of small, sharp teeth, which had been caught near Bristol. She thought she would read some more from the magazine tomorrow.

'You will be interested in some new experiments in electricity described here, Mary,' Mr Cox said. 'It tells how a person stood on an electric stand, so that he was well electrified. He then threw his hat to another person and it was found that the hat carried so much electricity with it, that a flaxen thread, floating in the air, was attracted to the person who received it.'

There was so much Mary wanted to learn, that sometimes she did not know where to start. Soon Grace brought in supper, but Mary was too tired to eat much. When she retired soon afterwards, Brune followed her upstairs. Mary lifted him up on to her bed and he went to sleep by her feet.

During the night, the snow fell heavily; by morning it was impossible to take the carriage to Corfe Castle, so that none of John's family attended his wedding. Mr and Mrs Cox were unable to leave the following day, as they had intended. Much to Mary's delight, they stayed until after Christmas.

You delve into the chest once again. Tucked down in a corner is a small, soft package wrapped in what looks like a piece of old wallpaper...

Chapter 5
The Pocket

When you unwrap it, you find what you realise is a lady's pocket, made of cream linen, with a simple leaf design embroidered in green silk; attached to the top, is a cord, which would have been tied around the waist, under the wearer's petticoats. You notice there is something inside and take out a plain white cotton handkerchief. What, you wonder, is so special about such an ordinary looking object?

Mary is now eighteen and has continued to increase her knowledge of all the natural sciences. She is enjoying the frequent visits of Mr and Mrs Cox, who still encourage her in her studies. Lewis has, at last, become officially engaged to Ann Best, and Mary is delighted that they plan to marry next summer. In August, Hannah, her brother John's wife, gave birth to a son, also called John. Shortly afterwards, Mary and Lewis went to Corfe Castle to see the new baby, but their father still refused to visit his son. Mr Cockram is now quite frail and leaves the running of the estate entirely to Lewis and Thomas.

Today, Mary and Lewis have travelled to Iwerne Steepleton, the home of Lewis's friend, Peter Beckford, to hear a young musician from Italy, Muzio Clementi, give a recital on the harpsichord.

As their carriage came up the drive and stopped in front of the entrance, Mary thought she had never seen such a large imposing house. They were shown into a huge central hall and were greeted by Peter Beckford.

'My dear Cockram, how good to see you after all this time.'

'We are greatly looking forward to hearing your young protégé,' Lewis said. 'May I introduce you to my sister, Mary.'

After briefly acknowledging her, Peter Beckford turned back to Lewis. As he led the way into the drawing room, Mary decided he was a rather arrogant young man; his voice was too loud, his gestures too expansive. Two enthusiastic dogs bounded up to greet them. Mary stepped back in alarm. 'They will not harm you,' Peter said. 'They are my house dogs. All my hounds are kept outside. Sit!' At his command, the dogs went over and sat in a large basket in the corner.

Mary began to look around the room, which was dominated by a large marble fireplace. Half a dozen gilt chairs were set out facing a harpsichord. She thought that, although the room was impressive, with portraits and paintings of landscapes and hounds covering the walls, she would not enjoy living in such a large house.

'My father would have greatly enjoyed this occasion,' Peter Beckford was saying to Lewis.

'I was sorry to hear of his death,' Lewis said.

'He was in Jamaica at the time, visiting our estates. He had scarcely recovered following the death of my mother, three years previously.'

'My father is also still mourning my mother's death. I now run our estate. But, my dear fellow, I must congratulate you on becoming a member of parliament.'

'I am finding I do not enjoy the political life. I much prefer being here, where I can spend most of my time hunting. Now, may I offer you and your sister some refreshment after your journey? Once the other guests have arrived, we shall start the recital. You will be pleased that I have also invited your friend, Samuel Baskett, and his wife to join us.'

Mary was relieved that the two men were taking no notice of her, for she could feel herself blushing at the shock of hearing Samuel's name. She had never met his wife, as she did not attend their wedding, but Lewis had told her that she was very pretty. Mary was afraid her hands would be trembling so much that she would spill her tea.

Then she heard Samuel's voice in the hall. Her heart gave a little leap of recognition. She looked up as the door opened, and there he was. The same dark chestnut hair, the same smile. And coming into the room with him, one of the most beautiful women, Mary thought, she had ever seen. She immediately knew why Samuel had married her and why she, Mary Cockram, would have had no chance of ever winning his heart. Her own hair was dark, and somewhat unruly, not fair and neatly arranged. Her own face was slightly tanned from the sun, not pale with delicately rosy cheeks.

'It gives me the greatest pleasure to meet you at last, Mrs Baskett,' Peter Beckford was saying, taking her hand. Mary Baskett smiled and immediately the room seemed to light up. Samuel greeted Lewis and then turned and saw Mary.

'My dear Mary, I am so pleased to see you once more. I hear from Lewis that you are becoming very knowledgeable in natural philosophy.'

'I have been keeping myself occupied in papa's library.' Mary could scarcely find her voice and was sure Samuel must think her very foolish.

'Excellent! You must tell me more after we have listened to the recital.'

Peter Beckford went to stand beside the harpsichord. 'If you will all take your seats, I shall go to fetch my young friend, Muzio Clementi. I believe you will be amazed how talented he is. He has set himself a rigorous programme and practises eight hours every day, without fail, and it is the first time he has played for anyone but myself since I brought him here from Italy. Today he will play music by Johann Sebastian Bach, George Frideric Handel and Domenico Scarlatti.'

Mary found herself sitting between Lewis and Samuel. She had imagined Clementi would be elegant, tall and confident, so she was surprised when Peter returned, followed by a sallow-skinned boy, with a high, sloping forehead and long nose. He immediately sat down at the harpsichord, fidgeted about a little, then started to play. Although Mary had learned to play the spinet as a young girl, she had not continued to practise once Miss Clarke had left Newton Manor. She enjoyed occasionally attending concerts in Swanage, given by the local musical society, but she had never heard anyone play like Muzio Clementi.

To her embarrassment, she felt tears coming into her eyes. Seeing Samuel again made her realise how much she had been thinking of him since she last saw him. She had imagined conversations she might have had with him; that he regretted his marriage; that he had loved her ever since he first met her. What would he think of her if he knew? She looked down at her lap. Out of the corner of her eye she could see that Samuel had turned to his wife, who was smiling affectionately at him.

Clementi rose and bowed stiffly to acknowledge the applause and murmurs of appreciation. He sat down again and started to play once more. Mary recognised the piece as one she had attempted to play herself, by Johann Sebastian Bach. Samuel's wife, she was sure, was a talented pianist and singer;

she was undoubtedly very clever and probably knew everything about the plants and herbs Samuel needed to mix his medicines.

When Clementi had played his final piece, Peter Beckford rose to his feet and went to stand by the harpsichord. 'Now my young maestro will play one of his own compositions for you. While he lived in Italy, he wrote an oratorio and a mass. He composed this sonata in G major while living here at Steepleton and plans to dedicate the work to me. I am sure you will all agree that he has a great future before him as player and composer.'

All this time, Clementi had not once smiled or looked directly at his small audience. Before sitting down once more, he gave a shy, sideways look at Peter Beckford. The music he played was simpler than the previous pieces, but Mary was sure she would never have been able to compose anything like it, especially when she was only fifteen.

When he had finished playing, Clementi rose from the harpsichord, bowed, then, at a nod from Peter Beckford, shook hands in turn with each of them, then quickly left the room.

A servant almost immediately came into the room, and announced that dinner would be served in the dining room. Peter Beckford led the way out of the room and down a dark corridor. Samuel came up to Mary and walked beside her.

'It seems a long time since I saw you at Newton Manor, Mary.'

Mary could see Samuel's wife walking with Lewis in front of them, in her elegant blue gown. Her own gown suddenly seemed shabby and she wished she had asked her father if she could have a new one for her visit.

'I believe it was nearly ten years ago,' she said, although she knew it was actually nine years, two months and six days. 'I was only nine years old and you were about to go to London to study.'

'A lot has happened since then. I enjoyed my studying but would prefer to forget everything I saw when I went with Mr Hunter on the hospital ship.'

'My life is very unadventurous, but I find learning as much as I can of the natural sciences keeps me occupied.'

'I remember your dog was a good companion and followed you everywhere.'

'My old dog, Brune, died but Mrs Cox gave me a new puppy. I have called him Brune also. He is nearly three years old now. I love him very much.'

'I look forward to meeting him one day. Now, tell me more about your studies.'

'I have become interested in the properties of light. I have learned why a rainbow appears when there is sunshine and rain at the same time. And why the colours are always in the same order – red at the top and violet at the other end.'

By now, they had reached the dining room, so there was no further opportunity to speak with Samuel alone.

'Is our young friend not joining us?' Lewis said, as he sat down beside Mary.

'Muzio takes his meals elsewhere,' Peter Beckford said, sitting down at the head of the table. 'He would find it difficult to converse with us, as he is not yet fluent in English.'

Samuel and his wife were sitting at the other side of the table. Samuel turned to his wife as they sat down, and asked her quietly if she was feeling better. Mary thought she looked perfectly well.

When the food was brought in, Mary thought she had never seen such a variety of dishes. At Newton Manor, their meals were usually quite modest, even when they had guests. Today, the first course included a roast leg of lamb with carrots and turnips, stewed carp and a haunch of venison. A servant came around the table, offering a choice of wines. Mary noticed that Peter Beckford had finished his first glass of madeira, before his guests had taken their first sips.

The second course was just as elaborate – including roasted pigeons, lobster, a dish of asparagus and a gooseberry tart. Samuel's wife ate very little. Mary thought that, perhaps, if she herself ate less, she would also be slender and graceful.

Peter Beckford was telling them about his travels in Italy. 'I first saw Muzio Clementi playing the harpsichord in Rome and was very impressed by his talent, which I felt would greatly improve if I took him to England. I suppose you could say that I bought the boy from his father. I make quarterly payments to him and will continue to do so, until Muzio's twenty-first birthday.'

'Is his father pleased with this arrangement?' Samuel said, taking a sip of his wine.

'He was pleased to encourage his son's talent – and the payments will help him support the rest of his family.'

Mary remembered Lewis telling her that Peter Beckford had not previously seemed interested in music. He had told him that he thought it merely a charming talent, of little use in life, so it seemed strange to her that he had taken such an interest in Clementi.

'If I had a son, I would not want him to be taken away,' Samuel said. He turned and looked affectionately at his wife, who smiled and blushed. Mary wondered if she were the only one noticing this.

The servants cleared away the remains of the food, then brought in the dessert – a variety of fruit and cheeses. Samuel's wife cut up an apple and took a few dainty mouthfuls.

Once everyone had finished eating, Peter Beckford stood up. 'Tea and coffee will be served in the library. Gentlemen, do you agree we should join the ladies immediately?'

Mary was very relieved she would not be left alone with Samuel's wife. She would not know what to say to her. In the library, she went up to look at the books on the shelves. Unlike her father's collection, the volumes mostly seemed to be on subjects of little interest to her. Three volumes entitled *The Compleat Sportsman,* by Giles Jacob; large volumes of parliamentary reports; a shelf of books on political economy. But there were also some travel memoirs – even one written by a woman, Lady Mary Wortley Montagu. Mary was still hoping that one day she, too, would be able to travel on the continent of Europe. On the wall by the fireplace were numerous paintings of horses, dogs and hunting scenes. Samuel came up beside her.

'You have not yet told me more about your studies. Perhaps we will have an opportunity tomorrow, before we depart. I believe you and Lewis are also staying for the night?'

'Yes, it is too far for us to travel back this evening.'

'I hope you will join us on our morning ride tomorrow, Samuel,' Peter Beckford called from across the room. 'Lewis is keen to ride my new mare.'

'I have little opportunity to ride now. I am too busy looking after my patients and my apothecary shop. I shall stay here until it is time to depart.'

'At least allow me to show you my plans for some new kennels.'

Samuel smiled at Mary and went to join Peter Beckford and Lewis. They were all soon absorbed in looking at the plans. Mary sat down to take her tea.

'I am so pleased to meet you at last, Miss Cockram,' Samuel's wife said, sitting down beside her. Mary realised it was the first time she had heard her speak. Her voice was low and quiet, so Mary had to strain to hear her. Perhaps her own voice sounded shrill and unattractive in comparison.

'I first met Samuel when I was scarcely six years old, when he visited us at Newton Manor.'

'Then you have known him longer than I. We were both fifteen when we met. I went to Sherborne School to see my brother in a play, but we did not speak to each other that day. He says he fell in love with me then, although I, of course, did not know that.'

Mary could not think what to say. So, all the time Samuel had been in her thoughts, even when she was a small girl, he had already fallen in love with his future wife. She took a sip of her tea; once again her hand was trembling. Samuel came over and sat down beside them.

'I am very weary, Samuel,' his wife said, rising from her seat. 'I shall retire now.'

'My love, it is early. Perhaps you can join us again, once you are rested.' Samuel stood up and took his watch from his pocket. As he did so, his handkerchief dropped to the floor at Mary's feet. Her first thought was to return it to its owner. But she bent down, picked it up and put it into her own pocket, beneath her skirts. At least then she would have something of Samuel's to keep for ever. She glanced over to where Lewis sat and saw he was looking at her, a half-smile on his face. He had seen what she had done, but immediately turned away. He said nothing.

Mary suddenly longed to be back at Newton Manor, with her dog, Brune. For the remainder of the evening, she sat quietly by the fire. Samuel's wife did not join them again. Lewis was telling his friends about the farm and his forthcoming marriage; Samuel spoke of his patients in Wareham; Peter Beckford of his hounds and horses. She told herself not to cry, to be strong. Her life would go on as before. She would continue her studies, add to her collections, start to paint again.

The following morning, Samuel and his wife left early, immediately after breakfast, so Mary had no further opportunity to tell him about her studies. Lewis went riding with Peter Beckford and she was left alone to wander through the house and garden. She and Lewis returned to Newton Manor in time for dinner.

There are still many objects in the chest; Mary's story is by no means over yet. At first, you think the book you bring out from the chest could be another of her journals. But then you see it is a dictionary...

Chapter 6
The Dictionary

Tuesday, 3 April 1770 – Newton Manor, Swanage, Dorset

The "Universal Etymological English Dictionary" has a dark brown leather cover, now worn at the edges. On the inside is a label, so you can see it was originally sold by Joseph Braffet, a bookseller in the Dorset town of Poole. On the opposite page, Mary Cockram has written her name several times, together with that of Lewis. To your surprise, the name Mary Baskett also appears; over the page, in large, confident script, is inscribed "S. Baskett of Wareham Dorset, Surgeon, Apothecary and Man-midwife". The ink is now brown and faded in places. You think, perhaps, it is an original Samuel Johnson dictionary, but, turning the page, you see it was compiled by N Bailey and dated 1766.

It is over two years since you last met Mary. She is now twenty and has lost the plumpness of her youth. In May 1768, as preparations for Lewis's wedding to Ann Best were being made, they received a letter from Samuel telling them of the birth of his son, William, followed shortly afterwards by news of the death of his wife. Mary was immediately ashamed of her first reaction. Would Samuel now realise that he belonged at her side? She told no one of her hopes, expressing only her shock. Samuel did not attend Lewis and Ann's wedding in June, although Lewis tried to persuade him to come.

Everyone is once again worried about Mary's brother, John. A year ago, his wife, Hannah, gave birth to a second son, Thomas. It is rumoured that John has once again started to drink heavily and has again been consorting with women in the town. Hannah has now left John and gone back to live with her father and stepmother.

Ann has taken over managing the household at Newton Manor, and Mary is helping her to organise work in the garden, which has become rather neglected. Her brother, Thomas, continues to work on the farm, and her other brother,

William, has now left school and is at university. Her father at last seems to be recovering from the death of his wife, and was delighted when, last summer, Lewis and Ann told him they were expecting a baby. Their son, John, is now three months old and Mr Cockram visits the nursery every day.

Today, Samuel is bringing his son, William, to Newton Manor for the first time. The little boy is nearly two years old and Samuel has brought him back from his father's rectory, together with Sarah, his old nursemaid, to live with him in Wareham. Mary is trying, unsuccessfully, to hide her excitement and continue with her daily routine.

Mary could hear her little nephew crying as she climbed the stairs to the nursery. Rose, the nursery maid, was bending over the cradle.

'Mrs Cockram says she will be up shortly. She is speaking to cook about dinner.' Mary knew that Samuel thought mothers should suckle their own babies, so was pleased that Ann was feeding little John herself.

'He has been awake for some time and has been such a good little boy.'

Ann had taken Samuel's advice about not swaddling young babies and John was able to kick his legs and flail his arms about freely. Rose picked him up and handed him to Mary. He stopped crying and stared at her. He already had the dark hair and eyes of the Cockram family. Mary carried him over to the window. It had rained in the night, but now the sun was out. She could see Lewis talking to George, the gardener, who was beginning to get quite stooped. He was now known in the family as "Old George", as his son "Young George" now worked as under gardener at the Manor.

'Where's my lovely boy?' Ann always added an air of cheerfulness whenever she came a room. 'Here I am to give you your breakfast, little one.' She took the baby from Mary and sat down on the nursing chair.

Downstairs, Mary's spaniel, Brune, greeted her enthusiastically. She put on her cloak and went out to join Lewis and George in the garden. That morning, there had been a late frost, which was only just disappearing from the grass.

'Ah, Mary,' Lewis said. 'George tells me you are eager to grow more vegetables this year. I believe he has already planted some seeds.'

'So far, the year has been colder than usual, so we have delayed some of the sowing.'

Old George nodded his head in agreement. 'I have put dung on the earth ready for your beans, sir. 'Tis an odd year. Young George, he have kept the fires going in the greenhouse. You will be pleased with your pineapples this year, sir.'

Last year, her father had taken Mary to visit a bookseller in Poole, and said she could choose two books for herself. She decided on a dictionary and *The Gardener's New Kalendar*, which listed what should be done each month in all parts of the garden. In the back of the shop, were all manner of other things. Her father bought himself a new razor and some shaving powder. She bought some drawing paper, some Indian ink, a new journal and an account book. She had continued to keep her diary, noting not only the plants she grew, but also the birds seen in the garden and the woods, the weather each day and the stars she could see on clear nights through her father's telescope. Between the pages, she had pressed examples of flowers from each season.

'You will be able to show Samuel your plans for the garden,' Lewis said, smiling at Mary. 'He should be arriving shortly.' Lewis had never said anything, but she suspected he knew of her feelings for Samuel. 'Now, it is too cold to stay out here any longer.'

Inside, Mary went into the library. Last year she had found an old book on the shelves, written by a garden designer called Batty Langley, which included a plan for "a compleat kitchen garden". She had measured their own vegetable plot and carefully drawn it to scale, dividing it into squares. Each area would be planted with different vegetables and herbs, producing enough to supply the kitchen in the manor all the year round. She took the plans from her desk and spread the paper out on the library table. She hoped Samuel would be impressed.

'Now, Brune, what are we going to do until Samuel arrives?' The dog looked expectantly up at her and wagged his tail. 'We shall be meeting little William for the first time. He will love you, I am sure.' The clock in the library struck one. Mary sat down on the window seat and looked out on to the garden. Eventually, she saw a small carriage turn into the drive and stop in front of the house. Young George took the horse's reins, while Samuel climbed down from the driving seat. He reached up and lifted his little son to the ground, then helped the boy's nursemaid to climb down.

Mary did not move from her seat. She just wanted to watch Samuel, to recognise the way he moved, the way he looked. She wanted to see his little son, William. Above all she wanted to know whether he resembled his father. The boy had the same dark chestnut coloured hair, the same shaped mouth. She could imagine that, as a small boy, Samuel had looked exactly like his son. And she realised she felt immensely happy.

As she watched, Lewis came out of the house to greet his guests and bent down to say something to the little boy, who turned away, burying his head in his nursemaid's skirts. The two men laughed and shook hands, then turned to go inside. The nursemaid followed, holding little William's hand. Mary still did not move from her seat.

From the hall, she could hear the voices of her father and Ann, then Samuel himself.

'And where is Mary? I am looking forward to introducing her to William.'

She rose from her seat and went to stand in the doorway. Her heart was beating quickly and her legs were feeling shaky.

'Here I am, Samuel!'

'How good to see you again, Mary.' Samuel smiled at her and bent down to pick up his son. As the little boy looked at Mary, she could see his eyes were pale blue, like Samuel's. He pointed to Brune. 'Wow-wow,' he said. Samuel put him down again and the little boy went over and put his arms round the dog. He looked up at his father. 'Wow-wow,' he said again.

'He has made a new friend already,' Samuel said.

'He is most likely ready for his sleep, sir,' Sarah said.

'I will take you up to the nursery,' Ann said. 'Rose is there with my baby, John, and she will show you where William can take his nap. Samuel, I'm sure you would like some refreshment after your journey.' She rang the bell, then turned to go upstairs.

'Now, my dear fellow,' Lewis said, 'come into the library. We have much to talk about after all this time. And Mary is eager to show you her plans for our vegetable garden.'

Mary followed Lewis, Samuel and her father back into the library. Her father picked up a copy of the *Gentleman's Magazine*. 'I should like to discuss the American problem with you, Samuel. I remember you have an American friend.'

'Yes, sir. Billey Shippen studied with me in London and has founded a medical school in Pennsylvania. He writes that his father is very involved with the unrest in America and is a supporter of Benjamin Franklin.'

Grace soon brought in tea and some of cook's gingerbread cakes. Ann came downstairs again.

'William is nearly asleep already. I am pleased he has returned to you, Samuel. I believe he was living with your father in the rectory.'

'Yes. He has settled very well, especially as Sarah is still with him.'

Samuel went over to the table, where Mary's garden plans were spread out. 'This plan is excellent. It could also be used for a smaller garden.'

Mary felt herself blushing. 'Have you a garden?'

'Yes, but is very small and behind my shop and surgery. There is a house a short distance away which I hope to purchase.'

Lewis joined them. 'You must by now have many more patients and customers in your shop.'

'Yes, I am almost too busy, which I believe is a blessing. I have no time to think of how my poor wife died.'

Mary turned away and went to pour the tea. She had imagined that after nearly two years, Samuel might have recovered his spirits, especially as he now had his son with him again.

Her father joined Samuel. 'Who is this fellow, Junius, do you suppose?' he pointed to an article in the *Gentleman's Magazine*. 'It is said that his letters were the main reason the Duke of Grafton resigned. And now we have Lord North as our prime minister.'

Mary knew that once her father started to discuss political matters, it would be difficult for anyone to stop him. Her mind began to wander. Dinner would not be served for some time. She wanted to talk to Samuel, to find out about his life, to get to know his little boy. And of course, find out whether he planned to marry again. Had he someone in mind? Could it possibly be her?

Ann's voice made her start. 'Mary, I am going to check how the preparations for dinner are progressing. The men seem far too occupied to notice if we leave them. Perhaps you could go up to make sure everything is well in the nursery.'

Upstairs, little John was still asleep after his feed, but William had woken up. 'Wow-wow,' he said when he saw Mary.

'Brune is downstairs,' Mary said, not knowing whether William would understand. 'We can see him again soon.'

'He is a clever little boy,' Sarah said. 'He already recognises the animals in his picture book. It belonged to Mr Baskett when he was a boy and we brought it from the rectory when we moved to Wareham.'

The little boy took the book from Sarah and gave it to Mary. It was called *A Description of Three Hundred Animals*. She sat down and lifted William on to her lap and, to her delight, he seemed happy there. She opened the book. William pointed to a picture. 'Meow,' he said.

'Yes, that is a cat.' She turned the page. 'And what is that?'

'Grrr,' he said.

'Yes, a tiger.'

Mary was surprised that many of the pictures in the book were of mythical creatures – a unicorn and something called a manticora, which had a human head with sharp teeth and the body of a lion. Further on, in the book were pictures of insects – a beetle, a wasp and a spider. She thought she could show the little boy her journal. In it, she had painted pictures of animals and birds he would know – cats, dogs, cows and chickens.

William climbed down from Mary's lap. Ann had asked Rose to get some toys out of the cupboard in the nursery in preparation for his visit. The little boy was still unsteady on his feet and was wearing his "pudding" cap to protect him if he fell over. He went over to a little horse on wheels and took hold of its string to pull it along. Rose went into the night nursery to pick up baby John, as he had woken up and begun to cry.

'I remember playing with the horse when I was small,' Mary said to Sarah. 'I was not in the least interested in dolls, although I think I was given one when I was about five.'

'We had only boys' toys at the rectory, as all Mr Baskett's little sisters died as babies. It was very sad.'

Mary could hear the clock downstairs strike four. 'It is time for dinner. Grace will bring your meal up shortly.'

Downstairs she was just in time to join Samuel and her family as they went into the dining room. 'Did you know, Lewis,' Samuel was saying, 'that I received a very strange letter before Christmas. It was from a Farmer Williams. He asked me for some jollop for his wife as she had the colic and a belly as big as a barrel. This Farmer Williams was certainly not well educated, as the spelling in the letter was very poor.'

'How strange,' Lewis said. 'I seem to remember you used to call me Farmer Williams.'

'He also wrote later to say that his wife was better. Your letter telling me of the birth of little John arrived at the same time.'

Lewis had shown Mary the letter he had written, hoping Samuel would enjoy the joke. 'Did you believe it really was from Farmer Williams?' she said, sitting down next to Samuel at the table.

'Not for a moment,' Samuel said. They all started to laugh. Her father looked puzzled. He sat down at the head of the table.

Thomas came in to join them, looking somewhat unkempt. He briefly apologised to his father for being late and took his place at the table.

'It is so good to see you, Samuel,' Lewis said. 'We have missed you.'

'You must visit us whenever you can.' Ann looked across the table and smiled at Mary.

'I have been making friends with William upstairs in the nursery.'

'I am so pleased.' Samuel looked at Mary, sitting beside him. 'I knew he would like you.'

'He seems a happy little boy. I should like to show him my journal, where I have drawn pictures of all the animals on the farm – and of Brune of course.'

Mary saw Lewis and Ann look at each other. Were they match making? Did they know something she did not? She could not help feeling that Samuel was very much part of her family, totally at ease with them all.

After they had finished their dinner, Thomas again went outside. He rarely took part in family life; he had once told them that he preferred the company of the animals. Mary went to fetch her journal. Sarah brought William downstairs to the drawing room and he immediately went over to Brune, who was sitting at Mary's feet. 'Papa wow-wow,' he said.

'No, William, Brune is Mary's.'

'Mary wow-wow,' William said, looking up at Mary.

'Yes,' she said, opening her journal. 'Look, William, who is this?'

'Broo wow-wow.' He laughed and climbed up on to her lap.

'I have to go up to the nursery,' Ann said. 'It is time for John's feed.'

'And I forgot to show you an article in the *Gentleman's Magazine*, Father,' Lewis said. 'I have it open ready in the library. A large brown eagle was caught alive near Wareham. It says it is eight feet from wing to wing.'

Suddenly, Mary found herself alone with Samuel and his little son. She turned another page. 'Here is my cat. She is called Kitty. And here are Lottie and Daisy.'

'Moo cow,' William said.

Samuel, sat down next to her. 'I think,' he said, 'we have been left alone for a purpose, Mary.'

'Why is that, Samuel?' Mary could hear her heart beating.

'Because William needs a mother. And I need a wife.' Samuel was silent for a while. 'I have to tell you, that I shall never forget William's mother. I loved her very much. But I have to start a new life without her.' He paused. 'I have been very fond of you, Mary, ever since I first met you and we went for a walk on the beach and collected shells. But you were just a child, so I did not feel for you then, as I realise I do now. And how I hope you also feel for me, Mary. You would make me very happy if you agreed to become my wife and a mother to my son.'

William was still on Mary's lap, but had now fallen asleep, his thumb in his mouth.

'I have waited years for this day, Samuel. I thought I had lost you for ever, first when you went to London, then when you married. And now I have met little William, I have two people to love. I suspect Lewis has told you of my feelings. I think he has known for some time.'

'I wrote to Lewis, telling him of my intention. He replied saying he and his father were very happy for us.'

William woke up, struggled to the floor and sat down beside Brune.

As she rose from her chair, Mary realised she had tears running down her cheeks. 'I am sorry, Samuel.'

Samuel smiled and stood up beside her. He reached for his handkerchief and gently wiped away her tears. 'My dear Mary, I hope these are tears of happiness, not regret.'

'Of happiness and relief, Samuel.' There seemed no reason to say anything else.

That night, as Mary prepares for bed, she takes out her dictionary. On the first page, she had written her name, Mary Cockram, several times. Now, she picks up her pen and writes, as she has longed to do many times, "Mary Baskett, her book".

Is this, then, the "happy ever after" end of the story of Samuel and Mary? Of course not. There are still many objects in the chest, and at the bottom, you find a small oblong box...

Part 3
Samuel Baskett

Chapter 1
The Dental Forceps

Monday, 15 April 1771 – East Street, Wareham, Dorset

When you open it, you realise you are looking at a set of dental forceps of various kinds, used to extract molars, incisors and roots, each placed in its own, shaped, slot. The handles are curved at different angles enabling them to be used for upper or lower teeth. When his patients with toothache began to come to him, Samuel wrote to John Hunter to ask his advice. Upon returning to England, from his time as ship's surgeon, Hunter had worked with James Spence, one of the first people in England to call himself a dentist. Hunter wrote back to say that he was preparing to publish a book called The Natural History of the Human Teeth *and promised to send Samuel a copy. It would be illustrated by van Rymsdyk, whom Samuel had met while studying with Hunter.*

After Samuel proposed to Mary, there was a flurry of preparations for the wedding, which took place in Swanage parish church, just over two months later. Samuel moved before the wedding to his new house in East Street. Mary was pleased she did not have to live in a house filled with memories of the other Mary. Little William was delighted to find that not only Mary, but also Brune was to live with them, and he soon began to call Mary "Mama".

Betty Brown, Samuel's servant from North Street, is now assisted in her duties by Hester Squib, a cheerful girl, who is always willing to please. Old Henry Hobbes comes in to work in the garden. Samuel is as busy as ever and has decided to employ someone to help him in the apothecary shop, giving him more time to visit his patients. Young Richard Hobbs is a conscientious young man, who keeps meticulous records. He has recently married and he and his wife, Rebecca, have set up home behind the shop.

Today, you find Samuel and Mary in the dining room, eating breakfast.

'My dear Samuel, you must wrap up warm. William was very excited this morning to see that there was snow on the grass. Sarah is taking him outside to play with Brune.'

'The weather is certainly strange this year. It seemed to be warming up yesterday.'

'Henry will not be able to sow anything in the kitchen garden today – just like last year at Newton. My *Gardener's Kalendar* says that by April the gentle fans of sweet-scented Zephyrs should be ushering in the goddess Flora!'

Samuel laughed. 'It is a very fanciful book at times!'

Not for the first time, he thought how much he enjoyed Mary's company. William's mother would always be the love of his life, but she didn't have the same sense of fun. He scarcely admitted it to himself, let alone to anyone else, that he sometimes wondered if she would have managed to run the much larger house and greater number of servants. And now his childhood friend, as his wife, was sharing his life and, in about two months, was to present him with his second child. He could not help being apprehensive. He would do his utmost to make sure she had an easy, safe birth.

Outside, in the garden, he could see his son throwing a ball for Brune and squealing with laughter when the dog nosed into the thin covering of snow on the grass and brought the ball back for him to throw again. Sarah stood beside him and Samuel could see she was beginning to look quite elderly.

'I wonder, my love, whether we should get some help for Sarah in time for the new baby.'

'I was thinking the same. Sarah says she will be able to cope perfectly well, but I can see she is not as agile as she was when I first met her last year.'

'I will make enquiries in the town. Now, I must go. I am teaching Richard to mix some of the medicines, but he is not yet able to do so without me. And then I shall visit poor Joseph and Jane Goodwin. I had feared little Joseph would not survive much longer. He was such a sickly baby.'

Samuel's friends had now lost three of their five babies. Their second daughter, Jane, had died three months after William's birth and their next baby, another Joseph, was only six months old when he died. Last year, Jane had given birth to a healthy daughter, whom they also called Jane, followed a year later by another Joseph. But then, a week ago, the little boy had become feverish and, at only two months old, was too small for Samuel to treat him with any of the medicines for older children. He was buried yesterday.

'Will you tell them I shall pay them a visit tomorrow?' Samuel knew Mary had become very fond of Jane Goodwin and was very distressed when she heard the news of the baby's death.

'I shall send them both your good wishes. And you must rest, my love. I shall be home in time for dinner.'

'I shall continue to read Benjamin Franklin's book on electricity. This new edition is so much larger than the one I read in my father's library. His experiments with the Leyden jar are most interesting. He found that the glass holds the charge of electricity and not the water.'

'My love, I must go. You can tell me later. You are the only woman I know who is able to lecture me on natural philosophy!'

Samuel smiled to himself as he put on his woollen frock coat, buttoning it up against the morning chill. He had scarcely gone a few yards from his house, when he heard his name being called. Turning around, he was delighted to see his brother, Thomas, hurrying towards him. He had recently moved to Wareham from London, where he had met a fellow law student from Wareham, Thomas Bartlett, who invited Thomas to join him to work at the legal practice of his father in North Street, near Samuel's own shop.

'My dear brother, I believe we shall be seeing you later. Ruth tells me we have been invited to dinner.'

'Yes, of course. I had almost forgotten. We are looking forward to seeing you. Is Ruth recovered from her cold?'

'She is completely better now, thanks to your advice. She found the smell of liquorice and linseed very soothing when she rubbed it on her chest and the syrup helped her sore throat.'

Thomas and his wife had been married for eight years and had no children. Ruth took great delight in her little nephew, William, and now visited the house several times a week.

'I trust Mary is keeping well so near to her confinement?'

'I am having difficulty stopping her doing too much. The only time she rests is when she is reading.'

They walked on together, until they parted as they reached Samuel's shop. Inside, Richard was sitting at the desk catching up with the accounts.

'Nathaniel Bestland did come in about an hour ago, Mr Baskett. He have got a very bad toothache. I did tell him to come back later, sir.'

'Thank you, Richard. I fear I shall have to pull the tooth. I have already filled the hole with wax.'

John Hunter had advised Samuel to fill the cavities in his patients' teeth with lead or wax; if the tooth were broken, then extraction was the only solution. He also wrote of his work transplanting healthy teeth from homeless people into the mouths of his wealthy patients, something Samuel was not prepared to do.

Samuel could hear the loud cry of a child approaching from down the road and the door burst open. He recognised Mrs Grady, who was dragging her little boy by the hand into the shop.

'He be such a stupid boy, Mr Baskett. He have put his hand in the fire and have got such a bad burn. Show Mr Baskett, George.'

Little George held out his hand, tears still running down his cheeks. The wound was only superficial, but obviously very painful.

'You will not do that again, will you George?'

'No, Mr Baskett.'

'I shall give your mother something to put on your hand. Richard, give Mrs Grady a box of camphorated ointment. That will sooth his burn while it heals. It will cost you six pence.'

'Thank you, Mr Baskett. I have only got three pence today.'

'Richard, make a note Mrs Grady owes us three pence.'

Samuel knew that her husband spent a good part of his wages at the Bricklayers Arms before they reached his wife. He was not prepared to reduce the cost of the ointment, as he might have done for someone living in genuine poverty.

Samuel began preparing more medicines and showing Richard how to make up some of the simpler recipes. When Nathaniel Bestland returned an hour later, Samuel could see his face was very swollen on one side.

'I fear there is no more I can do to save your tooth, Nathaniel. I shall have to pull it out.'

Samuel opened a cupboard behind the counter and took out his dental forceps and keys together with a lance, which he would use, if necessary, to cut into the gum to make it easier to extract the tooth. He noticed Richard turning somewhat pale. Samuel realised he had not yet seen the operation taking place. He said nothing; Richard would have to grow accustomed to watching unpleasant operations, if he were to remain as his assistant.

Nathaniel sat down and opened his mouth. Samuel was relieved to see the offending tooth was already quite loose. He picked up his forceps and gave a sharp tug.

'There, Nathaniel, it will not give you any more trouble. Your gum should soon heal. And you should care for your remaining teeth by rubbing them with tooth powder.'

'Thank you most kindly, Mr Baskett.'

'Richard, add two shillings to Mr Bestland's account for pulling the tooth and six pence for a box of tooth powder.'

Nathaniel went out of the shop holding his handkerchief up to his mouth. Samuel put on his coat.

'I shall be back in about an hour, Richard. I can deal with any messages when I return.'

The town was bustling, as he walked towards Joseph and Jane Goodwin's house. Mrs Hutchins was just coming out of the haberdashery shop as he went past.

'Good day to you, Mrs Hutchins, I trust you and your husband are well.'

'Good day, Mr Baskett. When I have bought my bread, I shall come to your shop for some more medicine for my rheumatism and also for Mr Hutchins' gout. We are both not getting any younger and this weather does not help.'

'I am on my way to visit poor Joseph and Jane Goodwin. As you know, their baby was buried yesterday at St Mary's. My assistant in the shop, Richard, will give you your medicines and add the cost to your account.'

'I thank you, Mr Baskett. Please convey my condolences to Mr and Mrs Goodwin.'

'Indeed, I shall. I thank you, Mrs Hutchins.'

Samuel continued on his way, wondering what he could possibly say to his friends on their loss. They had been a great support to him after William's mother died and were delighted when Samuel told him he was to marry Mary Cockram. When he arrived, their four-year-old daughter, Mary, was eager to tell him about her new kitten.

'Mama says that Jane can also have a kitten when she is bigger.'

Jane Goodwin, looking pale and tired, came down the stairs carrying her other daughter.

'We are so blessed to have our two healthy girls, Samuel. It seems we are not meant to have a son.'

'There is still time for you to have a healthy boy, Jane.'

'We shall pray you are right, Samuel. Joseph is out at the moment. I shall convey your best wishes when he returns.'

'Then I shall bid you good day. Mrs Hutchins sends you her condolences. And Mary has asked me to say she will visit you tomorrow.'

'I shall look forward to seeing her. Perhaps she could bring William with her. Mary loves to play with him.'

'And Brune,' added little Mary, looking up at her mother.

'Yes, and Brune.'

When he returned to his shop, he found Mr Collins' farm labourer waiting for him.

'One of Mr Collins' horses have got a bad cough again, sir. He do want some more of the powder you gave him last year.'

'I still have more of the mixture. I shall add the cost to Mr Collins' account. Remind him to give some of the medicine in two quarts of ale and keep the horse bridled and warm.'

'That I shall, sir.'

Mr Collins' man left the shop, shutting the door loudly behind him.

'I shall return home now, Richard. If I am needed urgently, please come to fetch me.'

Thomas and Ruth arrived shortly after Samuel got home. Ruth and Mary went straight up to the nursery.

'Come, Thomas, I have my latest purchase to show you.' Samuel took Thomas into his study. On his desk were three large volumes, bound in dark brown leather. 'I had intended to take out a subscription for unbound copies of the *Encyclopaedia Britannica* as they were issued these last three years. But now I have bought the complete publication.'

Samuel opened one of the volumes. 'See, here it explains everything there is to know about astronomy. It has been one of Mary's great interests since she was a small girl. And I plan to buy her a copy of a new edition of *The History of Shells*, by Dr Lister. I helped her start her collection when I visited Newton Manor and there was an original copy of the book in her father's library. But do not mention it to her, Thomas. I shall give it to her after our first baby is born.'

'I have never seen you happier than you are now, Samuel.' Thomas smiled at his brother. 'I do believe you were always meant to be together.'

'Mary certainly believes so. She says she was determined I should marry her after our very first meeting, when she was only six years old!'

'Samuel, I read in the *Gentleman's Magazine* that Mr Gill, master of the Grammar School at Sherborne, has died. I believe they have misread the name.'

'I certainly remember Mr Hill, our headmaster. How can we forget?'

Thomas laughed. 'He must have been very elderly when he died. I remember him as old when we were at the school. He suffered badly with the gout I seem to recall.'

Mary and Ruth came downstairs from the nursery and dinner was served shortly afterwards.

Samuel took his place at the head of the table. 'Jane Goodwin seemed in good spirits, although she did say that she doubted they would ever have a son.'

'I hope you told her not to despair yet,' said Mary.

'Of course. She asked if you can bring Brune when you visit them tomorrow and little Mary wants to show you her new kitten.'

'William would love to see it too. Perhaps we should think of getting one for him.'

Thomas took a spoonful of his soup. 'Do you remember our kittens at Owermoigne, Samuel?'

Samuel knew that Mary enjoyed hearing reminiscences about his childhood, before she was born and before he knew Lewis.

'Father at last allowed us to keep one each, after drowning them all the previous year. Mine was black and white.'

'And mine was marmalade, black and white, like their mother, Tabatha. I think William had the black one.'

'Or did he say he did not want one? He thought he was above such sentimentality, even then.'

'And Father said John and Robert were too young.'

'Father is far less strict with little William than he was with us. He was delighted to have his grandson living at the rectory. I believe it has given him a new lease of life. He is very much looking forward to seeing our new baby when it arrives.'

'I shall ask Jane tomorrow if she knows of someone who could help Sarah,' Mary said. 'I believe her nursemaid, Martha, has a younger sister.'

Hester brought in the second course and cleared away the dishes.

'Tell me, Thomas,' Samuel said, passing him a dish of stewed beef, 'when will the first assize court be held in the town hall, now it is fully restored?'

'Mr Bartlett tells me the first hearings will be next month. He is pleased all the money for rebuilding the town after the fire has finally been allocated. He has been involved in working on the committee for nearly ten years and is a trifle weary.'

'Mary, this stewed beef is delicious,' Ruth said. 'I should very much like to have the receipt.'

'Betty has shown she is a good cook, and Hester is helping her in the kitchen. I brought my mother's cookery book from Newton with me when we married. It says it is for Good Wives, Tender Mothers and Careful Nurses. I hope I am all three! I shall copy out the receipt for you. I grow a great many herbs in the garden, which make all the difference to the flavour. It has thyme, parsley and marjoram in it and the gravy has claret added.'

As Samuel was helping himself to some apple pudding, Hester came in once more.

'Thomas King have come, Mr Baskett. He do say his wife's mother have been taken very ill with a high fever and could you come, sir.'

'Of course, Hester.' Samuel got up from the table. 'Do excuse me, everyone. I shall return as soon as I can. Mary King's mother, Mrs Sleet, has been visiting the family. I believe she lives in Wimborne.'

Samuel had treated Mrs Sleet last year and knew she was becoming very frail since the death of her husband. He walked with Thomas King to his house in East Street, where he found the old lady scarcely conscious.

'I do worry that our little boy is also a little feverish, Mr Baskett,' Mrs King said.

'I am very sorry, but I believe there is little I can do for your mother.' Samuel knew Mrs Sleet would probably not last the night. 'But if Mr King will come back to my shop, I will give him something for your baby. In the meantime, bathe his feet in cool water.'

When Samuel returned home, Mary and their guests were taking tea in the parlour. Shortly afterwards, Sarah brought little William downstairs from the nursery, before he went to bed. Samuel watched his family with affection. Mary, Brune lying at her feet, lifted William on to her lap and turned the pages of the book she had made for him. She had painted pictures of animals William knew, and had written their names underneath. He liked it much more than *A*

Description of Three Hundred Animals she had shown him at Newton Manor. Ruth turned to Samuel and smiled.

'My sister, Jane, is visiting us next week. She is greatly looking forward to meeting you all.'

'She will be most welcome here. Thomas has told me she has been unwell recently.'

'I believe it is because she has not recovered from the death of the man she was hoping to marry, although he died several years ago now. We are hoping the change of air will improve her health.'

'I will give a tincture to take which should improve her spirits, together with good, nourishing food.'

Sarah returned to take William up to bed, and shortly afterwards Thomas and Ruth left.

Later, upstairs, Mary sat before her mirror and removed her cap. Samuel could see his own reflection beside hers as he bent to kiss her dark curls. She smiled up at him and took his hand.

'The baby is very active tonight. Feel how his little legs are kicking out against me, Samuel.'

'He could be a girl of course!'

'I shall just be happy with a healthy baby.'

Once again, Samuel's final thought before falling asleep, was the fear of once again losing his wife in childbirth and that he was the only one who could protect her and their unborn child. His talisman, his fossil, was safely put away in a drawer. He was not superstitious, but he hoped it would help him protect those he loved.

You have been looking at a typical day in Samuel Baskett's life. He is once again a happy man. His practice is thriving, and his reputation in the town is growing. But his hopes for the future are inevitably tinged with anxiety, as he looks forward to the birth of his second child.

You look into the chest once more. Tucked down at the bottom you find a small, well-worn book, bound in brown leather...

Chapter 2
The Children's Book

Saturday, 18 June 1774 – East Street, Wareham, Dorset

When you open it, you see it is the one of the books Samuel was reading when he was a boy at the rectory, A Description of a Great Variety of Animals and Vegetables. *The inscription inside reads: "Samuel Baskett's book, the gift of his father". On the next page is a drawing of animals and birds in an idyllic landscape. Above is a quote from the psalms: "The works of the Lord are great, sought out of all of them that have pleasure therein"; underneath, is a quote from the book of Job: "Lo, these are parts of his ways: but how little a portion is heard of him?" The animals chosen are an odd selection – a bezoar goat, a cross between a goat and a deer, from the East Indies; a man-tiger, from Africa, which looks like an ape and is "bold and fierce"; a shagreen, a horse common in Turkey and Poland, where they use its hard, dry skin for pocket utensils, watch cases and toys.*

Mary's baby, born in July three years ago, was indeed a girl, whom they called Jane, after Samuel's mother and his dead sisters. She was followed in March nearly two years later by another little girl, Anna Maria. Mary's third child, four months old, is a boy, whom they have called Samuel. William is now nearly six and is a bright, happy little boy. Molly Brine is now helping Sarah to look after the children as assistant nursery maid.

Samuel and Mary were delighted when their friends, Joseph and Jane Goodwin finally had a healthy baby boy. The Reverend Hutchings completed his History of Dorset *a few weeks before he died a year ago. The work has now just been published with the help of Dr William Cuming from Dorchester, whom Samuel and Lewis met nearly ten years ago.*

Today, Lewis and Ann Cockram and their son, John, who is now four, are travelling from Swanage to Wareham for an overnight visit.

Samuel came out of his shop and looked up at the sky. The overnight rain had stopped and the sun was just coming out from behind the clouds. It was going to be a fine day. Richard Hobbs had told him there were no messages for him, so he was returning home to greet his visitors.

'My dear Mr Baskett!' Samuel turned to see Mrs Hutchins hurrying to catch him up. 'I hope you have received a copy of my dear husband's book.'

'I have indeed, Mrs Hutchins. I am greatly looking forward to reading it. It is very sad that Mr Hutchins did not live to see it published.'

'I have to thank Dr Cuming and Mr Gough and all the subscribers. My daughter and I are so very grateful to all our friends in the town for helping us at this difficult time.'

Mrs Hutchins showed no sign of continuing on her way and Samuel knew Mary would be expecting him at home.

'I hope to see you again soon. Please give my regards to your daughter.'

'And my regards to your wife, Mr Baskett.'

When Samuel got home, he could hear Mary's voice coming from the kitchen. He had lost count of how many people she had invited for dinner. She had told him yesterday that she hoped they could eat in the garden if the weather were warm enough. Mary came out of the kitchen, a list in her hand.

'Samuel, I am glad you have returned early. We need to ask Henry to take a table and chairs into the garden. I have asked Hester to help him.'

'I presume when you say we, you mean me?'

'That would be most helpful.'

Samuel smiled affectionately at his wife. She was never happier than when she was organising other people.

'Lewis warned me years ago, that I would become your slave if I was not careful!'

Mary ignored his remark. 'All the children can come down from the nursery when we have finished eating.'

'All the children? How many are you expecting?'

'There will be little John of course. And I have asked the Goodwins to dinner, so there will be their three. Then Rebecca Hobbs is already here helping in the kitchen, so Sarah and Molly are taking care of her three.'

Soon after marrying and settling into the rooms behind the shop, Richard's wife, Rebecca, had given birth to a daughter and they now had another daughter and a son.

'And how many seats do we need in the garden?'

'Eight, I think. I have also asked Thomas and Ruth to come.'

'You never cease to amaze me, my love.'

Samuel went out in search of Henry, their gardener. He found him in the vegetable garden, picking some peas, and gave him Mary's instructions. Back inside, he went into the parlour and sat on the window seat, Brune lying at his feet. Mary's energy seemed unending; he felt exhausted just watching her. Soon, a carriage drew up in front of the house and he could see Lewis climbing down. He took Ann's hand to help her down and then lifted his little son to the ground. Samuel went into the hall, followed by Brune, as Hester opened the door to their visitors.

'How good to see you all! Mary has so been looking forward to your visit. She seems to have invited half the town to dinner today.'

Mary came down the stairs and embraced Ann, then knelt down to greet John, who was sitting on the floor, his arms around Brune. 'William is upstairs in the nursery. He wants to show you his collections.'

William more and more reminded Samuel of himself at about the same age as his son was now. How he had delighted in looking at his father's collections of butterflies and birds' eggs. William loved looking at the drawings Mary had made in her journal at Newton Manor and had started his own collection of pressed leaves and flowers.

Ann was holding a small parcel. 'We have brought a doll from Newton for Jane and Anna Maria. Lewis says it was your mother's, but you did not ever want to play with it.'

'Oh, yes, I remember it very well. I think my mother was quite upset that all I wanted to do was be outside with my brothers, climbing trees if I could. I think it was called Jemima. I'm sure Jane will love it.'

Mary and Ann went upstairs to the nursery with John.

'I have been reading about the unrest in Boston,' Lewis said, as they walked into the parlour. 'My father is following events closely and wonders if you have heard from your American friend recently.'

'I received a letter from Billey Shippen last month. He is very occupied with his work in the hospital in Pennsylvania. He writes that his father is more involved in the unrest. Billey has also been worried about his wife. She has been very depressed following the death of so many of her babies. She went to the seaside to recuperate and has now started to occupy herself with charitable works. Fortunately, their other children, Nancy and Tommy, are still thriving.'

They were interrupted by the arrival Thomas and Ruth, followed shortly afterwards by Joseph and Jane Goodwin. Jane and Ruth immediately took the children and their nursemaid upstairs to the nursery. The excited cries of the children could be heard from downstairs as the door opened.

Thomas and Joseph joined Samuel and Lewis in the parlour.

'Lewis, allow me to introduce you to my good friend, Mr Joseph Goodwin.'

'Delighted to meet you, Mr Goodwin.' Lewis turned to Samuel. 'Exactly how many people has my sister invited today?'

'I have completely lost count. I love Mary dearly, but sometimes she completely exhausts me with her enthusiasm for life!'

'She also exhausted all her brothers at Newton!'

'Tell us the news from the manor, Lewis.'

'You will recall my brother John's wife, Hannah, left him to return to live with her father, John Kent?'

'And John continued to drink and associate with the young girls of Corfe!'

'Now we hear John Kent has made a will, leaving Hannah and her children two shillings a week and part of the remainder of his estate, but only if she does not dwell or cohabit with her husband! John seems to have accepted these conditions. He is now living with his uncle and continues to work at the quarry.'

'And how is your father?'

'He has completely disowned John, of course. He is now eighty and rarely leaves the house. He spends much of his time with his nose buried in the *Gentleman's Magazine* and insists on reading aloud to us anything which particularly engages him. In addition to the political articles, he also reads out reports of disastrous fires, murders of parents by children, children by parents, husbands by wives and wives by husbands. I must confess that, after a tiring day, I often nod off to sleep. Fortunately, he does not seem to notice, even if I leave the room and return sometime later.'

Their peaceful talk was interrupted, as their wives came in, chattering to each other.

'Dinner will be ready in an hour,' Mary said. 'It is very sunny now, so we can all go out into the garden. The children have come down already.'

Outside, the children were running around on the grass. Samuel and Lewis walked down to the small orchard Mary had started at the end of the garden. The table was already laid for dinner.

Samuel took a letter out of his pocket. 'I have received news from my friend, John Hunter. As usual, it is difficult to read – his writing and spelling are not of the best! He and his wife, Ann, now have three children.' Samuel looked through another page of the long letter. 'He says here that one of his favourite pupils, Edward Jenner, has left the household and is now working as a country doctor. Jenner had been helping him to catalogue the specimens his friend, Joseph Banks, brought back with him from his voyage with Cook.'

'My father was interested in the journal of Cook's voyage round the world when it was reported in the *Gentleman's Magazine*,' Lewis said. 'I shall tell him about your letter.'

'Hunter's book on childbirth has at last been published and he writes that he has performed another caesarean operation. Although, as before, the mother herself died, the child survived. I am not sure if I would be so bold. I would hesitate to perform a caesarean operation myself.'

'Have you continued to inoculate people in the town, Samuel?'

'I am still offering to do so, especially young children, but some parents are still very reluctant. I have inoculated little William and both my daughters without any ill effects.'

'I ask you now because a friend of my father, the Reverend Morgan Jones, visited us at Newton Manor last week. He knows of a farmer, Benjamin Jesty, from Yetminster, who employs two dairymaids. They both developed cowpox after milking cows with the disease. And he observed that they did not contract smallpox when they nursed some relations a few months later.'

'Did Mary not contract cowpox when she was a girl?'

'Yes, we feared she had smallpox at first, but she made a full recovery. She had also milked two of our cows at that time.'

'The symptoms are very similar at first, but cowpox is a much milder disease.'

'Mr Jones told us that Benjamin Jesty then did a very bold thing. He went to a neighbour's farm where he knew some of his cows had signs of cowpox on their udders. He used one of his wife's stocking needles to take some material from a lesion on to the tip. He then inserted it into his wife's arm and repeated the procedure on his sons. Unfortunately, his wife's arm became very inflamed and he had to seek medical assistance from a local physician, Dr Trowbridge, but she made a full recovery. Neither of his sons showed any ill effects.'

'I should very much like to meet Mr Jesty,' Samuel said. 'It seems to be a much safer procedure than using smallpox itself to inoculate people. Did he meet with local opposition to the procedure?'

'Mr Jones says he has become the object of derision and has met with abuse when he attends local markets. Then there are those in the church who say it is against God's will to introduce matter from a beast into a human being.'

'I also met with opposition when I started inoculation here.'

Little Jane came running down the garden. 'Papa, I have a new doll. She is called Jemima.'

Samuel knelt down beside his daughter. 'You are a lucky girl. I believe she was mama's when she was little.'

'Mama says it is time for our dinner. We must go up to the nursery. And you must sit down at the table, papa.'

Lewis laughed. 'Now who, I wonder, does she remind you of, Samuel?'

At the age of three, Jane had her mother's dark curls and brown eyes and her tendency to organise everyone. Her sister, Anna Maria, at fifteen months, had Samuel's own chestnut coloured hair and was content to sit in her highchair and watch everything going on around her.

Sarah called to the children and they followed her into the house. Hester and Rebecca came down the garden, with dishes of food to put on to the table. Lewis and Samuel were soon joined by the other guests. For a while, everyone was occupied in passing dishes up and down the table and filling their plates.

As the chattering went on around him, Samuel was thinking about Benjamin Jesty. What would his father think if he knew he was considering following the same procedure on his patients? His father had been delighted when two of his sons, William, the eldest, and John, his youngest, entered the church but had been bitterly disappointed that Samuel himself had not followed that path. But he had become very close to his father while little William was living at the rectory and he would not want to upset him in any way.

'You are very quiet, Samuel,' Ruth said. 'And you have scarcely touched your food. Are you not well?'

'I must apologise. I am quite well. I was lost in thought.' Samuel smiled at Ruth. She was always first to notice if there was anything wrong with anyone in the family.

Thomas turned to Samuel. 'Do you remember that a man called William Knapp visited the church when were boys?'

'Yes, I do. He came to teach us some hymn tunes and Father insisted we all joined the singers every Sunday when we were old enough.'

'I have been reading Mr Hutchins' book. He writes that William Knapp was born here in Wareham before he went to live in Poole, which is why he named one of his hymn tunes after the town. He died about six years ago, but his hymn tunes remain very popular.'

Samuel took his family to church every Sunday out of habit, rather than conviction. He enjoyed the singing and the distraction from his busy life but had admitted to Thomas that he would probably describe himself as an atheist. He still wanted to save lives, not souls.

Mary, at the other end of the table, laughed at something Lewis said to her. Samuel looked at her and smiled. She was his rock, his beloved companion. He saw her put her hand down under the table to give Brune a piece of chicken. She thought no one noticed, but Samuel always did. He wanted to tell her about Benjamin Jesty's inoculation experiments. He knew she would encourage him if he decided to use the method himself on his patients.

Hester brought out the dessert and Samuel noticed that there was a dish of pineapple; he guessed it had come from Newton Manor. He remembered how proud their gardener, George, had been of his glasshouse and his pineapple bed. His son, young George, had now taken over from his father.

After they had finished their dinner and the plates were being cleared away, they could hear the chattering of the children as they came out of the house and into the garden. Little William came up to his father carrying a book. Recently, Samuel realised that days had gone by without his thinking about his other Mary, William's mother. But then he would see his son's blue eyes, Mary's eyes, and in a moment of guilt, realise she was fading from his memory.

'See, papa, Sarah says this belonged to you when you were a little boy.'

The book was *A Description of a Great Variety of Animals and Vegetables.* Samuel was instantly taken back to the rectory kitchen, where he used to sit quietly, away from the bustle of the nursery, to the sound of Martha, the kitchen maid, shelling peas – the pop, as she opened the pod, followed by the sound of the peas falling into a basin.

'Yes, that is right, William. Can you read it for yourself?'

'I try, papa. But some of the words are difficult. Mostly I look at the pictures.'

Then another memory. An orange butterfly landing on his sleeve as he watched his baby sister's coffin being lowered in the ground. His brother telling him it was the baby's soul.

William ran off, carrying his book. Brune followed him to the bottom of the garden. The little boy lay down on the grass, looking up into the apple tree. The dog lay down beside him.

Samuel went to join Mary, where she was in deep conversation with Lewis and Ann. Their little boy, John, was clinging to his mother's hand, holding a piece of blanket up to his face. He was obviously feeling overwhelmed by the noise of the other children around him. Lewis and Ann had not been able to have any more children and the little boy was a shy, only child.

'I have been telling Mary that I have had a letter from Peter Beckford,' Lewis said. 'He tells me he married the daughter of George Pitt last year. I would think she has brought a fortune with her to Steepleton. He also says that Clementi is no longer living there and is now in London.'

Mary was flushed with indignation. 'I remember Peter Beckford as a very arrogant man when we went there to listen to Clementi. And now he writes that his estates in Jamaica are no longer profitable. And listen to this, Samuel, he says the price of a negro slave has doubled in less than twenty years. How can it be right that a person is actually owned by another person?'

'I recall Father talking about a court case reported in the *Gentleman's Magazine* some time ago,' Lewis said. 'A slave here in England escaped, which meant he was then a free man. But his master found him and forcibly put him aboard a ship to send him to Jamaica. The court ordered he should be freed. And I believe there are some who say all slavery, even in the colonies, should be abolished.'

'I would be most interested to hear more, Lewis.'

'My dear Mary, surely you are far too occupied with the family to worry about such matters,' Ann said.

'I believe it is our duty to learn about the wider world.' Mary was becoming visibly upset and Samuel was relieved when their daughter, Jane, trotted down the garden, carrying her new doll.

'Mama, Jemima has been a naughty girl.'

Mary smiled at the little girl. 'What has she done?'

'She would not eat her dinner and threw it on to the floor.'

'Just like Anna Maria yesterday?'

'Yes, mama. And Jemima should have a new dress. This one looks very old. I shall ask Aunt Ruth to make her some new clothes.'

Ruth was always delighted to be involved in the lives of her nieces and nephews. Jane ran up to her aunt, who greeted her warmly.

Samuel stood quietly by himself, watching his family and friends. Everything seemed well in his world. But he knew that the people he loved most could suddenly be taken from him, leaving an irreplaceable gap in his life.

You wonder how long it will be before you next see Samuel. Will he have an opportunity to meet Benjamin Jesty? And will Mary find out more about the slave trade? Then there is the American question. Will Samuel's friend, Billey Shippen, become more involved in the unrest?

You decide to bring out the next object from the chest to learn more of Samuel's story. Tucked down the side of the chest is a long, narrow book...

Chapter 3
The Account Book

Thursday, 21 October 1779 – East Street, Wareham, Dorset

When you open the book, you see it is Samuel's accounts ledger. The first entry, in what you guess is Samuel's own hand, was made early in 1765, charging Nathaniel Bestland nine pence for two emetic powders. Each entry notes the date, to whom it was sold and cost of the medicine or treatment. The inhabitants of Wareham suffered from many things, including gout, scalds, coughs, inflammation of the eyes and stoppage of urine, in addition to more serious ailments, such as the measles, scarlet fever and cancer.

In a separate section, Samuel lists the births he has attended, noting whether it was natural, laborious, involved forceps or resulted in the death of the child. He charged according to the wealth of the patient, varying from a guinea to nothing. Later in the book, many customers have a separate page. Mr and Mrs Hutchins frequently bought powders for his gout and her rheumatism; Farmer Collins regularly requested medicines for his animals; the Bestland family suffered from a variety of ailments, but often required purges. In 1767, the hand becomes much neater and smaller; this must be Mary's writing before she died. After that, until 1771, Samuel kept his own accounts. Then, once again the hand changes to that of Richard Hobbs. Searching through the book, you find a section headed "Inoculation", but you can see nothing obvious to indicate whether Samuel had used Benjamin Jesty's method.

Samuel was right to feel uneasy about those he loved. A few months after you last saw Samuel and Mary, their baby son developed a high fever and died; Samuel blamed himself for not being able to save him. Eighteen months later, Mary gave birth to twin boys, Thomas and Samuel, but once again, the baby called Samuel died. Then Samuel's own younger brother, Robert Russell, died and was buried in Shapwick. Mary's father had become increasingly frail and confused in his last years, wandering around the garden, searching for his wife, not realising she had died over twenty years before; he died in March. It was only in July, when another little girl, Charlotte, was born, that Mary started to become her usual cheerful, enthusiastic self. The little girl is a healthy, happy baby.

The household has expanded in the last few years. Their nursemaid, Sarah, who is now in her late fifties, is now governess, teaching Jane and Anna Maria; Molly is now assisted in the nursery by Lizzie Cribb. Mr Harding, who had been tutor in Swanage to Mary's brothers, is now living in Wareham and teaching William.

Today, you see Samuel leaving home to walk to his shop. It is a misty, early autumn morning and he walks briskly, wearing his warm coat and thick breeches.

Two figures were emerging out of the mist. Samuel recognised the scarlet jackets of soldiers from the militia. They raised their hats to Samuel as they passed by. There had been great excitement among the young girls in Wareham, when the South Battalion of the Lincolnshire Militia arrived in the town to camp by the river. Mary had told him that Lizzie, their nursery maid, had been seen walking over the bridge towards Stoborough, arm in arm with one of the soldiers.

When he arrived at his shop, Richard was already measuring out some syrup of poppies for Mrs Savage.

'Little George have got a bad cough, Mr Baskett.'

Samuel recalled he had delivered the baby in the summer, just before his own daughter, Charlotte, was born, so he was only about three months old.

'There have been several cases of chin cough in the town recently. Is your baby able to breathe easily, Mrs Savage?'

'No, he do catch his breath and do cough with a strange noise, like a dog barking.'

'I shall call to see him in half an hour and bring some more medicine.'

Mrs Savage hurried out of the shop looking anxious.

'Richard, please measure out some testaceous powder for me to take to Mrs Savage. It may do some good, but I very much fear that such a young baby will not survive the disease.'

Later in the morning, Samuel was to visit Farmer Collins. Some of his cattle had developed cowpox and Samuel planned to collect some material from the lesions on their teats. Earlier in the year, Samuel, accompanied by Lewis and the Reverend Morgan Jones, had eventually met Benjamin Jesty at his farm in Yetminster, to learn about the method of inoculation using cowpox. Jesty was adamant that he was not intending to inoculate anyone apart from his own family; the opposition in the town had been too strong. Before using this new method on his patients, Samuel wanted to inoculate his own baby daughter. Mary and he had discussed whether to conduct the experiment on Charlotte and had agreed it seemed a far safer method than using material from a smallpox patient.

Samuel decided not to tell his father of his intentions. He had visited Owermoigne in the summer, when an elderly relation, the Reverend Brinsden, was staying at the rectory. Charles Brinsden had told them he intended to leave his entire estate to Samuel's father in his will, and that it would please him greatly if Samuel would name the baby Mary was expecting after him; and so, they had called the baby Charlotte Brinsden. From the conversations between the two elderly men, it was obvious to Samuel that they both still held firmly to the conventional views of the church. He remembered that some of the opposition in Yetminster was due to the view that matter from a beast should not be introduced into a human being.

Samuel set out to visit baby George Savage. It was as he feared; the baby had the whooping cough and a high fever. All he could do was give his mother the powder and advise her to bathe the baby's face with cool water.

The walk to farmer Collins' land took him about half an hour, which gave him enough time to consider the implications of inoculating baby Charlotte. If she suffered no ill effects, he would inoculate his patients in the same way. But would he tell them? Perhaps it would be wise not to comment, just to make a note in his ledger. Could he trust Mr Collins to say nothing? He had already inoculated the farmer's wife and children in the conventional way, with no ill effects. He knew the family worshipped at the Old Meeting House; what was their belief concerning the introduction animal matter into humans? He had not yet told Mr Collins the purpose of his visit, merely sending a message by his man to say he was bringing the sheep wash he had requested. The further he walked, the more questions came to his mind.

The mist began to clear, but he could see dark clouds approaching from the west. He was glad he had remembered to bring his umbrella. By the time he arrived at the farm, it was beginning to rain.

Mr Collins greeted him at the door of the farmhouse. 'Tell me the real reason you are come to visit me on such a wet morning, Mr Baskett. I know you would not have come yourself merely to bring me some sheep wash!'

Samuel smiled. 'You have read me like a book, my dear Mr Collins. Can I trust you not to tell the townspeople about the purpose of my visit – at least not yet.'

'Of course, sir. I am curious to know what you mean.'

The two men sat in Mr Collins' parlour, while Samuel explained why he was there. To his relief, Mr Collins immediately embraced the project.

'If the method is successful, I shall send my man with more of the matter whenever you need it. I shall be honoured to be involved. Now, come outside. The infected cattle are in the barn.'

An hour later, Samuel was walking back home, feeling happy with his morning's work, the stocking needle he had brought with him, carefully placed in an ointment box. As he went into the house, Brune, now aged twelve, got up slowly from his basket in the hall, wagging his tail in greeting. Mary was coming down the stairs from the nursery.

'Charlotte has just woken up and she has had her feed. I have explained to Molly what we intend to do. I hope that was right, Samuel?'

'Of course, my love. Charlotte might be slightly unwell following the inoculation, or her arm might be swollen.'

Up in the day nursery, Jane and Anna Maria were sitting at the table. Jane jumped up to greet Samuel.

'Papa, Anna Maria knows all her letters. And I can read my new book. It is about a little girl called Goody Two Shoes.'

'That is excellent, Jane.'

'And Sarah says we can play with the dolls' house after we have had our milk. It is raining so we cannot go out in the garden.'

Little Thomas was sitting on the floor playing with the puzzle Samuel remembered from his childhood at the rectory. William was sitting quietly in the corner arranging his collection of stones and shells. Molly came out of the night nursery, carrying baby Charlotte. Samuel looked around the room. Here were all the people he held most dear. Was he right to be experimenting on Charlotte? He would never forgive himself if anything went wrong. Mary took the baby from Molly and led the way back into the night nursery. Samuel knew she would always support him, whatever the outcome.

Mary gently put the baby down in her cradle and removed her dress. Samuel took the needle from the ointment box and inserted it into her arm just above her elbow. Charlotte screwed up her face and let out a sharp cry.

'I am so sorry, my little one,' Samuel said. 'It is all for your good.'

Mary picked her up and walked round the room, quietly singing to her daughter, who gave her mother a puzzled look.

'Have you told Molly what method we are using, my love?'

'I have told her we are inoculating Charlotte, but not that we are using the matter from cowpox.'

'That is sensible. The news could easily spread around the town if the maids talk to each other about it.'

Mary put the baby back in her crib and went back into the day nursery. 'Can you stay with Charlotte until she falls asleep, Molly?'

Before Molly could answer, Lizzie, the assistant nursery maid, stood in the doorway, turned pale and fell to the floor. Samuel bent down to examine her. Molly stood beside him, wringing her hands.

'Oh, sir, she have fainted again. And this morning she did vomit when she woke up.'

'I very much fear she is with child, Molly. I believe she has been seen with one of the soldiers from the camp.'

'Yes, sir. Hester did see her yesterday.'

Lizzie opened her eyes, sat up and started to struggle to her feet. She looked bewildered, then put her face in her hands. Molly helped her up and sat her on a chair. Mary came and sat down next to her.

'Who is the father of your child, Lizzie?'

The girl started to cry. 'Oh, madam, 'tis Roger Boardman.'

'Does he know of your condition?'

'No, madam.'

'Then you must tell him without delay. Now, go to your room and rest.'

'I shall leave everything in your hands, my love,' Samuel said as they went downstairs. 'I must go back to the shop to find out if I have any messages.'

'We shall have to look for another nursery maid, Samuel. Let us hope this Roger Boardman is in a position to marry her. She has been a very foolish girl. I believe one of the other soldiers had to marry another girl from the town in the summer.'

It was still raining as Samuel walked to his shop. Thomas had told him that the militia would shortly be going to fight in the American war, no doubt breaking the hearts of many of the girls in the town. Samuel had not heard from Billey Shippen for some time. How stupid it was, that two such old friends were now on different sides. The thirteen states had declared their independence three years ago, but the fighting continued. Last year, Billey wrote to say he had become a chief surgeon in the army and, in October, had been appointed head of all the hospitals of the Hudson River. At the same time, he had become involved in a long argument with another surgeon, resulting in his being charged with malpractice and dishonesty. Samuel was appalled to hear this; he knew Billey would never do anything to harm his patients. He had written back to Billey but had received no reply.

When he arrived at the shop, Richard was busy pounding some oak galls in a pot.

'We need some more ink, Mr Baskett. If I start making it now, it will be ready for when the ink is used up.'

'Thank you, Richard. I believe you will be leaving early for your glee club, will you not?'

'Yes, sir. I do not want to be fined for being late. Did I tell you that there was a dispute at our last meeting?'

'Yes. You told me Daniel Baker kicked someone downstairs?'

'He did say that Luke Waterman had accused him of singing out of tune, which greatly displeased Daniel Baker. I do not think he meant for him to fall down the stairs. But I am wondering if either of them will be at the meeting this evening.'

The door opened and an agitated young boy ran into the shop.

'Oh, Mr Baskett, sir, 'tis my sister. She be very bad, sir. My mother do say her baby be nearly born.'

'I shall come with you to help her. What is her name?'

'Mary, sir.'

'And yours?'

'George, sir.'

'Well, George, I shall deliver your sister's baby safely. Richard, I shall go straight home afterwards for dinner. I hope the singing goes well!'

Samuel picked up his bag and followed young George out of the shop and down towards the river. Two hours later, he was walking back home, having delivered not one, but two healthy baby girls. It had become obvious that their mother was not married and that their father was yet another soldier.

At home, he explained to Mary why he was late for his dinner. 'The arrival of the army has done nothing for the town. The sooner they leave, the better. But tell me, how is little Charlotte?'

'She is sleeping, but I believe she has a slight fever. I have told Molly to let me know if she wakes.'

'I really hope I have done the right thing. I will never forgive myself if I have harmed her.'

'We both made the decision. I am sure we have done the right thing, Samuel. Now, we should have our dinner.'

For once, they had no guests. Neither of them said anything for a while.

'I forgot to tell you, Samuel,' Mary said, after they had finished their soup. 'I received a letter from Lewis today. He and Ann send you their best wishes. He asks me to tell you that he has heard that Peter Beckford has money problems again and has mortgaged two of his plantations to Baron Rivers.'

'And he seemed so prosperous when we saw him.'

'But the best part, Samuel, is that his wife has left him for his cousin William. And there is even gossip that she became much too fond of Clementi before he left to go to London.'

'I suppose he will be even more involved with his dogs and horses now.'

'As you know, I have never liked him, so I am not sorry about his misfortunes.' Mary helped herself to some chicken and took a sip of her wine. 'And Lewis says we will be most welcome to stay with them when we go to my brother William's wedding next month. Now tell me, I believe you received a package from John Hunter yesterday. You have not told me what it contained.'

'He thought I would be interested in a pamphlet about a German doctor called Meyerbach, who lived in London until this summer. The man was a rogue. He was taking advantage of the folly of the public and making about a thousand guineas a month.'

'I would not want you to become a villain for double that money, my love. I would rather lose everything than know you were dishonest. How did he deceive people?'

'He said he could cure diseases by inspecting a patient's urine. But it was discovered that he could do nothing of the sort.'

'How did they find out?'

'When people began to suspect him, they decided to make some experiments to test the doctor's skill. One young man took a vial of cow's urine to the doctor, instead of his own. He was told it showed he was suffering from a high fever. Another time a gentleman took the urine of a seventy-year-old woman to the doctor, who said the patient was pregnant.'

'So where is he now?'

'John Hunter wrote a note at the front of the pamphlet. He says that once the doctor realised this summer that he had lost his reputation, he suddenly quit the country and retired to Germany to enjoy his ill-gotten wealth!'

Mary took an apple from the bowl in front of her and began cutting it into quarters. 'Do you remember, Samuel, that Lewis used to call you a quack and you called him Farmer Williams? I thought, when I was little, it meant you were going to keep ducks. I am very relieved you did not turn into a quack yourself.'

'Thank you, my love, I do my best. Let us hope that if I admit to using cowpox matter to inoculate my patients that they won't consider me a quack.'

When they had finished their dinner, they both went up to the nursery. It was already getting dark and the lamps had been lit. Charlotte was still sleeping peacefully and her slight fever had left her. The other children were still in the day nursery. William was spending more and more of his time looking through the microscope, which had belonged to his mother. Once again, Samuel saw his younger self in his son, as if he were looking into the past. And Jane was becoming more and more like her mother. Anna Maria seemed quite happy to be told what to do by her elder sister. Now, she was sitting on the floor, watching Jane arrange the animals in their Noah's ark.

'The giraffes must go behind the lions. Then the cows should go behind the goats. They are farms animals.'

'Come, Thomas, it is your bedtime,' Molly said to the little boy, who was sitting on the floor, turning the pages of the picture book Mary had made for William.

'No, not bedtime.'

Mary knelt down beside her son. 'Yes, Thomas, you must drink your milk and get into your bed. You can look at your book tomorrow. Tell me, Molly, how is Lizzie?'

'She be better, madam. She have gone to see Roger Boardman to tell him about her condition.'

'We shall need someone else to help in the nursery soon, Molly. Let me know if you know of a reliable girl willing to take on the position.'

Downstairs, Samuel and Mary settled down to an evening together by the fire. Samuel could not help remembering the times he had sat with Mary, William's mother, the love of his life, looking forward to his future with her. She would sit quietly by his side, sewing or writing letters. It was difficult to prevent himself thinking of what might have been. But now, Mary, the mother of his other children, with Brune sitting at her feet, occupied herself reading, commenting on scientific topics and expressing her thoughts on the matters of the day. And he told himself to reflect on how lucky he was to have the support of such a loving, lively wife and companion.

You decide to look at the account book once again. Did Samuel give any indication, however secret, of inoculation using cowpox? You can still see no sign, so perhaps he only used the method on his own children. You delve into the chest again. At the bottom, you can feel quite a large object. When you lift it out, you see it is a leather bag...

Chapter 4
The Medical Bag

The bag is worn, especially at the corners. The clasp is stiff and when you manage to undo it and look inside, you are disappointed to see it appears to be empty. But delving down to the bottom, you find what seems to be a small saw, with its blade missing. This must be Samuel's medical bag, which he took with him when visiting his patients.

The Lincolnshire militia left Wareham for America and were replaced by soldiers from the Surrey militia, until they too left. Lizzie married Roger Boardman; that year, three other girls from the town also married soldiers; the following year, two soldiers from the Surrey militia married local girls.

Charlotte was not affected by her inoculation and is now a cheerful, affectionate four-year-old. She has her mother's dark curly hair. It seems that Samuel and Mary are not able to keep any of their sons other than Thomas; two more little boys, Charles Brinsden and another Samuel, were born and survived no more than a few months. But now there is another healthy baby girl, Sarah, in the nursery, born in January.

William is fifteen and now attends Sherborne School. His cousin, Lewis's son John, is also at the school. Thomas and Charlotte are being taught by Sarah, now over sixty; but Mary decided that Jane and Anna Maria should join Joseph and Jane Goodwin's daughters at a boarding school in Hampshire. All their school fees are paid by Samuel's father, with the money left to him by the Reverend Brinsden.

Lizzie's cousin, Martha, is now assistant nursemaid and Henry Hobbs, the gardener, has been joined by Jamie Twine, a strong, willing lad from the town. Their old dog, Brune, died a year ago. A year before that, Lewis and Ann had given the family another spaniel puppy.

It is the day before Good Friday; William, Jane and Anna Maria are expected home for the Easter holidays. It is a fine, cool April day, with a light, southerly breeze. You find Samuel and Mary at breakfast in the dining room.

Mary took another bread roll and poured herself some more chocolate.

'Thomas and Charlotte are so much looking forward to seeing William and the girls.'

'In his letter, Lewis said they should arrive with William before dinner.'

'It will be so good to see Lewis and Ann again. It was kind of them to bring William home.'

'And we are lucky Joseph and Jane will bring Jane and Anna Maria back.'

'So, all we have to do is wait!'

'Well, my love, I shall have to go to see if any of my patients need me before I can do that.'

'And I shall help Betty and Hester prepare dinner for us all.'

Samuel finished his coffee and got up from the table and gave Mary a quick kiss.

'I shall try not to be too late.'

As Samuel walked to his shop, he thought once again about Billey Shippen. He had written to his friend after the King had spoken to parliament saying that he had no further objections to the Declaration of Independence by the thirteen American states and that he had given orders for all fighting to stop. It had been a relief to know that his friend was no longer in danger. He had last received a letter from Billey nearly three years ago, saying he had been appointed professor of anatomy and surgery at Pennsylvania University. Almost as an afterthought, he had added that he had escaped conviction by one vote on charges of neglecting the soldiers in his charge. Had Billey perhaps changed from the caring student he had known twenty-five years ago? He very much hoped not. And had he himself changed? His purpose in life was still to save people and now, of course, to look after his family.

As he opened the door of the shop, he could hear a baby crying. His assistant, Richard Hobbs and his wife Rebecca, now had a son and five daughters, the youngest a few months old. Samuel wondered how they all fitted into the rooms behind the shop.

'I must apologise for all the noise, sir. 'Tis the baby's teeth. She were awake all night.'

'Rebecca must know what to do by now!'

'Yes, sir. Her mother have given her a necklace to put on round the baby's neck. She do say it charms away the teething pains. What do you think, Mr Baskett?'

'I do not think it will help, Richard. I have heard of its use, but there is no proof it works. The best thing is to let the baby chew on a teething ring or a crust of bread, as I am sure Rebecca will know. Or perhaps rub her gums with a mixture of herbs and ginger.'

Samuel was thinking he was to have a quiet morning, when the door opened and an agitated young man came into the shop. Samuel recognised him as Thomas Savage, the son of an elderly woman he had treated about two weeks before. She had fallen down whilst visiting her family and had broken her right arm. It was not a simple fracture, and part of the bone had pierced her skin. Samuel had had difficulty setting the bone and binding the wound, but he had learned, while studying with John Hunter, to avoid amputation of a limb if at all possible.

'Mr Baskett, I would be most grateful if you could examine my mother again. She is still in great pain and I am fearful that the wound is not healing as it should.'

'I will come with you immediately, Thomas.'

Samuel followed the young man down the street and around the corner to a large house in West Street towards the outskirts of the town. Immediately Samuel saw Mrs Savage, he knew her condition had deteriorated. He gently unwrapped the bandages binding the leather splint. The stench from the wound was overpowering. Samuel knew that gangrene had set in and there was now nothing he could do to save his patient's arm.

Samuel took Thomas to one side, so the old lady could not hear what he was saying. 'I shall need you to assist me, Thomas. The only way to save your mother's life is to amputate her arm. But first you need to explain what I intend to do. I shall return to the shop for the implements I need and some laudanum to ease the pain.'

Samuel knew that Thomas and his wife, Betty, had lost their baby nearly four years ago and it seemed they were unable to have more children. It was not an easy time for them. Back in the shop, he put a bottle of laudanum and his amputating saw into his bag.

'Richard, I need you to come with me, to act as my assistant. Do you think you will be able to withstand the sight of the blood?'

'I have seen many of the wounds you have treated in your surgery, sir.'

Hurrying once again along West Street, Samuel could not help thinking of the sailors on board the hospital ship nearly twenty years ago. The images of men screaming in pain, the blood pouring from their wounds, had stayed with him ever since, and had become his regularly recurring nightmare. Would he be able to perform a successful amputation after all this time? It would very much depend on whether he would be able to bind the wound and stop the flow of blood after the amputation.

'Richard, I shall need you to help Mr Savage hold his mother down, while I perform the operation. And you can hand me my saw when I am ready to cut through the bone.'

Richard looked apprehensive. 'I shall do my best, Mr Baskett.'

As they prepared for the operation, Samuel tried to hide his anxiety. He remembered how he had often felt physically sick before operating, whilst on the hospital ship. But once he had the knife in his hand, his uneasiness ceased. They gently lifted Mrs Savage on to the large kitchen table and Samuel gave her a few drops of laudanum.

'This will help to ease your pain, madam. I promise I shall perform the operation as quickly as I can.'

The old lady nodded, shut her eyes and gripped her son's hand tightly. Samuel picked up his knife and cut through the skin around her right arm, then through the fat and muscle down to the bone. Handing the knife to Richard, he saw his assistant was trembling. But there was no time to lose. He had to tie his patient's blood vessels to prevent a haemorrhage occurring.

Richard handed Samuel his amputation saw and he quickly removed the bone below the elbow. Lastly, he pulled the skin over the bone and bandaged Mrs Savage's arm. Thomas helped his mother to sit up and he and Richard lifted her from the table and sat her in a chair.

'I shall come back tomorrow to change the dressing and examine the wound. In the meantime, your mother should rest and try not to move her arm.'

'Thank you, Mr Baskett. My wife will prepare a little nourishment for her. We shall see you tomorrow.'

Walking back with Richard to the shop, Samuel wondered if there was anything he could have done to prevent Mrs Savage's arm becoming septic.

Perhaps he should have returned sooner to examine the wound. He decided to write to John Hunter for his advice. He noticed Richard looked pale and shaken.

'I am sorry I was not more help to you, Mr Baskett. 'Tis the sight of the blood.'

'You did well, Richard. Do not worry.' Samuel thought that perhaps he had asked too much of the young man. 'Let us hope no one else needs us today.'

Samuel was very relieved the operation appeared to have gone well, but he knew there was still a chance that the wound would not heal properly. When they got back to the shop, Samuel decided that Richard had done enough for one day.

'Go and be with your family, Richard. I shall go home now, but let me know if anyone needs me urgently. Anything else can wait until tomorrow.'

When he got home, he could hear a great deal of noise coming from the parlour. As he opened the door, he was immediately greeted by his daughter, Jane.

'Papa, it is so good to be home and to see Little Brune again.' She bent down to fondle the little dog's ears. He wagged his tail and licked her cheek.

Mary was talking animatedly to Jane Goodwin, while their daughters were chattering and giggling excitedly. Joseph Goodwin came up to Samuel.

'My dear fellow, you look exhausted. Have you had a busy morning?'

'I have indeed. It is very noisy in here. Perhaps we could take a turn round the garden.' As they walked, Samuel explained to Joseph what he had been doing. 'So, I hope no one else needs me for the rest of the day.'

'My role as mayor seems very unimportant after hearing what you do every day.' Joseph had already been mayor seven years ago and his father, Robert, had been mayor twice. 'I shall be glad when someone else takes over next year. I get weary dealing with all the petty matters in the town.'

They had reached the vegetable garden, where Henry was planting out some lettuces and Jamie was weeding the herb beds.

'I see the strawberry plants have plenty of flowers already, Henry.'

'Yes, sir, they be doing well this year.'

As they turned to go back inside the house, Samuel could hear William's voice, now that of a young man. His son was the same age as he had been when he had first seen Mary Templeman. He felt in his pocket for his ammonite, his talisman. It was time to pass it on to William. To tell him how he had first met and fallen in love with his mother.

'Father! There you are. It is good to be home again.'

'Precisely what your sisters said!'

'Now,' Joseph said, 'I shall fetch my wife and daughters and return home, if I can drag them away. Our dinner will be ready soon.'

Samuel shivered. 'It is getting cold out here. I shall come in now. I feel considerably refreshed. Thank you once again, my dear fellow, for bringing my daughters home.'

After Joseph, Jane and their daughters had left, Molly brought Thomas and Charlotte down from the nursery. Charlotte threw herself at William, who picked the little girl up in his arms, laughing.

'William, you must come upstairs.'

'Why is that, my Little Mouse?'

'I have done some drawings. You will like them.'

'Later. After we have had our dinner,' William said, smiling and putting his little sister back down on to the floor.

'I see yet another Mary,' Lewis said to Samuel.

'At least Anna Maria does not want to organise anyone.' Samuel looked over to where his daughter was sitting quietly by herself, absorbed in her embroidery. 'I sometimes worry that she is too quiet, that she is in Jane's shadow.'

'Ann and I also worry about John. He is very unhappy at school. He finds it very difficult to make friends. Even when his cousins came to Newton when he was small, he would never join in their games. The only thing he really enjoys is helping on the farm.'

'Perhaps you should consider taking him away.'

'I have already spoken to Mr Cox. You remember Mrs Cox was Mary's governess until she married?'

'Indeed. And Mr Cox taught her to read Latin. Mary still speaks of them both with great affection.'

'They moved from Langton to a small house in Swanage last year, and Mr Cox said he and his wife would be delighted to tutor John at home.'

Molly took the younger children back to the nursery and Mary went with them to feed baby Sarah. It was nearly time for dinner. Samuel and Lewis remained sitting by the fire in the drawing-room.

'Samuel, I have been reading about something you will find most interesting. As you know, I have continued to take the *Gentleman's Magazine* ever since my father died. In the February issue, there is a review of a book containing an account of how Mr Herschel has discovered another planet, which he had at first thought to be merely a comet. He has called it the Georgian star, after the King.'

'I know Mary will also be interested in hearing this. You must tell us more at dinner.'

The conversation around the dinner table was lively. As they had all just returned home, William, Jane and Anna Maria joined them instead of having their dinner in the nursery. Samuel sat and listened with affection to the chatter of his family. William was telling Lewis about his frustration over the lack of natural philosophy and mathematics teaching at his school and how he thought Mr Toogood, the headmaster, was becoming vague in his old age. At the other end of the table, he could hear Jane complaining to her mother that all they did at their school was sewing, spelling, French and playing the spinet.

'We learnt so much more at home with Sarah and you, mama. And I know Mary and Jane Goodwin feel the same.'

'What do you think, Anna Maria?'

'She enjoys the sewing, as you know, mama. Do you not, Anna Maria?'

Her sister blushed and nodded. 'Yes, but I would prefer to be at home, mama.'

'Lewis, tell Mary about the new planet. You say Mr Herschel thought at first it was another comet.'

'Yes. He was looking at double stars at the time.'

'What are double stars, sir?' William looked puzzled.

'They are merely two stars which appear to be very close together in the sky. Their movement, getting closer or further apart, can then be observed. I remember, Mary, you were always eager to look at the sky at night through Father's telescope. I believe Mr Herschel's sister assists him in his studies.'

'I remember Father saying I had to go to bed and not stay up when Samuel was visiting us.' Mary turned to Samuel. 'Perhaps we could buy a telescope. I'm sure William would enjoy examining the night sky when he is home.'

Samuel smiled at his son, remembering how he himself had looked through Mr Cockram's telescope during his visits to Newton. 'I shall make enquiries.'

'Before I forget, I have heard from Peter Beckford,' Lewis said. 'You remember his wife left him and went to live in Bath, so he was living alone at Steepleton.'

'I remember thinking it was no more than he deserved.' Mary helped herself to some apple pie.

'You are probably right, Mary. But now he has heard that Louisa has tuberculosis and he has decided to take her to Italy in the hope the warmer climate will help her. So, you see, Mary, he is not all bad.'

Mary continued eating and said nothing. Samuel knew that once she had made up her mind about anyone or anything, it was very hard to make her change her mind. He caught Lewis's eye and they smiled ruefully to each other.

In the drawing-room after dinner, while they drank their tea, Samuel could not stop himself thinking of the operation he had performed that day and hoped he would not dream again of his time on the hospital ship. Looking around the room, he thought once again how lucky he was to have such a loving, close family. Mary was sitting by the fire with their daughters, William was deep in conversation with Lewis about the discovery of the new planet and Ann was telling John he could leave school and stay at home. But he knew only too well how everything could change in a moment, with no warning.

Lewis, Ann and John were to stay the night in the coaching inn, the Black Bear, in South Street, before returning to Newton Manor in the morning. As Samuel said goodbye to his guests, there was a full moon lighting up the street outside. He watched as they walked towards the centre of the town until Lewis turned to raise his hand as they rounded the corner.

When will you next see Samuel and Mary and their family? Will Mary and Jane Goodwin decide to take their daughters away from school? Will John Cockram be happier remaining at home? And you wonder if Mrs Savage will recover from her operation and hope Samuel will not have nightmares about his time on the ship.

You decide to look for a further clue and open the chest once again. Tucked down the side of the chest is a mahogany-framed looking glass...

Part 4
Mary Baskett

Chapter 1
The Looking Glass

Wednesday, 20 November 1776 – East Street, Wareham, Dorset

The looking glass is about eighteen inches high and twelve inches wide, with carved scrolling on the top. The silvering on the back of the glass has deteriorated in places and there is a small crack at the bottom of the mahogany frame. You look at your own reflection in the glass and try to imagine all the faces from the past reflected in it. The mirror was left to Mary's mother, Sarah, in her father's will and after she died, Mary hung it in her own chamber. She would gaze into it and imagine her mother's smiling face looking back at her. When she moved to Wareham, the mirror was one of the few items she brought with her.

Three months ago, Mary gave birth to twin boys, Samuel and Thomas, named after Samuel's brother. Thomas is thriving, but little Samuel, much smaller than his brother at birth, is giving cause for concern. Mary is finding it more difficult to recover from her latest pregnancy and is perpetually tired. Their nursemaid, Molly, is now assisted by Lizzie Cribb, who is only fifteen.

William has become an enthusiastic pupil of Mr Harding and is getting more and more like his father, keen to learn as much as he can about the world around him. Jane is now five and still eager to organise everyone, especially her sister, Anna Maria.

It is a stormy November day and this morning you find Mary sitting by herself in the parlour, a volume of the Encyclopaedia Britannica *open on her lap, Brune asleep at her feet.*

Mary looked up, as a particularly heavy shower of rain lashed the window. The children would not be able to go out today. Later, she would show William the article on astronomy she was reading. It included an illustrated section

145

explaining how the moon causes the ebbing and flowing of the tides. She was finding it difficult to concentrate and had read the same paragraph several times.

Samuel had already left for his shop, saying he would be back as soon as he could. Mary thought that sometimes, recently, he seemed very quiet. She knew he was worried about his friend Billey Shippen after the Americans had declared independence and he had read about the fighting between British and American forces. And she wondered whether he was thinking of the other Mary, William's mother.

The doorbell rang. She could hear Ruth's voice in the hall talking to Hester. Mary wondered how she would have coped recently without Ruth's almost daily visits. She got up from her seat to greet her. Ruth looked wind-blown and was handing her wet umbrella to Hester.

'My dear Mary, I would have been here earlier, but I met Mrs Hutchins while I was in the haberdashery.'

'I know it is difficult to get away once she starts talking!'

'She was telling me she has just received a letter from her daughter. Her wedding in Bombay Cathedral seems to have been a very grand affair.'

In June, Mrs Hutchins' daughter, Anne, had married John Bellasis, a Lieutenant in the East India company. Anne had met her husband-to-be at the home of a friend of her father and had travelled to India a year ago.

'She seems to be enjoying life in India, but finds the weather in Bombay very hot and tiring.'

They went into the parlour and sat down. Ruth turned to Mary and took her hand. 'Now, Mary, tell me how you are feeling today.'

'I am still very tired, and worried about little Samuel. He is not feeding as he should. Thomas has a splendid appetite.'

'I am sure he will be thriving soon. We know Anna Maria was slower than her sister in all respects, but she is a healthy little girl now, is she not?'

'That is true. In fact, she is learning her letters already and is quicker in that respect than Jane!'

'Jane seems to find it difficult to concentrate on her lessons.'

'Grace used to say I was always looking out of the window instead of listening to what she was saying. But once Miss Clarke arrived, I was always eager to go to my lessons.'

Ruth got up and smiled at Mary. 'I will go up to the nursery to see if there is anything I can do. It will do you good to sit here quietly.'

'No, I shall come with you. The babies will be ready for their feed. Samuel says that feeding them both myself is the reason I am so tired. But I am reluctant to pass them over to a wet-nurse. Molly and Lizzie give them a bottle of milk and water at night, so I am able to sleep.'

Upstairs, it was far from peaceful. They could hear both twins crying for their feed in the night nursery. Jane rushed up to her mother.

'Mama, Anna Maria has taken all the animals out of the ark. I must put them all back now. They have to be in the right place.'

Anna Maria was sitting on the floor, tears running down her cheeks. Molly picked up the little girl. 'They be very restless today, madam. 'Tis the weather I should think.'

Ruth took Jane by the hand. 'We can soon put all the animals back. But you must learn to share your toys with your sister.'

Samuel took a little milk, then soon fell asleep. But Thomas took his feed greedily, looking up at Mary as he sucked. Once Mary had finished feeding them, she felt exhausted. In the day nursery, Sarah was sitting with the girls, reading to them from *A Pretty Little Pocket Book.* Mary remembered Grace reading the book to her at Newton Manor. Sometimes she longed to be back there. She still missed all the animals on the farm, especially her pony, Hodge.

She stood in the doorway, watching her daughters. She had never imagined she would ever have felt anything but total joy after marrying Samuel. She still loved him dearly, of course, but now all her time seemed to be occupied by domestic activities. What had happened to her dreams of travelling to the countries she had only read about? Or her wish to be like Samuel and help to cure people? None of that would ever happen now. She had felt recently that she had nothing to look forward to. She knew that was nonsense, of course. She was part of a loving family and had many good friends. Ruth broke into her thoughts.

'Come downstairs again, Mary. Perhaps the rain will stop later. We could go for a walk. I am sure the fresh air will cheer you up.'

'You are right, Ruth. I just feel a little down today.'

As they started to leave the nursery, Mary noticed their nursemaid, Molly had tears in her eyes.

'What is wrong, Molly?'

'Oh madam, my cousin, Thomas, he do say his mother has taken to her bed ever since his father died just two weeks ago.'

'I shall ask Mr Baskett to call to see her, Molly. Do not worry.'

'Thank you, madam. I shall tell our Thomas when I see him later.'

Downstairs, Mary turned to go to the kitchen. 'I must see Betty about dinner.'

'I shall go, Mary. Betty will have already decided what she will cook for dinner. You should forget about trying to organise everyone and everything.'

Mary smiled ruefully. 'You are quite right, Ruth. Samuel is always telling me the same thing!'

Back in the parlour, Mary continued to read the article on the moon and tides. She stood up and took her orrery out of the cabinet beside the fireplace. It always reminded her of another time in her life, when she had felt she had little to live for. Her father had given her the orrery for her birthday in September. Earlier, in February, Miss Clarke had married Mr Cox. Her dog, the first Brune, had died that summer. And in October she had learnt that Samuel was to marry Mary Templeman.

'Then at Christmas, Mr and Mrs Cox gave me a present. And it was you,' she told the second Brune, who was lying by her side. 'And suddenly I began to feel happy again.'

The dog got up, wagging his tail, laid his head on her lap and licked her hand while she fondled his silky ears. Ruth came in and sat down next to Mary.

'Betty has already been to the butcher. She is making a good beef stew and an apple pie for dinner.'

'What would I do without you, Ruth?' Mary could feel her eyes begin to prick with tears. 'I was never like this when the girls were born.'

She got up and went to the window. There was no sign that the rain would stop soon. The garden looked bleak and grey. She remembered how she had been so proud of her little garden at Newton Manor and how she had been so eager to plan the garden here. Now she left all the work to Henry, who had recently been complaining of his rheumatism.

'I think,' Ruth said coming over and putting her arm around Mary, 'that you need to see more of your friends.'

'Jane Goodwin called yesterday, but I was tired and I think she found me a poor company.'

'Nonsense. I know she will understand. You were such a good friend to her when she lost her babies.'

'We walked in the garden for a while. It seems a very long time since I made the plan for the vegetable beds and started to plant the orchard. Everything looks so dead now.'

They stood watching the rain run down the windowpane.

'It will not be long before the snowdrops begin to appear and soon after that you will be able to see the spring blossom in the orchard.'

'I know you are right, Ruth. I am just being foolish.'

'Where are your plans for the garden? I do not think I have seen them for a while.'

'I think they are in here somewhere.' Mary went to a cabinet and opened a drawer. 'Yes, here they are.'

When Samuel arrived back from the shop an hour later, Mary and Ruth were still sitting at the table, examining the garden plans.

Mary sprang to her feet. 'See, Samuel, we thought we could add a flower bed here, so we would be able to see it from the window in the summer. I should like to plant some hollyhocks and foxgloves at the back, and then some pinks and candytuft in the front. I shall speak to Henry about it. I believe he is in the kitchen. He usually takes the vegetables in for dinner about this time.'

'I am so pleased to see you are more cheerful, my dear Mary.' Samuel turned to Ruth. 'What have you been saying to her to change her mood?'

'I merely asked to see the plans.'

'You are both speaking as if I am not here. I shall be back in a few minutes.' Mary picked up the plans, gave Samuel a quick kiss on the cheek and went out of the drawing room.

In the kitchen, Betty was chopping carrots, parsnips and turnips for the stew, and Hester was stirring a pot on the range. Henry was sitting at the table, a plate of biscuits in front of him. He struggled to his feet as Mary came in.

'Henry, I believe I have been neglecting the garden recently.'

Mary laid the plans out on the table. 'See, I think we should have another flower bed here.' Henry bent over to look at them.

'I have been doing as much as I can in the garden, madam. Last week I did sow your peas and beans for next year. And yesterday, I did dig over the flower beds. The rain do come down very heavy today, so this morning I did work in the greenhouse.'

'That is splendid, Henry. We will speak more tomorrow if the rain clears.'

Back in the parlour, Ruth was sitting by herself.

'I think I may have offended Henry. I did not mean to say he had not been working hard recently. And he is beginning to look quite old.' Mary sighed. She folded up her garden plans and put them back in the cabinet drawer. 'Where is Samuel? I have scarcely seen him today.'

'He has gone to his study. He said he needed to refer to one of his medical books. He is worried about little Abner Symonds.'

'He is the son of John and Frances Symonds, is he not? I remember they lost another baby about a year ago. He was also called Abner.'

'Yes. Samuel said their other baby died of smallpox. He believes it was because they refused to allow him to be inoculated. Now they are saying they will not have their new baby inoculated either. But he is looking very sickly and has a rash.'

'I have told Molly to examine the babies carefully every day. I fear for them so much.'

'Samuel has inoculated them both, has he not?'

'Yes, but there are so many more illnesses. Very many babies do not survive measles or the whooping cough. And my other lovely little baby, Samuel, died of a fever.'

'You worry too much, my dear Mary.' Ruth rose and went to the window. 'The clouds are lifting. I do believe we shall be able to take a walk soon.'

Mary turned towards the door as Samuel came into the room, carrying one of his medical books.

'I believe I am right in thinking little Abner may have scarlet fever. The spots are broader and less regular than the measles. But I hope he may have the milder form of the disease.'

'Is there no way to prevent the measles and scarlet fever in the same way as you inoculate babies against smallpox?'

'I am not aware that there have been any experiments. I shall write to John Hunter to enquire, my love. It would be a great relief.'

Mary remembered her promise to Molly. 'Could you visit Mrs Brine, Samuel? She is Molly's aunt and has taken to her bed since Obadiah Brine died. Molly's cousin is very worried about her.'

'Of course, my love. I shall go tomorrow morning. I know his death was a shock for her.'

Ruth came over to Mary and took her arm. 'I believe the rain has stopped. I shall return home after we have taken a turn round the garden. Thomas is playing his violin in the musical society concert this evening. They will be celebrating St Cecilia's day, which is on Friday. I believe they are to perform part of Mr

Handel's Ode to St Cecilia and a new symphony by Dr Arne. Can I persuade you both to come with me? It will do Mary good to leave the house for a little, will it not Samuel?'

Samuel turned to Mary. 'Yes, my love. The babies will be quite safe with Molly and Lizzie for a while. Joseph Goodwin told me he is to play the flute and I believe Mr Bartlett will be playing his violoncello, will he not, Ruth?'

'Yes. And Thomas is very pleased that he has agreed to become treasurer to replace his father.'

When they came from London to live in Wareham five years ago, Thomas and Ruth had started a musical society. The first concert was held in the Town Hall, which had recently been rebuilt after the great fire. The society was now flourishing and put on a concert each month.

Out in the garden, it was a relief for Mary to feel the cold air on her face. She drew her cloak closely around her. As she and Ruth took the path down to the orchard, she could feel the hem of her skirt becoming wet as it brushed against the damp grass.

'It seems so long since we sat under the apple trees having our lunch. Do you remember, Ruth? I had invited half the town to eat with us. It must be over two years ago. I was so happy that day. My little Samuel was only a few months old and seemed such a healthy baby.'

'We will have more happy, sunny days soon, Mary.'

'Tell me, Ruth. Do you think Samuel regrets marrying me? I sometimes believe he is still missing William's mother – the other Mary.'

'I do not think for one moment he regrets marrying you, my dear Mary. Thomas says he has never known him to be as happy as he is now. And it would be strange if he did not think sometimes of his other Mary. He must be reminded every day when he looks at William. But I know you are the reason he is so contented now. And William has never known a mother other than you.'

Mary once again felt tears coming to her eyes. 'Thank you, Ruth. You always say the right things when I am feeling low.'

'Now, I must return home. And I shall see you at the concert this evening, shall I not? I know you will enjoy listening to the music.'

As they turned to go back into the house, William came running down the path.

'I have finished my lessons for today. Mr Harding has returned home. Papa says he believes you have something to show me in one of your books, mama.'

Mary smiled. 'Yes, William. We were talking the other day about tides, were we not? I have found an article in the encyclopaedia, about how the moon influences the sea. And I have got my orrery out for you. Come, let us get out of the cold.'

It was getting dark. Back in the sitting-room the fire was burning brightly and the lamps were lit. William soon became absorbed in turning the handle on the orrery and seeing how the moon circled the earth.

He went over to the table to look at the open encyclopaedia and frowned. 'I cannot read all the words, mama. It looks very difficult.' He turned a page. 'And I do not understand the diagrams.'

'I also find it difficult. Perhaps you will be able to explain it to me when you are older! We do not need to know all the details, just to remember that the tides rise and fall to a greater degree when there is either a full or new moon.'

'I think the moon today is neither new nor full, so the tides will not rise or fall as much. Is that not right, mama?'

'Exactly, William. Now, it is nearly dinner time. We shall put the orrery away for today.'

After dinner, Mary agreed to accompany Samuel to the musical society concert and to leave the babies with Molly and Lizzie. Although she enjoyed listening to the music, Mary found herself starting to nod off towards the end and it was late by the time they returned home.

Leaving Samuel downstairs in his study, Mary went straight up to their chamber. She picked up her mother's looking glass, as she always did before going to sleep, and examined her own image. Lately, she had noticed slight wrinkles starting to appear at the corners of her eyes and one or two white hairs among her dark curls. She imagined her mother's face smiling at her and telling her not to worry, that she would always be with her. In bed, she soon fell into a deep sleep, stirring only slightly when Samuel joined her an hour later.

You hope that when you again see Mary, her black mood will have lifted. But you know she has more sorrow to come before she becomes happy and optimistic once more. You know Henry will eventually get help in the garden before his rheumatism gets any worse and hope that Mary's plans for the garden can be put in hand.

You decide to delve into the chest again. Tucked down at the bottom you find something wrapped up in brocade fabric...

Chapter 2
The Wooden Doll

Wednesday, 18 July 1781 – East Street, Wareham, Dorset

When you unwrap the fabric, you find a small, wooden doll. Her dress is made of cream brocade; it has long sleeves, trimmed with pale pink ribbon and fine cream lace; perched on her dark brown hair, is a matching cap; over her skirt is a narrow apron in cream silk, embroidered with pink flowers and green leaves. She has rosy red cheeks, a small red mouth, curved eyebrows above large, dark eyes and a small nose, slightly chipped at the end.

Baby Charlotte is a cheerful, friendly little girl. She is two years old; today is her birthday, which she shares with her sister, Jane, who is ten. Anna Maria is now eight and is still a quiet, self-contained child, her pale face sprinkled with freckles. William is twelve and will start attending Sherborne School after the summer holidays, his fees paid by his grandfather with the money left to him by his friend, Charles Brinsden. As you know, Samuel and Mary have lost yet another baby when he was only two months old. And now Mary is pregnant again; the new baby is due to be born at the end of January.

Henry now has help in the garden; Jamie Twine is a tall, strong lad and does all the heavy digging and pruning. When Lizzie Cribb married Roger Boardman, her cousin Martha replaced her in the nursery.

Today, there is to be a meal to celebrate the birthdays. Lewis, Ann and John will arrive by dinner time from Newton Manor. It is a fine but windy day, with flying clouds. You find Mary in the kitchen.

Betty looked up from stirring a pot on the stove, her face flushed from the heat. 'I have made a good jelly for Miss Jane, madam. And she did specially ask me for strawberries. Henry did pick them for her this morning.'

'Excellent, Betty. And Mr Cockram will bring a pineapple from Newton Manor.'

'And I have made a chicken pie, madam. I know how Miss Jane do love her pies.'

'William, Jane and Anna Maria will eat at the table with us today, Hester. But Thomas and Charlotte will have their dinner in the nursery as usual. It is not warm enough to eat outside.'

Hester was standing at the sink, peeling potatoes. 'Betty have told me there will be ten at the table. May I ask Jamie to help me bring more chairs to the dining room, madam?'

'Of course, Hester. And I shall ask Martha to come down from the nursery to help you carry the food from the kitchen.'

The door from the garden opened and Jamie Twine stumbled into kitchen, carrying an armful of vegetables.

'Put them down there, on the table, Jamie.' Betty went over to look at what he had brought.

'I shall need more cabbage if we are to feed everyone. And where are the carrots, Jamie?'

Jamie took off his cap and went red. 'P'rhaps I did drop them. Henry did give them to me, I know.'

Betty looked exasperated. 'Just go and get the rest of the things, Jamie. And tell Henry I shall need lettuces, radishes, beetroot and more tomatoes for the salad. And then come in and help Hester carry some extra chairs into the dining room.'

Jamie shambled out again, muttering to himself.

'I don't suppose he will remember what I have told him, madam. He be very good at digging, but not much else.'

Mary turned to go. 'I am sure the dinner will be splendid, Betty.'

Recently, she had taken Ruth's advice and had come to rely more and more on the servants to arrange domestic matters themselves. She climbed the stairs up to the nursery where everything seemed unexpectedly peaceful. Molly no longer had a tiny baby to care for at the moment, but of course that would change in the new year. Would this new baby thrive or would he or she be another sickly child? Mary prayed every day for a healthy baby, but often her prayers in the past had been unanswered. In her heart she knew Samuel was right. God took no part in saving lives; only physicians and surgeons could do that.

Lessons were finished for the day. William was showing Charlotte and Thomas his collection of stones and shells. Mary had given William her own collection from Newton Manor, together with the book, *The History of Shells*, by Dr Lister. Jane and Anna Maria were sitting at the table with Sarah.

Jane jumped up when she saw Mary. 'Mama, Sarah says my sums are much improved. And Anna Maria can read from *Goody Two Shoes* now.'

'That is excellent. And which book are you reading, Jane?'

'Sarah has given me this one to read, mama, but I am not enjoying it very much.'

Mary went over to the table to examine the book; it was called *The Governess or Little Female Academy*. 'Mrs Goodwin gave it to us. She says her girls have enjoyed reading it.'

'Well, mama, I think it is very tedious. So, I have decided I shall write my own story and then read it to Anna Maria.'

Mary smiled fondly at her daughter. 'What will it be about?'

'It will be the story of Brune, mama, and I want you to help me draw the pictures.'

'Of course, my love. Do you remember the pictures of Brune I painted for William when he was a little boy? I believe he has been showing them to Charlotte.'

'Brune was much younger then, mama. I tried to call him this morning, but he did not hear me until I got really close to him.'

The dog was now almost completely deaf and getting very frail. Mary wondered whether she should prepare the children for his inevitable death. When her father died two years ago, she and Samuel had agreed that the children should be told the truth and they knew of the death of their own little brothers. Samuel had said that one of his first memories was standing at the graveside of his baby sister and it was then that he began to question his own father's conviction that the souls of the dead rose up to heaven.

'Molly, where is Martha? Hester will need her to help her in the dining room.'

'She be tidying the nursery, madam. I shall tell her.' Mary could hear voices coming from downstairs. 'I do believe our visitors have arrived.'

Jane ran to the door and hurtled down the stairs, followed more slowly by Anna Maria, holding her brother, Thomas, by the hand.

'I will bring Charlotte down, mama,' said William, taking the little girl by the hand.

Downstairs, Jane rushed over to Ann. 'Have you brought a present for my birthday, Aunt Ann? And one for Charlotte?'

Ann laughed. 'Perhaps. You will have to wait.'

'I am so sorry, Ann,' Mary said, frowning at Jane. 'You must think my daughter has very bad manners.'

As Mary went to greet Lewis, she saw he was carrying a wicker basket.

'We have brought a present for all of you, not only for the birthday girls. Mary, will you open it so you can all see what it is?'

Mary suddenly knew precisely what would be inside. She remembered the basket; she remembered how low she felt all those years ago and she remembered the feeling of joy when Mr and Mrs Cox arrived with her Christmas present. And yes, when she opened the basket now, another little furry brown and white head appeared, as she knew it would.

'We thought Brune would like a new friend. He is just eight weeks old.'

'It is the best present you could have brought us. Is it not, children?'

The children crowded round as the little dog scrambled out of the basket. Mary bent down and picked him up. 'What do we call you, little one? We already have a Brune. Perhaps we could call you Little Brune.'

And so Little Brune he became.

'I shall go and fetch Old Brune to meet his new friend, mama. Do you know where he is?'

'I believe he is in his basket in the kitchen, William.'

John had been standing quietly beside his mother and now bent down to stroke the new puppy.

'We also have his sister at Newton,' Ann said to Mary. 'We have called her Lottie. John is training her himself. And he still very much enjoys riding your old pony, Hodge.'

'I miss all the animals at Newton. Did you know that one of my cows was called Lottie?'

'I had forgotten you had your own cows!'

'The other one was Daisy. We have called one of our cats Daisy.'

'What are you all doing standing around in the hall?'

Lewis turned to greet Samuel. 'And what are you doing creeping up on us so quietly, you old quack?'

Samuel laughed and shook Lewis warmly by the hand. 'And how is Farmer Williams today?'

William returned from the kitchen, followed slowly by Brune. The old dog wagged his tail and gave the puppy a lick on his nose.

'He is a present for us all, papa,' Jane said. 'We are calling him Little Brune.'

Samuel smiled down at his daughter. 'How splendid!'

Lewis took something from his pocket. 'I have received another letter from Peter Beckford. He says his wife, Louisa, is visiting London and having her portrait painted by Sir Joshua Reynolds. But he thinks the real reason for her visit is to see his cousin, William. Peter suspects he is her lover.'

Samuel laughed. 'From what I know of Peter Beckford, he is probably accepting the situation and might even be pleased! He will now be free to concentrate on his horses and dogs. Now, come into my study, Lewis. I want to show you an article I read in *The London Magazine*.'

Hearing Peter Beckford's name, Mary wondered whether to bring up the subject of slavery again. But she knew that Ann did not approve of her occupying her time in reading about such matters. She had recently discussed the matter with Jane Goodwin and thought it best to wait until tomorrow, when she would see her friend again.

Mary and Ann took the children and the two dogs out into the garden and watched them all running around on the grass.

'How is your mother, Ann?'

'She misses my father still, of course. But she is always pleased to see my sister Sarah's boys when they come to visit.'

Mary noticed that John was standing by himself. 'Does John not want to join in the games?'

'He is still very shy. It does not help that he has developed a stammer, so is reluctant to talk to anyone he does not know well. We worry about him, but he seems quite content when he is working on the farm, helping Thomas. And he loves his animals.'

'Does Lewis still plan to send him to Sherborne School when he is old enough?'

'Yes. I am trying to persuade him that he would be far happier at home.'

Mary could hear Ruth's voice coming from inside the house and turned to see her coming down the garden, carrying two parcels.

'Where are the birthday girls?'

'Here we are, Aunt Ruth!' Jane ran up the garden, holding Charlotte by the hand. 'We have a new puppy. We are calling him Little Brune. He is asleep under the apple tree.'

'How lovely! I shall go to meet him in a moment.'

'Thank you for my present, Aunt Ruth,' Jane said. 'Look, Mama, I can use my new journal to write my story about Brune – and his little brother.'

'That sounds a splendid idea.' Mary was helping Charlotte open her present. 'Well, what a lucky little girl you are! Aunt Ruth has given you a new doll of your own.'

'I know Jane and Anna Maria have their own dolls,' Ruth said. 'So, I thought Charlotte would like one of her own too.'

Jane went over to look at the doll. 'Charlotte will not have to play with Jemima anymore. The new doll looks like one of the pegs Hester uses to hang up the clothes. We could call her Peggy, could we not, mama?'

'What do you think, Charlotte?' Mary bent down beside her little daughter. 'Shall we call the dolly Peggy?'

'Pippy,' Charlotte said.

Little Brune suddenly got up from under the apple tree and bounded up the garden towards the little girl, who dropped the doll on to the grass in surprise. The puppy took it in his mouth before Mary could stop him. When she was able to take the doll from him, she noticed it had a small chip on its nose.

'Charlotte Pippy,' the little girl said, taking the doll from Mary. 'No doggy Pippy.'

'Yes, my love. You hold her tightly.' Mary picked up her daughter. 'Will Thomas be able to join us for dinner, Ruth?'

'He should be here soon. He is attending a meeting with his partner, Mr Bartlett, who as you know is the town clerk. And the mayor, Mr Clavill, will also be there. They are discussing the town finances, so he does not know when he will be able to arrive.'

'I believe I have come just in time for dinner!' They both turned to see Thomas himself walking towards them. 'The meeting was very tedious. It is good to be here with you all.'

Mary went to greet him. 'Samuel and Lewis are in the study. They will be delighted to see you. Perhaps you could tell them it is nearly time for dinner.'

Molly came down the garden and took the two younger children up to the nursery. Everyone else went into the dining room. Betty's chicken pie, a beef stew and a cold salmon were already on the table, and when Martha brought in the vegetables, Mary noticed that the missing carrots had obviously been found.

Mary could hear Samuel, Thomas and Lewis discussing the situation in America. She knew Samuel was relieved that the conflict appeared to be coming to an end and that he and his friend Billey Shippen would no longer be on opposite sides. Even after over ten years of marriage, Mary still loved to watch Samuel when he spoke of something he felt deeply about. She remembered when he had come to Newton all those years ago, before he went off to study with John Hunter in London. He had been so enthusiastic about his new life. At that time, she did not yet recognise her feelings as love; she just knew life would not be the same without him. Today, his hair was still dishevelled from being blown in the wind as he returned from his shop. She wanted to go up to him to smooth it down.

On the opposite side of the table, Ann was trying to persuade John to eat his dinner. The boy was very pale and had pushed his plate away, looking very distressed. Ann herself had aged since Mary saw her last. She had put on weight and her hair was beginning to turn grey. Her cheeks no longer looked fresh and rosy, but merely flushed.

Jane helped herself to some more chicken pie, while Anna Maria had finished her food and was sitting quietly, her hands in her lap. Listening to William talking to Ruth, Mary realised his voice had become considerably deeper in the last few weeks; he was suddenly becoming a fine young man, not the small boy she had known ever since she married Samuel. When he smiled at something Ruth said to him, she realised, with a start, how much he resembled his real mother.

Mary suddenly felt very weary. Until recently, she had been very sick in the mornings with this new baby and even now had little appetite for the food on her plate. Samuel had told her ginger would ease her sickness, but it had been of little help.

She heard the sound of paws and turned to see Brune creeping under the table. She automatically put her hand down to give the dog a piece of chicken from her plate. The puppy had followed and put his head on her lap. She could feel his wet nose in her hand.

Hester brought in the bowls of strawberries and pineapple.

'Please take the dogs to kitchen, Hester.'

'Yes, madam. I will do my best, but the little one be very lively and will not stay in his basket.'

The cool fruit made her feel slightly better. Ruth was looking anxiously at her from across the table.

'Are you quite well, my dear Mary? You have scarcely spoken since we sat down.'

'You always notice when I am not quite myself, Ruth. I am merely tired, so I will be thankful to rest a little after dinner.'

Here were all the people she held most dear sitting around her, enveloping her in their love. But the noise of chattering from around the table made her feel slightly dizzy. She would have a short rest after dinner and then join them all again later. Perhaps Samuel would be able to give her something to help her sleep for a while. Why did she feel so weary? She knew that the children would be safe in the care of by Molly and Martha, and that Ruth would organise everything else.

After dinner, Samuel gave Mary some syrup of poppies, so she was able to sleep. She felt refreshed after waking a few hours later. The children were asleep upstairs; their guests had departed. Thomas and Ruth had gone home and Lewis, Ann and John had left to stay at The Black Bear Inn.

Mary seems to have recovered from her dark moods, at least for the time being. At the moment, she has a happy family life. You know that Mary and Samuel's family will continue to increase but they will not keep this new baby for more than a few months.

When you reach down into the chest again, your hand grasps a wooden handle…

Chapter 3
The Hand Bell

Tuesday, 8 February 1785 – East Street, Wareham, Dorset

When you lift the object out of the chest, you see it is a small brass bell with a wooden handle, about six inches high. Examining it, you see the clapper is missing and, reaching down to the bottom of the chest, you find it hidden under a book. You fix it back on and when you ring the bell, the sound is clear and mellow.

There was an epidemic of measles in the town last year and twenty-three babies and young children died. Samuel was very distressed that he was unable to save them, but he and Mary were thankful none of their own children caught the disease. The second regiment of the Dragoon Guards is quartered in the town at present; many of the soldiers have had permission to bring their wives with them and several babies have been baptised in the town.

Baby Sarah is now two years old and is happy to play with her sisters, especially Charlotte, who is six. Little Brune is still a lively dog and follows eight-year-old Thomas wherever he goes, much to the boy's delight. William is still at Sherborne School, but John Cockram has left, and is far happier now he is being tutored at home by Mr and Mrs Cox. Lewis has promised him that once he is sixteen, he can help to run the estate, which he will eventually inherit.

Mary and her friend, Jane Goodwin, did indeed decide to remove their daughters from the school in Hampshire. They have both been fortunate to have a wide-ranging education themselves, and are eager to pass on their knowledge to their children. When it became known in the town that they were teaching their daughters themselves, several other families asked if they would be willing to include their own children; Mary and Jane suddenly found themselves running a school. Jane Goodwin's daughter, Mary, who is now eighteen, together with

Molly, the daughter of their neighbours, William and Elizabeth Cole, have now started to teach the younger children.

Yesterday, there was a fall of snow and today is cold and bright. This morning, you find Mary, and her daughter, Jane, who is now fourteen, in the day nursery, preparing for today's lessons.

Mary took a pile of writing books out of the cupboard. 'Please put these on the table for the little ones, Jane.'

'What will we be learning today, mama?'

'Mrs Goodwin will be reading to you for the first part of the morning and I will take Anna Maria's class downstairs into the study to look at the orrery.'

Jane Goodwin came into the room, rubbing her hands. 'It is still very cold outside. I am sorry to be so late, Mary. Mrs Hutchins stopped me again.'

'Did she complain once more about what we are teaching the girls?'

Jane laughed. 'Of course! When does she ever speak to us about anything else? This time it was to warn me that the girls would never be able to find husbands if we filled their heads with such useless nonsense! And then she told me once again of how her own daughter has married so well.'

'I believe she is never happier than when she has something to complain about. When I saw her recently in the town, she told me that Mr Hawker was not looking after the church nearly as well as Mr Hutchins, and that if he had been, it would not have been necessary to have the church bells taken down and replaced by new ones.'

Jane got a book out of the cupboard and put it on the large table by the window. 'I shall continue to read to the girls from *Robinson Crusoe*. We are nearly at the end now, so I shall have to decide what to read next.'

Her daughter, Mary, came upstairs and began to arrange the writing books for the youngest boys and girls.

'Mama, I shall start by giving the older ones some arithmetic sums. Molly will continue to teach the little ones their letters and numbers.'

Mary could hear the sound of chattering coming from downstairs. First to come up, were the older of the two sets of twins in the school, Ruth and Priscilla Pollard, followed by the five daughters of Samuel and Elizabeth Hayter. Their brother, George, was at Sherborne School with William; the boys joked that they were pleased to be able to escape from their sisters at last.

Charlotte was already sitting at the table ready for her lessons. She was soon joined by little John Lawrence, who had been brought upstairs by his older sister, Sarah. Mary and Jane had decided they would accept some of the younger boys who were not yet being tutored at home, and Thomas was pleased to be joined by companions of his own age.

Samuel put his head round the door. 'I am going to the shop, my love, then I shall visit little Jenny Payne. Unfortunately, she has the measles and I am afraid she will not last much longer.'

'I am sorry to hear that, Samuel. You believed, did you not, that there were no more cases in the town?'

'Yes, I had hoped so.' Samuel started to go back downstairs. 'Did you know that Anna Maria has hidden herself away in the parlour again?'

Mary knew her daughter would much prefer to be sitting with her sewing than joining in the natural philosophy lessons, which she said she found uninteresting.

'I shall be downstairs in the study soon with her class. And do not worry, Samuel, I shall see that none of your papers are disturbed.'

Samuel had at first been uncertain about using their home as a school. But he was at his shop most of the time the pupils were in the house and told Mary he was pleased she seemed much more cheerful recently.

Martha Cribb came in from the nursery, holding baby Sarah by the hand. 'May I take the little one for a walk round the garden, madam? She do like to see the snow. And I can take Little Brune for his walk.'

'Of course, Martha. How is old Sarah this morning?'

'She be still in her bed, madam. This cold don't suit her at all.'

Until recently, Sarah Squire enjoyed being involved in the care of the children, but a year ago, she had developed severe arthritis. Samuel and Mary considered she was very much part of their household and she still had her own room.

Soon, the remaining pupils had arrived and classes were under way. Jane Goodwin much preferred to teach reading and writing, but Mary particularly enjoyed teaching natural philosophy. Yesterday, she had shown the older girls Mr James Ferguson's pamphlet, explaining how to predict solar eclipses, and was delighted that her own daughter, Jane, wanted to carry on reading about the solar system after the classes had finished. Today, Mary had decided to use her orrery to show the younger girls how the moon circled the Earth and the way the

Earth, Mercury and Venus rotated round the sun. She had to persuade Anna Maria to leave her sewing and join the class. Mary realised her daughter much preferred to be on her own and suspected some of her classmates teased her about the freckles covering her face.

Mary turned the handle of the orrery to show the moon's path. 'Does anyone know how large the moon will be this evening?'

'It will be nearly gone, Mrs Baskett.'

'Yes, Priscilla, and tomorrow there will be no moon. And what happens the next day?'

'It will be a new moon.'

Both the Pollard twins were always eager to answer the questions Mary put to their class. She always tried to encourage the quieter ones to join in. Betty Clench, at ten years old, was the youngest in that class and had hardly said a word since she arrived, unlike her older sister, Sarah, who would have taken charge of teaching the others, if she could.

After a while, they heard Jane Goodwin ringing the school bell. Ruth had supported the school from the start and had presented them with a handbell to ring at the end of each lesson. And she had agreed to take some of the older girls back to her house to play her pianoforte at the end of the school day, while the other girls were sewing their samplers. Mary had already begun to teach Jane and Anna Maria to play the family's own square piano and Charlotte was already picking out tunes for herself.

Mary took the girls upstairs and they took their places ready to begin the next lesson. Jane Goodwin was to set them a task of writing a story, while Mary took the older girls down to study the large globe. She was pleased they already knew where most of the countries in the world were situated, and she was starting to teach them about Captain Cook's voyages.

Later, it was time for Hester to bring up drinks and cakes from the kitchen. During the break, the youngest children became restless and Mary decided to let them go into the garden for a short while, accompanied by Mary Goodwin and Molly Cole. Inevitably, the little boys started to throw snowballs at the little girls, who squealed with delight and ran around, followed by an excited Little Brune.

Mary noticed Eleanora Tayler and Elizabeth Hayter were sitting in a corner, their heads together, reading from a small book. They were giggling and soon some of the other girls were gathered round them. Mary was curious to know what they found so amusing. Eleanora turned to the title page.

'My grandmother gave it to me when she knew I was to come here, Mrs Baskett. It is called *The Young Lady conducted from her leaving the School to her entering upon the World. A series of familiar dialogues.* We find it very foolish!'

Elizabeth took the book from Eleanora. 'Here, a mother is speaking to her daughter about being invited to a dance. She says "*My dear, the young men are always full of desires upon the girls; and dancing gives them too much familiarity together. They mean nothing by what they say; that you may be sure, because they speak in the same manner to everybody; but they have the nonsense of making love in their heads; and a young lady is no sooner too big for a frock, but they think it is a piece of complaisance to court her*". And we all know who Eleanora wants as a partner! My brother, George, spoke of you very warmly when he was last at home!'

'That is not true, Elizabeth.' Eleanora blushed deeply. 'But we all know you were seen in the company of Edward Clavill in the summer and have since spoken of him a great deal.'

'What nonsense you talk, Eleanora!' Elizabeth rose from her seat. 'Mrs Baskett, I do believe we should have a dance when our brothers are back from school.'

'Well, I hope they will not behave like that if we do have a dance, girls.'

Mary was relieved when Jane Goodwin went down into the garden to ring the school bell. Soon the little ones came rushing up upstairs, their cheeks rosy from the cold. They all took their places and Molly Cole picked up *A Little Pretty Pocket Book* and began to read to them. When the weather was warmer, Mary and Jane would often take them all outside at the end of the school day, so they could collect leaves and flowers to draw and paint. Today, all the older girls sat quietly and read their books, while Anna Maria's class worked on their sewing.

While the girls were occupied, Mary and Jane sat together, reading the stories the girls had written. Mary tried not to favour her own children but was secretly very proud of their progress. Over the past three years, Jane had continued to write the story of Brune and Little Brune, for Thomas and Charlotte. Today, Anna Maria had written the start of a story about two sisters, who set off on a journey by boat to America, were shipwrecked and washed up on an island inhabited by strange animals. Mary could see the influence of *Robinson Crusoe* and the mythical creatures described in *A Description of Three Hundred Animals.*

It would soon start to get dark; it was time for the pupils to go home. Leaving Mary Goodwin and Molly Cole to tidy the schoolroom, Mary and Jane Goodwin went down to the parlour to take tea. Little Brune followed them and lay down beside Mary, his head on her feet. Soon Samuel returned from the shop and joined them.

'My love, have you let Jane know what we were speaking about yesterday evening?'

'What is that, Samuel?' Jane looked puzzled.

'Well, I believe our house is not large enough to hold all your pupils, especially as Mary tells me several other people have approached her to take in their daughters. And the other thing is…'

Mary interrupted him. 'The other thing is that I have been feeling nauseous in the mornings recently and believe I am again expecting a baby later this year. If that is so, I shall not be able to carry on teaching after the summer.'

'We thought our family was complete, but we will always welcome another little one.' Samuel smiled affectionately at Mary.

'It would be good for Thomas if he could have a baby brother at last. And I'm sure Martha and Molly will be delighted to have another little one to look after.'

Mary had not confessed to Samuel that the thought of losing yet another baby filled her with dread.

Jane put down her cup and went over to Mary. 'My dear, of course I will do all I can to help you. Joseph and I realise I am no longer able to bear another child, so our house is less crowded than yours, but is no larger, so it would not solve the problem to move the school there. I shall enquire straight away if there are suitable premises in the town.'

'I shall always want to be involved in the school. I love teaching and will, of course, be able to carry on once the baby is born. I shall speak to Ruth, as I am sure she would be able to take my place for a while. And I believe Mary Hayter and Deborah Dugdale will be able to take on some of the teaching. They will both be eighteen by then.'

'You seem to have given the matter a good deal of thought already. I am sure the school will carry on. Now, I must go home, as it will shortly be time for dinner.'

Once Jane and her daughter had gone home, and Molly Cole had also left, Mary suddenly felt exhausted. Little Brune pricked up his ears and trotted out of the room when he heard Thomas's voice. Charlotte started to protest at something he had said. She could hear the nursery maid, Martha, taking little Sarah up the stairs and into the nursery. She sat back in her chair and shut her eyes.

'You need to rest, my love. I shall leave you in peace. I need to look something up in the study before dinner.' Samuel gave Mary a quick kiss on the cheek and left the room.

Left alone, Mary could feel tears running down her cheeks. She was determined not to let Samuel see how upset she was at the thought of another pregnancy. She loved all the children dearly, of course, and could not imagine life without them, but had hoped her family was now complete. She was only thirty-six, but when she saw herself in her looking glass, she could see the lines on her face getting deeper and more grey hairs among her dark curls. She often found herself wondering what the other Mary, William's mother, would have looked like if she had lived. She would have been well over forty by now. Would she still have her fair hair? Would she still be slender and elegant? And did Samuel also still think of her, still love her? He had told her that he had given William the ammonite, his "talisman", to keep alive the memory of the mother he never knew.

Her thoughts were interrupted by Hester coming in to tell her that dinner was ready and that she had already taken up the nursery supper for Thomas, Charlotte and Sarah. Sitting round the table with Samuel, Jane and Anna Maria, her spirits soon rose once more.

'Papa, we learnt about Captain Cook's voyages today, did we not, mama?'

'Indeed, you did, Jane.'

'And mama asked us to find all the places he visited on our globe. I think he was very brave.'

'Did mama also tell you that he took Joseph Banks with him on his first voyage to the Pacific Ocean? He brought back many botanical specimens.'

'I shall be talking about that in our next lesson, Samuel.'

'I'm sorry, my love, I shall leave you to tell the girls more.'

'Anna Maria, you must continue the story you started in class today and show it to papa after dinner.'

'Let me see it, Anna Maria. I can help you write it.'

'But it is my story! Mama, tell Jane I do not want her to help me.'

'You should write your own story, Jane. Let Anna Maria finish hers alone.'

Mary caught Samuel's eye. She knew what he was thinking. He and Lewis still joked that Jane was just like her. She decided to change the subject.

'How was your day, Samuel?'

'Busy, as usual. Little Jenny Payne is no better. I do not think she will last another day. But Robert and Mary Tuck had a healthy baby daughter this afternoon. They have called her Betty. His brother, George, also called his daughter Betty, as did his other brother, Harry, although both his babies called Betty died.'

'It sounds very complicated, Samuel. They are all part of the Tuck family from Stoborough, who attend the Old Meeting House, are they not?'

'Yes, old Samuel and Joan Tuck had six sons and I believe they are all married now. I met Mrs Hutchins as I came over the bridge from Stoborough and, of course, when I told her where I had been, she was very dismissive of the whole family. After getting married at St Mary's, old Samuel and Joan had all their children baptised at the Meeting House, much to her husband's disapproval.'

'She never forgets a disagreement. I suppose she has little to occupy her now apart from gossip!'

Mary pushed away her plate. Betty's fish pie, which she usually enjoyed greatly, made her feel slightly nauseous – yet another sign confirming her pregnancy.

After the meal, she went up to the nursery. It would soon be time for the little ones to go to bed. She stood in the doorway, quietly watching her children. Thomas was sitting at the table, reading, Little Brune lying beside him. Charlotte was on the floor, arranging a tea party for her doll. Sarah was sitting in her highchair, watching her sister.

'You must be a good girl and drink your milk, Pippy.' Charlotte held a cup to the doll's lips. 'And you must eat your pudding.'

Martha came in from the night nursery and picked up Sarah.

'It is time for your bed.' The little girl put her arms around her nursemaid, who gave her a kiss on the cheek.

No one had noticed Mary. She found tears coming to her eyes once again. She turned and quietly went downstairs. Samuel was in his study and she joined her elder daughters in the parlour. Beside the lamp, Jane was reading and Anna Maria was working on her sampler.

'See, mama, I have nearly finished all the letters and numbers. I shall soon be able to start on the pattern underneath them.'

'It is looking splendid, Anna Maria. Jane, where is your sampler?'

'It is upstairs, mama. Please do not ask me to work on it except during lessons.'

Mary smiled. 'I know, Jane. I felt just the same when I was your age. What are you reading?'

'It is a book belonging to Elizabeth Hayter, mama. It is called *Evelina*. Do you know it?'

'No, but I have heard of it. May I look?'

The five Hayter sisters ranged in age from seventeen to seven. Mary knew that Mrs Hutchins, among others, thought they were undisciplined, and, for once, she was inclined to agree with them. Elizabeth Hayter was fifteen and one of Jane's closest friends.

Mary thought her daughter might be too young to read a novel intended for young women who had already left school, but had not read it herself. On the title page, it said it was called *Evelina, or the History of a Young Lady's Entrance into the World,* and, turning the pages, she could see it was written in the form of letters. She decided to ask Jane Goodwin the next day for her opinion of the book.

Later, once all the children had gone to bed, Mary and Samuel sat together by the fire.

'I was thinking, Samuel, how different from each other all our children are. I do believe that little Sarah will be like Anna Maria and be quite happy to watch the others at play. And Charlotte seems to be happiest of them all. Nothing seems to upset her.'

Samuel smiled affectionately. 'We are indeed lucky, my love. And we can only hope this new baby will thrive and be happy. Now, you look tired. You should retire early tonight.'

Upstairs, Mary got into bed and fell asleep almost as soon as she blew out her candle.

You wonder whether Mary and Samuel will lose yet another baby boy. You hope Jane Goodwin manages to find premises in the town in which to hold the classes and that Mary will continue to teach at the school.

It is time to see what else is in the chest and what story it will tell. Delving down, you find another book...

Chapter 4
The Medical Book

Wednesday, 6 June 1787 – East Street, Wareham, Dorset

When you open the book, you see it is entitled "Medical Observations and Inquiries, by the Society of Physicians in London, Vol V, dated M.DCC.LXXVI". Turning to the contents page, you read that many of the essays were "communicated by Dr William Hunter", so you assume John Hunter would have sent the book to Samuel.

Mary's baby was a boy, Robert, born in November; he was followed almost exactly a year later by another boy, Charles. Both babies are flourishing, much to Samuel and Mary's relief. Molly and Martha are once again fully occupied in the nursery and they are now assisted by Hannah Smith who is sixteen, from nearby Organford. William, now nineteen, has left school; as his grandfather was eager to continue to pay for his education, he is now at Wadham College, Oxford. Jane Goodwin found premises attached to Holy Trinity Church to continue running the school. With baby Charles only eight months old, Mary has yet to continue teaching. Thomas and the four other boys at the school are now being taught by Benjamin Goodwin, Joseph Goodwin's nephew.

Today is quite cool after a period of warm weather; this morning the sun is shining, but distant clouds threaten to produce showers later. William returned home yesterday for the summer, and today Jane, Anna Maria, Thomas and Charlotte have left to go to school. You find Samuel, Mary and William at breakfast.

Samuel took a piece of toast and spread it with butter. 'What are you planning to do today, William?'

'It is so good to be home, Father. I shall walk round the garden after breakfast to see old Henry and young Jamie. Then I shall visit George Hayter. As you know, we travelled from Oxford together yesterday and agreed to meet today.'

Samuel smiled at his son. 'We shall see you at dinner, William?'

'Of course, Father. But first, I need to speak of something which has been on my mind recently.'

Mary rose from the table. 'I shall leave you both. I will go up to the nursery to feed baby Charles.'

'No, please, Mother, do not go yet. I should like to discuss the matter with you both.'

'What is it, my son?' Samuel looked anxiously at William.

'I know Grandfather hopes I shall follow him into the church. I believe that is the reason he continues to pay for my education.'

'He was very disappointed when I decided to become a surgeon. It was only when you were born that we became reconciled.'

'When we saw him at Christmas, he kept saying how pleased he was that my uncles, William and Robert, had decided to follow him into the church and how I was named after my uncle.'

'He is proud of you, William.'

'But, Father, that is not what I want to do. George Hayter understands. We have often spoken of it.'

'When I wanted to train as a surgeon, your uncle, Lewis, was my confidant. It helped me a great deal. It would please me a great deal if you decided to train as a surgeon, but I have always tried not to influence you in any way – you must decide for yourself what you want to do with your life. You could speak with your uncle, Thomas, about training to be a lawyer, perhaps. But William, whatever path you want to take, it does no harm to finish your studies at Oxford.'

'George and I have agreed that we do not feel we belong there. Many of our fellow students spend much of their time eating and drinking. They spend very little at their studies. And the dons are mostly no better.'

Mary sat quietly listening to their conversation. She had always treated William as her own son and he, of course, had known no other mother. As far as she knew, he had had no contact with his real mother's family, but she did know that at least one of the brothers of the "other" Mary was a clergyman in Dorchester.

172

Samuel finished drinking his coffee and rose to his feet. 'I have to go to the shop now, but first I must consult the book John Hunter sent me recently. I am anxious about the wife of Roger Courtney, who has been complaining of a severe stomach pain. She is about four months pregnant and I seem to remember one of the cases in the book was very similar. I met Mr Robert Carruthers yesterday and asked him if any of his patients had experienced the same problem and told him about a possible cure. We will speak more when I return, William.'

Mr Carruthers had set up in practice a few years ago and Samuel had at first become anxious that there was no room for two surgeons in the town. But his business had not decreased, mainly because Mr Carruthers was not an apothecary, and the two had become friends. Mary had been fond of his wife, Isabella, and was devastated when she died of a fever a year ago, leaving a little boy, George, who was only four years old.

Mary climbed the stairs to the nursery; she could hear baby Charles crying. As she went into the room, little Sarah, who reminded Mary of her sister, Anna Maria, with her solemn face and red hair, was quietly watching her brothers. Robert was sitting in his highchair and Hannah was feeding him his breakfast of bread and milk. Martha was standing by the window, trying to pacify baby Charles, who held out his arms towards Mary when he saw her.

'Martha, I am sorry I have been delayed.'

'I have fed him some milk-pottage, madam, but he will not stop his crying. And madam, I did see he have got another tooth when he did wake up today.'

Mary took the little boy and went into the night nursery to give him his feed. Samuel was still adamant that a mother's milk was the only nourishment a young baby needed until he was ready to take more solid food, and was especially against giving him the medicine or cordials favoured by some parents. He had told her that he sometimes found that babies had been given ale or wine in attempts to calm them when they were sick.

As the baby suckled, Mary once again wondered to herself whether he would be her last. Jane Goodwin was eager for her to return to teaching. But, having lost so many babies, Mary found she worried about the little ones every time she left the house. Even when she went outside to walk in the garden, she could not resist hurrying back inside again.

Baby Charles fell asleep in the middle of his feed, so Mary handed him to Martha, who laid him down in his crib. Mary returned to the day nursery. Robert was out of his highchair and sitting on the floor playing with the animals from the ark. Sarah was sitting beside him, turning the pages of the book Mary had originally made for William, before any of her own children had been born.

Sarah pointed to one of the drawings. 'See, Robert, here is a picture of mama's cows. They are called Lottie and Daisy.'

Mary knelt down beside them. 'Yes, that is right. And who is this?'

'Brune, mama.'

'Yes, I also had a dog called Brune when I was a little girl.'

Sarah turned another page. 'Here are your chickens, mama. See, Robert, they have laid some nice brown eggs.'

Mary had already taught Sarah her letters and she was now able to read from the book herself. She was slower at learning her numbers, as Anna Maria had been. She would soon be ready to join her sisters at the school, together with the little daughter of Samuel's friend, George Filliter.

For the rest of the morning, Mary was engaged in domestic duties. In the kitchen, Betty was preparing a shoulder of mutton for roasting. 'Hester have asked Henry to pick some peas and Jamie is digging up some carrots, madam. And Hester have made Master William's favourite chicken pie.'

'It will be good to have all the family sitting down to dinner once again now that master William is home. Mr Baskett's brother and his wife will also be eating with us today and master Thomas will also come downstairs.'

'There will be plenty for everyone, madam. And we be making a special pudding for master William as a surprise.'

The kitchen was hot and steamy, so it was a relief to go out into the cool of the garden. Old Henry was kneeling down by the strawberry bed and slowly got to his feet as she approached. 'I be picking some strawberries for your dinner, madam.'

'Splendid, Henry. Master William will be pleased.'

'And I have told young Jamie to make sure there are no snails or slugs eating your winter greens. We have planted some more after they vermin munched their way through the last lot. He be over there, spuddlin' around for the last of the taties.'

She went down to the bottom of the garden and sat under the apple tree. Brune had followed her outside and settled at her feet. She fondled his silky ears and he wagged his tail. The sun was warm on her face. She watched as a beetle went scurrying through the grass. A blackbird flew on to the branch above her head. She remembered how they had all eaten dinner outside all those years ago, when Jane and Anna Maria were small, and baby Samuel was still alive. Her energy then seemed unending. Where had all those years gone?

The sun suddenly went behind a dark cloud and she shivered. It looked as if there would be a heavy rain shower and she wondered whether Samuel had taken his umbrella with him. She hurried indoors and was relieved to find that he had already returned. He was sitting at his desk in his study, his head in his hands.

'What has happened, my love?'

'I have a slight headache. I have come from visiting Sarah Courtney. I was correct in my diagnosis. She had been unable to pass urine for several days. But I was able to insert a catheter and was greatly relieved that it quickly resolved the problem. Her pregnancy should now proceed as normal.'

'Thomas and Ruth will be here shortly for dinner. I shall leave you to rest a little until they arrive.'

Mary had noticed recently that Samuel's hair had some flecks of grey and was beginning to recede. It had become something of a joke between them. But then he would point out the white hairs among her own dark curls; at first, she had tried to pluck them out, but recently had given up as they had become too numerous.

She went up to the nursery to check that all was well. Baby Charles was still asleep and Molly was sitting quietly with Robert and Sarah. As she went downstairs again, the street door opened and William came in, rain dripping from his hair.

'I was halfway home when it started. I shall go to my room and change into some dry clothes. Then I shall come down to speak to Father before dinner.'

'Your father is tired, William. Perhaps it would be best for you to continue your discussion later.'

'I have been talking with Benjamin Goodwin. As you know, Mother, he is teaching the boys at the school. He called in to see George while I was there and said how much he enjoyed the work, but that he will be leaving after the summer. I am thinking I should like to take his place and not return to Oxford.'

'You must wait to see what your father says – and Mrs Goodwin, of course. I found my time teaching very rewarding and look forward to being able to return when baby Charles is older.'

The door burst open and her daughters ran in, laughing, shaking the rain off their bonnets. As usual, Charlotte threw herself at William, who picked her up and swung her round in his arms. Little Brune danced around them, barking in excitement, until William put Charlotte down.

'Mama, I can read nearly all the words in *Little Goody Two-Shoes* now.' Charlotte took the book out or her pocket. 'Her real name is Margery.'

'I remember reading the book with Jane when she was about your age. Now, girls, go up to the nursery and take off your wet clothes. Your uncle, Thomas, and aunt, Ruth, will be here shortly.'

'We saw them setting off as we went past their house.'

As Jane spoke, the doorbell rang and Thomas and Ruth stood on the doorstep, shaking their umbrellas. Ruth embraced Mary.

'I see everyone has arrived at the same time.'

Hester came from the kitchen to take all the wet cloaks and umbrellas.

'Dinner will be a bit late, madam. Jamie, he were very slow bringing in the vegetables and Betty did scold him and he did stomp out again.'

'Tell Betty not to worry. Let us know when it is ready.' Mary turned to Thomas. 'Samuel is in his study. He has had a busy morning, but I am sure he will be pleased to see you. Let us go into the parlour, Ruth, while the others all go upstairs.'

'Now, Mary, tell me how you are – and the little ones.'

'They are both thriving, Ruth. Feeding the little one always makes me tired, but I am trying to keep cheerful. But I am worried about William. He wants to leave his studies and teach at the school when Benjamin Goodwin leaves. Samuel suggested he could speak to Thomas about becoming a lawyer.'

'Of course. I will ask him. But he will need to complete his studies at Oxford first.'

'I must go upstairs and give baby Charles another feed before dinner. Thomas will be eating with us today, to welcome William home.'

'I shall come up with you. I should like to see the other children.'

When Mary came out of the night nursery, Ruth was sitting at the table, turning the pages of *A Description of a Great Variety of Animals and Vegetables* with Sarah and Charlotte. Anna Maria sat in the window seat, sewing her sampler. Thomas had recently been drawing an imaginary island, complete with towns and villages, farms, woods and a harbour; he was engrossed in painting the blue sea with his watercolours. Molly was putting Robert into his highchair, ready for his dinner. The rain had stopped and the sun was shining in through the window. Mary stood, baby Charles in her arms, watching her family. How could she have ever wanted anything else? She remembered how, as a young girl, she had wanted to travel the world, to see beyond her small, intimate, circle. She knew now that she would never have that opportunity.

She was interrupted in her thoughts by Jane. Her daughter had recently become involved in the domestic life of the family. Samuel had remarked that she was just like her mother – always wanting to organise everyone.

'Mama, Hester says that dinner is ready. Anna Maria, you must come down with us. And Thomas, put your paints away. You will also be eating with us today.'

The shoulder of mutton and the chicken pie were already on the table when they went into the dining room. Hester came in carrying bowls of vegetables. Martha had come down from the nursery and followed her in bringing a poached salmon and a bowl of salad. Soon everyone had full plates of food.

Samuel raised his glass. 'It is good to see you home again, William.'

William helped himself to some pie. 'I do believe Betty has baked this especially for me, Hester. Please thank her.'

Hester blushed deeply and looked embarrassed. 'I did make it myself, master William. I do know as how you like a good pie.'

'That is excellent, Hester. Thank you.'

As usual at family gatherings, everyone started to talk at once. Looking down the table, Mary noticed Samuel looked pale and was not eating. Ruth, sitting next to him, said something to him and he shook his head.

Suddenly, he stood up, his hand to his chest, and fell forward on to the table. Everyone stopped talking. A glass smashed. A knife fell to the floor. His brother, Thomas, leapt to his feet.

'Hester! Fetch Mr Carruthers. As quickly as you can. William, help me lift your father and get him into the parlour.'

Mary found herself unable to move, unable to understand what was happening. Her only thought was that William would not now have his surprise pudding. Then, Ruth was by her side.

'Try not to worry, Mary, my dear. Mr Carruthers will be here soon. He will know what to do.'

But Mary knew. She knew there was nothing to be done. She knew that he was already dead. That the love of her life, the reason for her to be alive, was dead.

Jane and Anna Maria were with her now. They were both weeping. And how was she to tell the other children? Sarah and Robert and Charles were all too young to understand. But Thomas and Charlotte, they would understand.

'I want to see him, Ruth. I want to be with him.'

'It is best to stay here, Mary. Thomas and William are with him. They will make him comfortable.'

It was only when Little Brune came up and put his head on her lap, that the tears came.

Eventually, Robert Carruthers arrived with Hester, who took him into the parlour. When he came out, he looked grave.

'My dear, Mrs Baskett, I am so sorry. There was nothing I could do to help him. His heart had stopped.'

'In my heart I knew, Mr Carruthers. But thank you for coming so quickly.'

'I shall give you something to help you sleep. You have a loving family who will help you, I know.'

For the rest of the day, Mary scarcely knew what was happening. People came up and spoke to her. They made no sense. When she eventually stood up, she could scarcely support herself. So, it was a relief when Ruth eventually helped her upstairs to bed. Outside, the rain once again was lashing at the window. Almost immediately, with the help of Mr Carruthers' potion, she fell into a deep sleep.

You realise how fond you have become of Samuel and Mary and their family, and how sad and shocked Samuel's death has made you feel. But you are curious to know how they kept going, so delve down once again into the chest, to see what the next object could be...

Part 5
Charlotte Baskett

Chapter 1
The Posset Pot

Monday, 20 February 1792 – East Street, Wareham, Dorset

You lift out a small ceramic pot, which you realise is a posset pot, used to feed invalids. It is about five inches high with two handles and a thin spout, decorated with blue flowers and leaves on a white background. There are some small chips on one of the handles, around the rim and below the spout.

At the time leading up to the French Revolution, members of the dissenting churches in the town supported the Republican cause. Two years ago, there was a heated argument between the Reverend Hawker, rector of St Mary's and the Reverend Reader of the dissenting South Street Chapel, when the Reverend Reader had greeted the Reverend Hawker as "citizen". The quarrel remained unresolved, as the Reverend Reader died, at the age of seventy-two, just before the execution of the French King, followed seven months later by the death of the Reverend Hawker.

Mary has never really recovered from Samuel's death and there was a further blow when her friend, Jane Goodwin, died about eighteen months later. She rarely leaves the house now and relies more and more on her daughters, Jane and Anna Maria, to run the household. Ruth has given the family all the support she can. Samuel's father and his brother, Thomas, have given Mary the financial help she needs and both have made wills to leave legacies to Mary, provided she remain a widow, and to her children for their education, until they reach the age of twenty-one.

William returned to Oxford after Samuel's death and completed his studies. He is now training as an attorney with his uncle, Thomas Baskett. Richard Hobbs now runs the apothecary shop, assisted by Joe Cake, who started to work there when he was sixteen. Robert Carruthers is now the only surgeon in Wareham. Young Thomas, now fifteen, is a pupil at Sherborne School. Mary Goodwin and

Molly Cole continue to run the school and they have now been joined by Deborah Dugdale and Mary Hayter, who are both former pupils. And old Sarah, who had continued to live with the family and who had been Samuel's nursemaid, died in her sleep a few months ago.

Last week, Sarah, who is now nine years of age, developed a high fever and it is feared she will not recover. Mary has been sitting at her bedside night and day.

After a frosty night, the sun is shining in a clear sky and it promises to be a delightful day. You find Charlotte, who is now thirteen, in the day nursery, together with her brothers, Robert, six, and Charles, five, and their nursemaid, Martha.

Charlotte jumped up as her mother came in from Sarah's sick room. 'How is she, mama?'

'I do believe she will recover, Charlotte. When she woke this morning, I realised her fever had left her at last.'

'Oh, mama, that is so good. I shall be able to go to school without worrying now.'

Martha stood up from the table where she was sitting with Robert and Charles.

'That be such good news, madam.'

'Martha, please go to the kitchen and ask Betty to prepare a posset pot for Sarah. And be sure to ask her to put an extra egg in it and plenty of cream. She needs all the nourishment she can get now.'

Martha hurried out and Charlotte looked anxiously at her mother.

'Mama, you look so tired. I'm sure Molly and Martha will take care of Sarah while you rest.'

'Perhaps I shall, Charlotte. Your father would have known what I should do, I am sure.'

Charlotte could see the tears once more coming to her mother's eyes.

'I must leave for school now, mama. I shall walk with William if he has not already left and tell him the good news about Sarah.'

'Will you ask Jane to come upstairs on your way, please, Charlotte? I need to make sure Betty knows what to cook for dinner today.'

'I will, but I am sure Jane will have already spoken to Betty, mama.'

Downstairs, she found Jane in the kitchen and told her that her mother wanted to see her.

In the hall, William was waiting for her. She put on her cloak, pulled up her hood and picked up her muff. Outside, the sun was clearing the frost from the grass and the roofs of the houses. She always looked forward to walking with William as far as the end of East Street, especially since she was not responsible at the moment for taking care of Sarah. She was able to tell him things she was reluctant to talk about with anyone else. She felt she was his favourite of all his sisters.

'It seems Sarah is recovering from her fever at last and mama can get some rest.'

'That is excellent, my Little Mouse. I am sure Father would have insisted she take care of herself for a change.'

William was striding out and Charlotte almost had to run to catch up with him.

'We will be learning about Captain Cook's voyages today. Would you like to go on voyages like that one day, William? We could go together. But I might be very frightened to sail on rough seas to such faraway places.'

'Yes, I have dreamt about seeing all the strange places in the world, but I think mama relies on me as the man of the house, now Father is no longer with us. But I am not sure that I want to be a lawyer for the rest of my life, Charlotte. Uncle Thomas and Mr Bartlett are very good to me, but I find the work tedious sometimes.'

They had reached the end of East Street already, where William turned right and Charlotte turned left. As she walked along South Street towards the river, she thought about what William had said. She would miss him greatly if he left home but was pleased he felt he could confide in her.

As she passed the road leading to St Mary's Church, Mrs Hutchins hurried towards her. 'My dear Charlotte. I heard your sister, Sarah, is ill with the fever. Do tell me she has recovered.'

'Her fever left her last night, Mrs Hutchins. Mama is most relieved.'

'Do give your mama my best wishes, my dear. I have heard a great many people have had the fever recently. My neighbour, Mrs Chapman, was ill after Christmas and is still weak and unable to go out. And my dear, as you know, my daughter, Martha, and her husband, Mr Bellasis, are visiting from Bombay. Please tell your mama that they are planning to erect a mural monument in my dear husband's memory in St Mary's church. And I am sure your mama will be pleased to hear that they are expecting another little one in the summer.'

'I certainly will, Mrs Hutchins.' Charlotte turned to go on her way.

'And remind your mama that Mr Bellasis is arranging a new edition of my dear husband's History of Dorset.'

'I will, Mrs Hutchins.' Charlotte wondered whether she would be able to remember all these messages and was relieved when she saw her friends, Eleanor Hayter and her sister, Sarah, approaching. Mrs Hutchins called after them as they started to walk towards the school.

'I believe your dear late father's friend, Mr Bartlett, is to assist in its publication.'

Charlotte wondered whether William had met Mrs Hutchins' daughter and her husband and whether he had spoken to them about their life in India. She would ask him when they got home. Mama had told her that Mr Bellasis was an important man in Bombay and that he and his family lived in a large house outside the city.

Once inside the school, Charlotte soon became involved in the chatter of her fellow pupils. Eleanor and Sarah Hayter were now in the top class and Charlotte would join them later in the year. She remembered when she was the youngest in the school, when classes were still at home, before Robert was born. Now, there were no boys in the school, but then, Thomas and his friends loved to tease the little girls. She remembered one cold, snowy day, when they all went outside to throw snowballs. Did she and her friends make as much noise as the youngest ones did now? The Haines triplets, Hannah, Sarah and Mary, were always the noisiest and today they came rushing in, complaining of the cold. Charlotte always had difficulty telling them apart. They wore different coloured pinafores but loved to change them around to confuse everyone.

Until lessons started, the girls huddled round the fire in the main classroom, still wearing their cloaks. Today, Mary Goodwin was to teach Charlotte's class in the adjoining room. They were following Captain Cook's voyage round the large globe on its stand by the window. Yesterday, Mary Goodwin told them how Captain Cook had reached New Zealand after sailing from Tahiti. Today, they were to learn about his arrival in New Holland at Botany Bay.

During the lesson, Charlotte found her attention wandering. Mama had already told her much of the story. She knew that, during the voyage, the natural philosopher, Joseph Banks, had collected many specimens of plants and animals unknown then in England. And mama had told her how she wished she could travel to the places she and her governess used to look at on her pocket globe, which was now on a table in the drawing room at home, in its fish skin case. Outside, through the frosty window, she could see a carriage drawn by two horses coming from the direction of the river. And Mrs Hutchins was in conversation with another elderly lady on the other side of the road.

'Charlotte, can you find New Holland on the globe for us, please?' Mary Goodwin's voice startled her. She jumped up from her seat and rotated the globe on its stand and pointed to New Holland. The shape of the country differed from how she had seen it on mama's pocket globe.

'That is correct, Charlotte. We have learned much about the countries in the South Pacific Ocean since Captain Cook came back from his travels. Can anyone tell me something about the creatures they found in New Holland?'

'Captain Cook found a leaping animal called a kangaroo, Miss Goodwin.'

'Indeed, he did, Charlotte.'

In front of her, Margaret Hall said something behind her hand to Henrietta Best and both girls giggled. Charlotte could feel herself blushing, as she was sure they had said something about her. She knew some of the girls regarded her as the teachers' pet, just because mama had started the school with Mary Goodwin's mother and because her own sister, Jane, was a friend of Mary Goodwin, whom she had to call Miss Goodwin at school. She knew she would be much happier when she could be in the same class as her friends, Sarah and Eleanor Hayter.

After the morning break, there was a drawing class with Miss Cole. Today, they had to draw one of the other girls. Charlotte knew she was the best in the class, as she was always able to sketch a good likeness. She decided her subject would be Margaret Hall. She had a long face and Charlotte noticed her eyes were quite close together, her mouth turned down and her nose was slightly crooked. The strand of hair escaping from her cap was a mousy colour. Charlotte was aware that she should not have unkind thoughts about her fellow pupils.

But then she knew Margaret often made unkind remarks about her, so felt she was justified in drawing a caricature of her. When Miss Cole collected up the drawings at the end of the lesson, she made no comment about the picture, but Charlotte noticed her smiling to herself as she looked at it. Before they went home, they took it in turns to read from *Gulliver's Travels*. They had already read the first part, and now Gulliver had left Lilliput and was in the land of the giants, Brobdingnag. Gulliver was just about to be squashed to death by one of the giants as he lay on the ground. Charlotte read the passage describing how he was taken in by a farmer and his family.

It was starting to get dark as Charlotte walked home. In the hall, Little Brune, who was getting quite elderly, got up from his basket in the hall to greet her, wagging his tail. She went upstairs to make sure Sarah was still recovering. She was sitting up in bed looking pale, but much better.

'Where is mama, Sarah?'

'I believe she is still resting, Charlotte. I have not seen her since this morning.'

Charlotte opened the door to her mother's room as quietly as she could and found her awake but looking flushed and exhausted.

'I do believe I have the fever, Charlotte.'

'Is there anything you need, mama?'

'Jane has brought me some water and has been sitting with me at times. I just need to rest. And your aunt, Ruth, is feeling unwell as well and did not come here today.'

There was over an hour before dinner and she decided to see if she could find a book about India in papa's study. William now used the desk for his own books and papers. She could find nothing about India in the bookcases; most of papa's books were on medical or scientific subjects. She was turning to leave the room, when she noticed a book on the desk, called *The Interesting Narrative of the Life of Olaudah Equiano*. She picked it up and began to turn the pages.

'Hello, Little Mouse, I see you have found the book George Hayter has lent to me.'

William stood in the doorway, still wearing his coat and hat.

'Sarah is recovering well, but mama believes she also has the fever.'

'I shall go and fetch Mr Carruthers tomorrow if she is not better by the morning.'

'What is this book about, William? I do not know how to say this name.'

'It is written by a black man who was a slave, until he gained his freedom. He was bought and sold many times and travelled to many countries, before settling in London. He is now involved in the movement in this country to stop slavery altogether.'

'I have heard mama say she thinks it is very wrong that someone can own another human being. Can that ever be right, William?'

'Never, my Mouse. That is why George and I support the movement. But it is difficult for us to get involved here in Dorset. Many people in this country have become very rich dealing in slaves – even clergymen.'

'I believe Uncle Lewis has a friend who owns slaves in Jamaica. I know mama dislikes him. I do hope grandpapa does not own any slaves, William.'

'That I do not know. But there are several members of parliament who support the abolitionist cause. George's father has met one of them, William Wilberforce. He has been successful in limiting the numbers of slaves carried in any one ship, but so far has not got a bill put through parliament making the trade illegal.'

'You should become a member of parliament yourself, William. You are so passionate about it.'

William laughed and shook his head. 'I think not.' Nevertheless, Charlotte thought he looked pleased at what she had said.

'I came in to see if papa had any books about India. I met Mrs Hutchins on my way to school and she told me Mr Bartlett is helping her daughter and her husband to publish a new edition of Mr Hutchins' book about Dorset. Have you met them, William?'

'Mr Bellasis came in today to see Mr Bartlett and, yes, I had a very interesting conversation with him. He and his wife live in Bombay and they will be returning next year. He is a major in the East India Company.'

'Would you like to go to India, William? I think it would be very hot there.'

'Mr Bellasis says that he and his wife have become accustomed to the heat. In some parts of India, it is possible to go up to the hills where it is cooler at the hottest time of the year. He also told me about a clergyman, Dr Bell, who has been appointed by the East India Company to become superintendent of an orphanage in Madras, in southern India. He is beginning to teach the boys their letters and numbers.'

'I think you would be a good teacher, William.'

'Perhaps so, Little Mouse. Now I think it is nearly dinner time.'

'I do hope mama will be well enough to come downstairs.'

William took his talisman, the ammonite his father had given him in memory of his mother, out of his pocket and placed it on the desk beside the book by Olaudah Equiano.

'Tell me the story of your talisman, William.'

'I do believe I have told you the story many times, Charlotte.'

'But I love hearing it. Tell me again.'

'Papa picked up the ammonite on the beach when he was walking with your mama and your uncle, Lewis.'

Charlotte smiled. 'Tell me the rest of the story, William.'

'But then he met my mama and fell in love with her while he had the ammonite in his pocket. He thought it brought him luck. He gave it to me in memory of my mother on my fourteenth birthday. I shall always keep it safe. But you know that he also loved your mother dearly, as I do.'

'There you both are!' They turned as Anna Maria put her head round the door. 'Jane has sent me to tell you that dinner is nearly on the table.'

'Is mama able to come down?'

'I think not. Hester will take some broth up to her and to Sarah, later.'

Charlotte was pleased that she was now allowed to take her dinner downstairs and not share it with Sarah and her little brothers in the nursery.

Today Betty had prepared a good beef stew and an apple pie – mama's favourite.

As Charlotte, William and Anna Maria sat down at the table, Jane came in, looking anxious.

'I have just come from seeing mama. Her fever is worsening, William. I think we should fetch Dr Carruthers after dinner.'

William got up from his seat. 'I shall go now, Jane. I can have my dinner when I return.'

Charlotte had been so relieved that morning to hear that Sarah was getting well. But now she had mama to worry about. Mama was never ill. She was the centre of all their lives, now papa was no longer with them. They could not lose her. Charlotte's world was falling apart.

No one felt like eating after William had left. Jane rang the bell and asked Hester to take the food away until William returned with Dr Carruthers. They went and sat down in the drawing-room. Even Little Brune seemed to sense their anxiety and lay down beside Charlotte, his head on her feet. William returned sooner than they expected.

'I met Dr Carruthers when I reached the end of the street. He has been visiting Aunt Ruth, who also has a high fever. He is with mama now.'

Jane got up and hurried upstairs.

Anna Maria, William and Charlotte sat silently in the drawing-room, until they heard Dr Carruthers and Jane coming downstairs.

'It appears that your mother has the influenza. I have given her a tincture to reduce her fever, but someone should sit with her tonight and sponge her face to keep her as cool as possible. I shall call in again in the morning to see how she is progressing. There is nothing more I can do tonight.'

Jane followed Dr Carruthers into the hall. 'Anna Maria and I will take it in turns to be with her all night, Dr Carruthers.'

None of them had any appetite for their dinner. Hester brought in some tea and biscuits. She drew the curtains and put more coal on the fire.

'Betty did ask if you would like some soup, Miss Jane.'

'That is most kind, Hester. Yes, I think that is all we shall need this evening.'

Jane went upstairs with Anna Maria, and Charlotte was left alone with William in the drawing-room.

'Mama will get better, William, will she not?'

'I very much hope so, Little Mouse. I am sure she will recover, as Sarah has.'

Charlotte went to her room early but found it difficult to sleep. During the night, she awoke to hear Jane and Anna Maria talking quietly in the passage outside her door, before dropping off to sleep again.

You hope both Mary and Ruth will recover from the influenza. As you look once again inside the chest, you wonder if the next object will give you a clue. From almost at the bottom of the chest, you take out a cylindrical leather bag...

Chapter 2
The Portmanteau

Tuesday, 24 June 1794 – East Street, Wareham, Dorset

You see that the brown leather bag is a portmanteau, used for carrying clothing and other belongings when travelling. It has a long shoulder strap, and the flap is secured by three more straps, one of which has broken off. The leather is scuffed and the edges are quite worn.

The whole family was devastated when neither Mary nor Ruth survived influenza; they both died within a few days of each other. In the town, Mrs Hutchins' daughter, Martha, gave birth to a boy and shortly afterwards, she and her husband returned to India. Last year, Samuel's father died in his sleep. He was eighty-four and had been quite fit up until a few weeks before his death. In his will, apart from small sums to his servants, he had divided his considerable estate between his four sons. Samuel's portion went to his children so they were well provided for and could continue to live in the house on East Street.

Jane took full charge of the day-to-day running of the household after her mother's death. She has inherited her mother's organisational skills and is always cheerful. Anna Maria assists her by keeping a meticulous record of all the expenditure. Charlotte and Sarah are still at the school in the town. Thomas has been at Sherborne but is now home for the summer and his intention is to go to Oxford. Robert and Charles are, at present, being tutored at home.

William became more and more restless working as an attorney. Earlier this year he learned from the new Rector of St Mary's church, the Reverend Hyde, that his friend, Dr Andrew Bell, needed an assistant at the orphanage he had set up in Madras. Once his uncle, Thomas, had assured him that he would always be around for his brothers and sisters if they needed help of any kind, he decided to apply for the position and was accepted. Today is William's last day at home before sailing to India.

Charlotte will miss William greatly, but knows it is the ideal opportunity for him to see the world. He has promised to write to her every week while he is away. Jane has organised a farewell dinner for him. Charlotte and her friends, Sarah and Eleanor Hayter, have written a play to be performed before the meal. Lewis and Ann are travelling from Swanage to join them.

Today is fine, with a blue sky and white clouds, after a showery afternoon yesterday. Charlotte is now fifteen and this morning you find her in the garden. Jamie Twine is setting out chairs on the grass, ready for the performance.

'We shall need all the chairs from the dining room, Jamie. And then you will have to take them all back again in time for dinner.'

'Yes, Miss Charlotte. Henry, he have told me to finish weeding the vegetable beds today.'

'You will have plenty of time for that while we are performing our play.'

'Yes, Miss Charlotte.'

Jamie trudged back inside.

Charlotte had not told William what the play was about. Now, she saw him coming down the garden with his friend, George Hayter.

'Well, my Mouse, George tells me I shall very much enjoy your play. As we came through the hall, there were several young girls arriving and asking for you.'

Charlotte reached up and gave William a quick kiss on the cheek and hurried inside. There was a considerable noise of chattering from the little girls, who were all in the youngest class at school. Mary Hayter, who had accompanied them, was about to lead them out into the garden.

'Thank you, Miss Hayter. We shall be presenting the play where the chairs are being arranged. Six little boys from the free school will be joining us soon. And Thomas, Robert and Charles will be down here shortly.'

Charlotte went upstairs to fetch her brothers. When they came down, the schoolmaster from the free school had just arrived with his pupils.

'Caps off, boys! And behave yourselves for Miss Baskett.'

The little boys filed out into the garden, looking somewhat in awe of their surroundings, and sat down in a group away from the little girls, who nudged each other and giggled.

'Now, William, I need you to go inside, as we are about to rehearse the play.'

William bowed to Charlotte. 'Come, George, we must obey my sister's orders. You can help me choose some books from the study to take with me.'

Sarah and Eleanor Hayter arrived, and the rehearsal got under way. Once she was sure that the children knew what they had to do, and that Thomas, Sarah, Robert and Charles remembered their lines, she went inside to ask Hester to bring drinks and biscuits out into the garden for the children. Jane and Anna Maria were in the hall, greeting Lewis and Ann, who embraced her fondly.

'How good to see you, Charlotte. Lewis and I cannot wait to see your play.'

'I hope you enjoy it, Aunt Ann.'

William and George came out of the study. 'Uncle Lewis, I believe you have not met my friend, George Hayter.'

Lewis shook his hand. 'We want to wish you a safe journey, William. I look forward to hearing about the work you will be doing. We can talk more over dinner.'

'We will wait until Uncle Thomas arrives and then go out into the garden for the performance. George's sisters have written the play with Charlotte, but I have no idea what it is about.'

Charlotte went out into the garden again and took the children down to the orchard, ready to start the performance. William soon came out of the house, followed by their two uncles, Lewis and Thomas, and their aunt, Ann. Charlotte had not seen Lewis and Ann for some time, and realised his dark hair was thinning and turning grey and that she had put on a considerable amount of weight. Her cousin, John, never joined in any family gatherings, making the excuse that he was too busy on the farm, but Charlotte knew he disliked meeting people and much preferred animals. Charles and Robert's tutor, Richard Jones, also joined them and was walking down the garden beside her sister, Jane.

Once everyone was seated, Charlotte stepped forward. Although she knew everyone very well, she felt nervous. She hoped her voice would not shake.

'William has told me what he will be doing in India, so our play is all about the orphanage in Madras. My brother, Thomas, is taking the part of Dr Bell, who is in charge, and Sarah is the housekeeper, who looks after the children.'

She went to sit beside the Hayter sisters, anxiously watching the action unfold, hoping no one would forget their lines. As the performance went on, she was relieved that it seemed to be going very well.

They had decided to base the play on a typical day at the school. The little boys, on one side of the garden, and the little girls, on the other, all lay down on the grass, as if they were asleep. Sarah walked among them, ringing the school bell. They all leapt to their feet and lined up in front of her. She pretended to scrub their faces and give them their breakfasts out of imaginary bowls.

Thomas, as Dr Bell, strode on, carrying a large book. Robert and Charles sat down in front of him and he recited the alphabet to them. Everyone laughed when Little Brune trotted up and sat at Thomas's feet, as if he, too, wanted to learn his letters. The youngest children then sat down in rows; Robert and Charles, both carrying long sticks, stood in front of them, reciting the alphabet and drawing the letters on the grass. Sarah bustled about, pretending to stir cooking pots, serving dinner and eventually sending the boys and girls back to bed.

Everyone clapped enthusiastically at the end of the play, and the performers all bowed and beckoned Charlotte and her friends to join them.

William came over and gave Charlotte a hug. 'That was so enjoyable, my Mouse.'

Lewis joined them. 'Well done, Charlotte. I know my sister would have been so proud of you.'

Once they had all recovered from the shock of her death, the family rarely spoke of mama. It was almost as if Jane had always been the mother figure in the household.

'I hope she would, Uncle Lewis. She told us a lot about when she was a little girl in Newton and how you were papa's best friend when he was young.'

'Your mama always loved your papa, but she was only a little girl when she first knew him.'

William smiled at them both. 'And he had already fallen in love with my mother. But I never knew her, of course.'

Charlotte felt tears coming to her eyes. Talking about mama and papa, just as William, her best friend, was leaving, was too much. She turned away and went over to the little girls and boys, who were lining up ready to leave with Mary Hayter and the schoolmaster.

'You did so well! Thank you. I hope you have enjoyed yourselves.'

One of the little boys threw his cap in the air and jumped up and down in delight.

'Now, Johnnie, settle down. And all say thank you to Miss Baskett.'

The schoolmaster led his charges away and Mary Hayter came over to Charlotte.

'They did indeed all enjoy themselves, Charlotte. Perhaps you and my sisters could write another play for us all in the school.'

'That would be good, Miss Hayter. I shall speak to Sarah and Eleanor about it.'

Charlotte went over to the vegetable patch, where Jamie was on his knees, weeding.

'We have finished now, Jamie. The chairs must all be put back inside. And mind you wipe your feet!'

Jamie struggled to his feet. 'Yes, Miss Charlotte.'

As she went back to join Lewis and William, she noticed that once again Jane was walking beside Richard Jones. He had started as tutor to Robert and Charles last year and was lodging with her uncle, Thomas. They were talking and laughing together as they went inside the house. What would they do if Jane decided to get married? They relied on her always to be around. She might ask Anna Maria. She seemed to know everything that went on. Charlotte ran to catch up with Lewis and William.

'Uncle Lewis, I should love to talk more about mama.'

'Of course, Charlotte. It would be good if you and Sarah could come and stay with us later in the summer, when school has finished. Your mama was very fond of helping to look after the animals on the farm and even had her own special cows, called Lottie and Daisy. And we could walk on the beach, where your mama started her shell collection.'

'Robert looks after it now. And our grandfather left his butterfly collection to him and Charles.'

Lewis turned to William. 'Now, I shall be most interested to hear more about your position in Madras.'

'I am to be Dr Bell's assistant and will be staying with him at his house at Egmore Fort. I shall attend all the regular board meetings and write the minutes. Beyond that, I shall have to wait until I arrive to learn in more detail of my duties.'

Charlotte followed them into the drawing-room and listened quietly to their conversation. Lewis sat forward in his chair. 'I believe the system of teaching in the school is most unusual, William.'

'Yes. Before he arrived in Madras, Dr Bell had visited the state of Kerala. He saw some children there teaching others the alphabet by drawing in the sand. So, when he was put in charge of the orphanage in Madras, he decided to use a similar method. A schoolmaster teaches basic lessons to a small group of older pupils and then each of them relates the lesson to a group of younger children. And Dr Bell is very much against corporal punishment, so he uses a system of rewards instead. After my experience at school, I believe that is a much better way to keep order.'

Lewis laughed. 'Perhaps Dr Bell should have been appointed as headmaster of Sherborne. My headmaster was Mr Hill. I believe yours was Mr Bristed.'

'That is right, sir. And Mr Bristed's elderly father was the usher.'

'How long will it take to reach India, William?'

'I should arrive by Christmas. We stop at the Madeira Islands and at Rio de Janeiro and it depends on whether we run into any storms on the way. I shall keep a journal and I have promised Charlotte I shall write regularly.'

'And I shall be most displeased if he does not!'

Lewis smiled at her. 'You sound just like your mama, Charlotte. She was always telling everyone what to do when she was at Newton.'

Jane came in from the hall. 'Did you ask Jamie to bring the chairs back inside, Charlotte?'

'Yes, I did. Are they not back in the dining room?'

'There are only two chairs at the table. Would you go out and see what has happened, Charlotte?'

When she got outside, she could see Jamie by the vegetable patch again, talking to old Henry.

'Why have you not brought all the chairs in, Jamie?'

'Henry were telling me what I had to do in the garden, Miss Charlotte.'

'Jamie can come straight out once he has taken the chairs in, Henry. But we need them immediately, as dinner will be ready soon.'

Henry twisted his cap round in his hands. 'Sorry, Miss Charlotte. Jamie, he didn't tell me about what you asked him to do, so I told him not to loppy about an' go an' do some'at.'

Jamie trudged off towards the chairs. Old Henry muttered something under his breath. Charlotte knew that he was not able to do much of the gardening now and that Jamie worked too slowly to get everything done. Jane had spoken of getting more help for them.

When she got back inside, George Hayter had joined William and Lewis.

'I shall take my leave, William, and wish you a safe voyage. I shall miss our discussions, and only wish I were coming with you.'

William shook him warmly by the hand. 'As do I, George. I have packed my trunk and my bag with everything I should need onboard the ship. And I visited Richard Hobbs at the shop yesterday, and he has put together a sea box of ointments and tinctures for me. I only hope the seas will be calm and that I shall not be seasick on the way.'

The chairs were all back in place when they went into the dining-room. Charlotte managed to sit next to William, with her uncle, Thomas, on her other side, and Lewis and Ann opposite. As it was a special dinner, Robert and Charles were eating with them and not in the nursery. Jane had asked Betty and Hester to cook William's favourite dishes and to be sure to include a curry in preparation for his time in India.

A roast leg of lamb, a large bowl of chicken curry and one of rice were already set out on the table. Hester brought in dishes of vegetables, and a buttered apple pie, followed by Martha, who had come down from the nursery to help, carrying a pickled salmon and a bowl of strawberries from the garden.

Charlotte looked at everyone sitting round the table and suddenly felt tears come to her eyes once again. If only her mama and papa were still with them. Her uncle, Lewis, would be joking with papa about something they had done when they were boys at school together, and her aunt, Ann, would be discussing receipts with mama.

Before they started to eat, her uncle, Thomas, got to his feet, a glass of wine in his hand.

'William, everyone here wishes you have a safe journey and that your new life is everything you hope for. We shall all miss you and look forward to when you decide to return to us.'

They all picked up a glass and took a sip. Even Charlotte, Sarah, Robert and Charles had been allowed a drink of watered wine.

William stood up. 'Thank you everyone for your good wishes and I shall miss you all. And Hester, please thank Betty for cooking all my favourite dishes.'

Sitting down again, William turned to Charlotte. 'You are very quiet, my Mouse. And you are not eating.'

'I do not want you to go, William. I believe you will not return to us.'

'Of course, I shall. I do not intend to spend the rest of my life in India. And I have papa's talisman to keep me safe on the journey. It is always in my pocket wherever I go.'

Charlotte pushed her food around her plate. Everyone else seemed to be enjoying the meal and there was a loud noise of chattering. At the end of the table, her young brothers' eyes were watering from eating curry for the first time. At the other end, Jane was once again laughing at something Richard Jones was saying. Through the window she could see old Henry and young Jamie walking across the grass towards the orchard.

Apart from missing her talks with William, Charlotte knew that the other reason she was so upset was that, as a girl, she would never be allowed the freedom to travel, even when she was older. None of her sisters seemed to want to be anywhere else but here. But it was obvious, when she looked at the globe with Mama, that she also wanted to see the world. But papa had asked her to marry him, which was something she had always wanted.

After dinner, Lewis and Ann left to reach Swanage before it got dark. Her uncle, Thomas, and Richard Jones also went home. Jane and Anna Maria went to the kitchen to speak to Betty and Hester. Sarah and her younger brothers went up to the nursery. Charlotte followed William and her brother, Thomas, out into the garden. They sat down on the seat under the apple tree and Little Brune got up from where he had been asleep and lay down at Thomas's feet. He bent down to stroke his ears.

'I have been wondering, William, whether there would be a place for me at the orphanage. Now I have left Sherborne, I am not looking forward to the prospect of another period of study.'

'I shall enquire on your behalf once I have arrived. It would certainly be good to have you with me.'

Charlotte knew it was useless even to think of going with him, so she said nothing. Today was going far too quickly. William had been part of her life for as long as she could remember. Papa had always been busy visiting his patients. Mama had lost two babies soon after she was born, and was often too sad to play with her. Then her little sister, Sarah, had arrived to keep mama occupied. Her two older sisters were busy playing together. But William always had time for her. One of her favourite games involved creeping up behind him as quietly as possible, while he pretended to be asleep. That was when he had started to call her his Mouse. He would pick her up and swing her round until she was giddy.

William was to leave early in the morning to travel to Portsmouth and would set sail for India the following day. Jane and Anna Maria joined them in the garden until the light started to fade, then they spent a quiet evening in the parlour. Hester brought supper into the dining room, but once again, Charlotte had no appetite. All too soon, it was time for them to retire. William would have an early breakfast and everyone else would rise in time to say goodbye to him.

Charlotte lay in bed, unable to sleep at first. Of course, she would continue to enjoy the company of her family and friends. And she looked forward to writing another play with Sarah and Eleanor Hayter. She thought about how her uncle, Lewis, had invited her to visit Newton Manor with her sister, Sarah, once school was finished for the summer.

You hope William will arrive safely in Madras by Christmas. You wonder whether Thomas will be able to join him. And will Charlotte learn more from Anna Maria about Jane's friendship with Richard Jones?

You look into the chest once more. At the bottom, you find a bundle of letters.

Chapter 3
The Letters

Wednesday, 7 September 1796 – Newton Manor, Swanage, Dorset

The letters are tied together by a narrow, faded red ribbon. You untie the knot and see they are all addressed to Charlotte. The first is dated July 1794, when William had just set out on his voyage to India.

Last year, following the outbreak of war with France again, extra men began to be recruited for the navy and in April, three men were enrolled in Wareham. In May, Mrs Hutchins died at the age of eighty-seven, surviving her husband by over twenty years.

Jane and Anna Maria continue to run the household in East Street and Richard Jones is still tutoring Robert and Charles. Sarah remains at the school, but Charlotte has left. In April this year, Thomas sailed for India to join William in Madras. A few days later, Little Brune, who was devoted to Thomas, died at the age of thirteen. Lewis and Ann have given the family a new puppy, which they have inevitably called Brune.

Yesterday, Lewis came to Wareham to bring Charlotte back to Newton Manor for a visit. She has brought Brune with her to meet the Cockram family's dog, Lottie, and today you find Charlotte and her uncle walking the dogs on the beach.

Lewis bent down and picked up a shell. 'Your mama started her collection here. This one is from a cockle and that one over there is a whelk.'

'I can understand why she was interested in them. They are all so different. Look, this one is a spiral.'

'And here is a razor clam.'

'Papa gave mama a book about shells just after Jane was born. I must look at it again when I get home.'

Brune trotted behind them, then picked up a pebble and put it down in front of Charlotte.

'He wants me to throw it for him. I am worried he might swallow it though.'

They walked further along the beach. 'This is where your papa found his ammonite. I believe he gave it to William.'

'Yes, he has taken it to India with him. He says it brought him luck on the voyage. I have brought some of William's letters with me. I shall show them to you when we get back to Newton. We have not yet had a letter from Thomas. I hope he is having a good voyage. We worry about them both. They are so far away.'

They watched as Brune and Lottie ran into the water, chasing the waves.

'Did you know that your papa inoculated you against smallpox when you were a tiny baby, Charlotte?'

When Charlotte was here in Swanage last year, Sarah, Robert and Charles were with her, so she had no opportunity to speak with Lewis about her mama and papa.

'Mama told me we had all been inoculated when we were young.'

'Did she also tell you the method your papa used?'

'No, Lewis. Was it remarkable?'

'Just after you were born, your papa and I went to see a farmer called Mr Jesty, who lived in Yetminster. He had inoculated his family with a stocking needle using matter from cows with cowpox, instead of from people with smallpox. Your papa was intending to use the same method when he inoculated his patients, but I do not know if he carried out his plan.'

'He never discussed it with me, Lewis. But then I was only nine when he died.'

'Earlier this year, Mr Jesty brought his family to live at a farm near Harman's Cross – not far from here. And now I have read that a doctor, Edward Jenner, has inoculated a young boy using material from a lesion on the hand of a dairymaid with cowpox. He is claiming to have been first to use this method.'

'Mama told us she caught cowpox when she was young after milking one of her cows.'

'Yes, we were worried about her. We thought she had smallpox.'

The dogs ran out of the water towards Charlotte, and shook themselves, making the bottom of her skirt wet.

Lewis laughed. 'Time to go home, I think. Your aunt will be waiting.'

As they walked up to the house, Charlotte's cousin, John, was coming from the farmyard. Without looking up, he greeted them with a quick wave and went inside.

'John is taking over more and more from your uncle, Thomas, on the farm. It is what he enjoys more than anything. He will eventually inherit the manor from me, of course. And before you ask, no, he shows no signs of wanting to marry and start a family to carry on after him. Come, Charlotte, we have time to go down to the bottom of the garden before dinner. Your mama's oak tree has produced acorns for the first time this year.'

'I should like to take one back to Wareham with me to plant in the garden. I am sure mama would be pleased.'

As she stood under the huge tree, Charlotte could imagine her mama carefully planting the acorn in the ground. She would have had no idea that, twenty-five years later, her daughter would be standing beneath it, tears coming to her eyes.

Lewis came and put his arm round her shoulder. 'You look very like your mama when she was your age, Charlotte. She had the same curly hair and rosy cheeks. When we were on the beach, I found it difficult to believe that it was not my sister walking beside me.'

George, the gardener, came round the corner from the vegetable garden, pushing a barrow. He was beginning to look quite old, in spite of still being called young George. Charlotte knew that his father, old George, had been gardener at Newton when her mama was a girl.

'Will you show me the pineapples in the hothouse, George?'

'I be going there now, Miss Charlotte. I be preparing beds for the new plants. They will have their fruit next summer.'

Her aunt, Ann, came out of the house.

'Dinner is nearly ready. I hope you had an enjoyable walk, Charlotte.'

'Yes, thank you, Aunt Ann. I feel much refreshed. I have to go in now, George, but I shall come and see you tomorrow morning.'

Charlotte found Newton very peaceful after life at home. Today there were just five of them at dinner. Her cousin, John, had obviously made an effort to look presentable. He had brushed his hair and was wearing a clean shirt. Her uncle, Thomas, arrived after they had been seated at the table for a while. His hair was somewhat unkempt, and Charlotte noticed he was still wearing his working boots.

'I must apologise for my lateness, Ann. I was working in the top field and did not realise the time.' He helped himself to some stew and vegetables. 'It is good to see you again, Charlotte. John, we must hope the weather stays fine tomorrow. Joe will need to finish the ploughing if we are to plant the wheat next week.'

John nodded, but did not say anything.

Ann got up from the table to ring the bell. 'Mr and Mrs Cox hope to visit us tomorrow, Charlotte. They both tutored your cousin John when he left school.'

'Mama told me so much about them, Aunt Ann. She said she so enjoyed being taught by Mrs Cox when she was her governess.'

The door opened and a young girl, looking anxious, came in, carrying a bowl of pineapple and an apple pie.

'Thank you, Kitty. You can put the dishes down here. And we will be taking tea in the parlour after dinner.'

'Yes, madam.' Kitty almost ran out of the door once the food was safely on the table.

Ann smiled. 'She only started here last week and is very young. But I am sure she will settle down soon.'

Charlotte took a helping of the fruit. 'I always love the pineapple you bring to Wareham when you visit. I have told George I should like to see them growing in the hothouse tomorrow.'

After dinner, Charlotte fetched William's letters from her chamber and brought them down to the drawing room. Once they were seated and Kitty had brought in their tea, she carefully undid the ribbon holding the letters together. The first one was sent by William from on board ship and posted once they reached the Madeira Islands. It began, "Dear Mouse", as did all his letters.

'This letter describes what life is like on board the ship, Ceres. He says, "My cabin ceiling is very low and I am writing this on my knee. The weather is calmer now, but the waves were enormous as we crossed the Bay of Biscay". He goes on to say that there were cows and goats on board to supply milk, and also sheep, pigs and chickens. Some of the passengers organised dancing and put on plays. And there were a few ladies on board going out to India to visit a brother, or look for a husband.'

Lewis smiled. 'I had no idea there would be so much going on. Does he describe what his life is like at the school?'

Charlotte looked through some more letters. 'This one was written shortly after he had arrived in Madras. He seems to think he will soon be acclimatised to the heat. At noon, it is much hotter than most summer days here, but it is cooler in the morning. He says there are about a hundred pupils at the school. They leave when they are sixteen and are either apprenticed or trained to be servants. He is the assistant schoolmaster. He also keeps the accounts for Dr Bell. The currency there is called a pagoda.'

'Does William say if the pupils are well looked after?'

Charlotte knew her aunt would want to know the domestic details at the school. She found a passage from another letter.

'They do seem to be well looked after. Here he says, "The boys have beer and rice or milk and rice at breakfast and for dinner either mutton broth or various curries. For supper, there is more rice and milk". I must say their diet does not seem to vary much. He says they wear long drawers and a shirt most of the time, with a white waistcoat and a leathern cap on special occasions.'

'When we spoke before he left, William explained the method of teaching to us. We still remember seeing the play you and your friends wrote for him. Does he elaborate on that?'

'Yes, Uncle Lewis. Let me find the passage. Here it is. "There is one particular pupil called John Friskin, who is still only about thirteen years old. He was the first to be taught how to teach the younger boys. He is now in charge of the teaching arrangements. Nearly every boy is both a master and a scholar".'

Charlotte looked through some of the other letters and picked out a more recent one.

'William says that Dr Bell is about to return to England, at least for the time being, as his health has been deteriorating of late. He wonders whether that is the reason that he has a bad temper at times. A Mr Kerr will replace him as head of the school.'

Her aunt looked anxious. 'Let us hope William remains in good health and that Thomas will not find the heat intolerable.'

Lewis stood up. 'Now, I must go outside. Joe will be milking and I need to check on the cows. I was a little worried this morning, that one of them was lame.'

'May I come with you, Uncle Lewis?'

'Of course. But I fear you will find it muddy in the farmyard.'

Charlotte followed her uncle outside, but decided to remain behind the gate to the farmyard. Lewis walked along the row of cows, which were waiting to be milked.

'Your mama would have milked her special cows here. And it was where she caught cowpox, of course.'

'William says in one of his letters that the pupils are all inoculated against smallpox by the physician there, Dr Baillie, although probably not by Mr Jesty's method.'

Once Lewis had examined the cows and spoken to Joe, they walked back through the garden towards the house. The dogs were running around together on the grass and Brune bounded up to them when he saw Charlotte.

Back in the drawing room, Ann was waiting for her.

'I found your mama's journal the other day at the back of a drawer and thought you would like to have it. It covers the year before she got cowpox and I suppose she stopped writing it when she became ill.'

Charlotte carefully opened the book. 'That is one of the best presents you could have given me, Aunt Ann.'

When she was little, William had given her the picture book mama had given him, when she married papa. And she treasured the dictionary with her mama's name written inside. Now, she had written "Charlotte Baskett's Book" inside. On the page opposite, her papa had written "S. Baskett of Wareham, Dorset, Surgeon, Apothecary and Man-midwife". She knew she would keep them all for as long as she lived.

'Now, tell me, Charlotte, how are your brothers and sisters?'

'They are all well, Aunt Ann. I believe Jane enjoys keeping house. She is very fond of the boys' tutor, Richard Jones. Anna Maria thinks they have secretly become engaged.'

Ann smiled. 'Did you know your uncle and I also became engaged secretly before we announced it to our families?'

'No, I did not! That is perhaps something mama did not know.'

'And Anna Maria?'

Charlotte laughed. 'She blushes a lot if a young man even speaks to her. I think she falls in love very frequently. There was George Hayter, William's friend. Then Robert Carruthers, the son of the surgeon in Wareham. And, most recently, Edward Clavill. But none of them seem in the least bit interested in her.'

'That is unfortunate! But it does not help that she always looks so serious. And you, Charlotte?'

'No, Aunt Ann. I have yet to meet a young man with whom I can imagine spending the rest of my life.'

'I am sure there is someone, somewhere, meant for you.'

Charlotte knew that her aunt would not approve if she told her what she really wanted to do. She wanted to go to visit William and Thomas in India. She wanted to learn how to be a surgeon, like her papa. She wanted to write another play and see it performed. They were all things her aunt would consider not fit for a young lady even to think of doing. But even if she could do none of these things, she was determined not to make domesticity the centre of her life, as her sisters seemed to want, nor to be forever looking back to the past. It had taken this visit, away from the house in East Street, away from Wareham, to make her realise this.

Tomorrow, she would go with George to the hothouse to see the pineapple plants. She also planned to ask Mrs Cox more about her mama when she was a little girl and if she remembered when her papa visited Newton Manor. Her uncle, Lewis, had promised to show her his telescope. Her mama had told her she loved to look through it at the night sky. And yes, she realised, she was happy.

You are getting to know Charlotte better and to see she is growing up to be a determined young lady, just like her mama. You are eager to learn whether any of her hopes will be realised. You decide there might be a clue in the next object, so you look in the chest once more. Lying flat at the bottom is a small picture frame…

Chapter 4
The Portrait

Friday, 23 November 1798 – East Street, Wareham, Dorset

In the small, oval frame is a sketch of a young Indian woman. She has a half smile on her face and her large, dark eyes are looking straight towards the artist. Her black hair is parted in the middle and is partly covered by a pale shawl, which falls over her shoulders. She is wearing a necklace, from which hangs a small pendant, and several bracelets on her delicate wrists.

In the town, as anxiety has grown about a possible invasion by the French, more men have had to be recruited, including twenty-one-year-old William Lambert from Wareham. The annual Court Leet is being held this month, when disputes will be heard and settled by a jury appointed by the Lord of the Manor. Bread-weighers, Chimney-Peepers and Ale-tasters will do the rounds of the local businesses, ending at various public houses, the fines being paid in ale.

Last year, Thomas Bartlett received news from Bombay, of the death of Mrs Hutchins' daughter, Anne Bellasis. In May, Jane and Richard Jones became engaged, after much speculation by the family. They have decided to wait until both the younger boys are at school before getting married. Robert will be going to Sherborne next year, and Richard will continue to tutor Charles, until he joins his brother the following year. Charlotte has become more and more involved in the life of the town. She now helps her uncle, Thomas, to run the musical society. Richard has become a member, and plays the bass in the orchestra. Sarah is still at school and her sisters are worried that she seems to be more and more withdrawn, finding it difficult to make many friends. Anna Maria continues to fall in love with any young man she meets, but has yet to find anyone who returns her affections.

Two months ago, the family received the devasting news that both William and Thomas had died within a few days of each other, in April, from cholera.

Then, yesterday, a small trunk was delivered to the house, containing their belongings, including all the letters the family had sent to them. When they found the portrait of the young woman, they could only guess who she was.

It is a foggy, November day, after showers yesterday. It is early morning and you find Charlotte alone in the drawing-room, staring out of the window at the dreary, damp garden.

Charlotte could hear Betty and Hester in the kitchen, preparing breakfast. It was very early and the rest of house was quiet. Last night she had dreamt about William. She had been uncertain who it was coming towards her, out of the mist, but then he had greeted her as "Little Mouse". William was the only person to do that. He told her she should be brave, for his sake, and not abandon what she believed in. She had known in her dream that he should not have been there and she had told him he would have to leave, that he was dead. She had awoken early and knew she had to get up, to look in the trunk once more.

Now, she was holding William's copy of *The Interesting Narrative of the Life of Olaudah Equiano*, the freed slave. She remembered talking to William about slavery and how strongly he felt that it was wrong. Later, after he had left for India, she had discussed the subject with her friends, Eleanor and Sarah Hayter. Their brother, George, had travelled to Bath to hear Olaudah Equiano speak. But last year, George told them that Olaudah had died. Surely, she owed it to William to learn more, even if she herself could make little difference. She opened the book and started to turn the pages. The first chapter described the country, Abyssinia, where Olaudah had been born, before being kidnapped, together with his sister, and sold into slavery.

The door opened quietly, and Sarah came in, still in her nightgown, followed by Brune. 'I woke up and found you were not in your bed, Charlotte. I was worried.'

Charlotte bent down to stroke the little dog, and he jumped up on to her lap. 'I am sorry, Sarah. I could not get back to sleep. I wanted to look at all the things in the trunk. We need to find out about the picture of the young woman.'

Sarah stood in the middle of the room, shivering, tears starting to run down her cheeks. 'I had thought that perhaps the letter from India was a mistake, that they had not died, that they would come back to us. But now we have their things, I know it is true.'

'Go upstairs and get dressed, Sarah. You will catch a chill. After breakfast, we will look through the chest again together.'

Sarah nodded and went upstairs again. Charlotte put the book down and went to fetch her cloak. She needed to take Brune for his morning walk. The little dog bounded down the garden to the orchard and Charlotte followed him. This was where, in her dream, she had seen William, coming towards her from behind one of the apple trees, dressed in a long, thin, white shirt. His deep chestnut-coloured hair had faded and he looked bewildered. She knew the image would stay with her for the rest of her life.

'Charlotte! Breakfast is ready. It is too cold to stay outside.' Jane's voice made her start. She called Brune and made her way up the garden again.

Robert and Charles were already at the table when she went into the dining-room and had helped themselves to a hot Bath cake each. Charlotte sat down beside Robert and poured herself some hot chocolate. Her sisters soon joined them. Sarah looked pale and her eyes were still red from weeping. Jane sat down at the head of the table and Anna Maria sat at the other end, as usual. Robert and Charles were the only ones eager to eat. Charlotte buttered some toast but knew it would stick in her throat if she tried to eat it. Brune sat under the table at her feet and put his head on her lap. It was as if he was aware how upset she was and was trying to comfort her.

After breakfast, Charlotte and Sarah went into the study. The chest was still open, on the desk.

'I think we need to take everything out, Sarah, and look through all the letters and papers.'

On the top were the few clothes which had been returned to them. Charlotte first of all took out a long white shirt. 'Oh, Sarah, I dreamt last night about William. He was wearing this shirt. I suppose I must have seen it when we looked at the things yesterday.'

Sarah lifted out a blue waistcoat. 'I remember Thomas packing this in his trunk when he left. And here is his cravat.' She held it up to her face. 'It smells of Indian spices.'

Charlotte took out a small leather bag. She opened the clasp. Inside was William's talisman, the ammonite her papa had picked up on the beach at Swanage all those years ago. Her first thought was that it had not kept him safe. Then she wondered whether she should hand it on to one of her brothers. But perhaps William would have wanted it to be passed to the next generation.

Sarah was starting to look through the letters. They had all written to their brothers in India, and it looked as if they had kept them all.

'Here is the first letter I wrote to Thomas, Charlotte. And here is one you wrote to William. But look, here is one to William from someone else. It is more like a note than a letter. It is from someone called Apana. Do you think that is the name of the young woman in the picture?'

'It could be. It will do no harm now to read it.'

'It says she will meet him in the usual place at noon. And she signs it, your Apana.'

'It must have been a secret from everyone. I do remember in one of his letters William said he had been asked by one of the merchants in Madras to teach English to his two young daughters. She could be one of them.'

Charlotte and Sarah both stared at the portrait again.

'Do you think William had found his true love, Charlotte? It sounds like a fairy story.'

'Let us hope it made him happy in his last days. I wonder if William drew the portrait of her himself. Thomas might have known, but now the secret has gone with them into their graves.'

There was nothing more in the chest apart from a few more items of clothing. Sarah went to find Jane, to tell her about the note. Then, as Charlotte was putting everything back into the chest, she noticed a small, leatherbound book tucked in between the letters. When she opened it, she realised it was a diary, in William's hand. Inside the cover it said, *'To my Mouse. If I do not return, this book will tell you everything that has happened to me since I left home. You should keep my talisman to bring you luck.'* The first entry was written on board the ship on his way to India, and the last one the day before he died, saying he was feeling unwell. For the first time since she heard the dreadful news, she wept. When Jane and Sarah found her, she was sitting on the floor, clutching the diary, tears running uncontrollably down her cheeks.

Jane bent down beside Charlotte and gently took the book from her fingers. 'Come, let us go into the drawing room. You can read it later. Richard has arrived and is upstairs with the boys, so we can go and sit there quietly. Sarah, go to the kitchen and ask Hester to bring in some tea.'

Jane always knew what to do to make things seem better. They would all miss her greatly after she had married Richard and set up her own home.

Charlotte could not imagine Anna Maria being in charge of the household. She was inclined to daydream and forget what she was supposed to be doing.

Hester brought in the tea and some of Betty's seed cake, together with a letter, which she handed to Jane. 'I believe this is from Uncle Lewis – I recognise his hand. I wrote to him as soon as we knew about William and Thomas.' She broke the seal and started to read. 'He expresses his sorrow at our news and says that he and Aunt Ann will drive over when the weather has improved. And our cousin, John, has become a Captain in the Purbeck Volunteers. I would not think he is very suited to be in that position, but I suppose he is the only person in the area to qualify.'

After they had finished their tea, Charlotte went into the study and sat down to read William's journal. Much of what he had written had been included in his letters. But he also wrote about his thoughts and feelings about life in Madras – the heat, the food, the poverty. Further on in the journal, he started to write about the lessons he was giving to the daughters of an Indian friend of Dr Bell – Savita, who was only thirteen, and Apana, who was eighteen. At first, the entries merely gave details of what he was teaching them. But then Charlotte read the entry for a day in May last year. *'Savita was unwell today and only Apana came to the lesson, accompanied, as usual, by an elderly servant. This evening, as I ate my meal, I kept seeing Apana's shy smile and her dark eyes looking at me.'*

Charlotte read on, eager to find out how their relationship had developed to the point where they were obviously sending notes to each other in secret. She found another entry for the end of the month. *'Today, as I arrived for the lesson, Apana was waiting for me by the gate. She told me that next week would be our last lesson, as the family would be going to their summer residence until October. I could see there were tears in her eyes. I said how much I would miss her. Then, I did something I know I should not have done. I took her in my arms and told her I loved her. To my surprise and delight, she responded to my embrace. Then we heard her sister calling to her and she immediately broke away and ran into the house.'*

In an entry the following week, William wrote that Apana had been waiting for him by the gate when he arrived for the next lesson. *'I took her into my arms once more and told her again how much I loved her and that I would wait for her return.'* Charlotte turned to the entries for October, when the family were due to return to Madras and found the entry referring to the note Apana sent to him. She supposed the gate must have been "the usual place".

When Jane came into the study, Charlotte was able to tell her how William had finally asked Apana to marry him and return to England with him the following summer. 'I am amazed that he said nothing of this in his letters to any of any of us. Was he planning to arrive with an Indian bride as a surprise for us? And I wonder whether her family knew.'

Jane took the journal from Charlotte. 'The poor girl must have been distraught when William died. I cannot imagine that she would have settled happily in Wareham. But now we shall never know.'

'If William loved her, we would have made her welcome, would we not, Jane?'

'Yes, of course. Now, I have to go to the kitchen to see Betty about dinner.'

Left alone again, Charlotte sat, Brune at her feet, thinking about what she had just read. So, William was planning to return home this year. All she knew was that she had to keep his memory alive by living her life as he would have wished. And Thomas? There was little mention of him in William's journal and it appeared Thomas himself had not kept one.

Her thoughts were interrupted when she heard the doorbell ringing and Hester greeting the visitors. She recognised the voices of her friends, Sarah and Eleanor Hayter, and their brother, George. Hester brought them into the study. Eleanor embraced her.

'Oh, Charlotte, we have only this morning heard your dreadful news. We have been away from home, visiting our aunt and uncle in Bath.'

George took her hand. 'I shall miss William more than I can say, Charlotte. He was my dearest friend.'

'We have discovered his diary, George. We have learned of his love for an Indian girl. Did you know of this?'

'I received a letter from him recently. By the time it reached me, he must have already died. He told me he was planning to bring her back here, but he asked me not to say anything about it yet. I suppose he wanted to tell you all when he knew it would be possible. I do not think they had told her parents of their plans.'

Charlotte did not know what to say. She thought she knew everything about William, but she did not know about the most important person in his life. She realised Eleanor was speaking to her.

'We saw Sophia and Elizabeth Carruthers on our way here, Charlotte. They told us that their brother, Robert, has just qualified as a surgeon and has returned to join his father. At last, we shall have another surgeon in the town.'

Jane came in and greeted their visitors. Charlotte sat by the window, only half listening to the conversation going on around her. Their new kitchen maid, Edith, missed her own family and was worried that the French would invade the town. Deborah Dugdale, who still taught at the school, had just got engaged to John Cole. Thomas Bartlett's wife had a fever and was not expected to live.

Charlotte picked up the book by Olaudah Equiano, which was lying on the desk. 'I believe this is your copy, George. It was among the things which were returned from India.'

'I gave it to William before he left, so it is yours now. When I heard Equiano speak in Bath, he was introduced by William Wilberforce as Gustavus Vassa. I believe he was called that when he converted to Christianity.'

'I know William would have been pleased for me to learn more about the anti-slavery movement. Is there anything I could do, George?'

'I can ask my father. We were introduced to a lady called Hannah More when we were visiting our relations in Bath. She is very opposed to slavery. She has written poems about the movement. And she and her sisters have set up some schools in Somerset villages, to teach poor children.'

Eleanor stood up. 'Come, George, we must leave. Father and Mother will be expecting us at home.'

Before dinner, Charlotte took William's journal and his talisman upstairs. She put them both safely away in her chest of drawers. She told herself that William would have wanted her to keep busy, to concentrate on all the things he felt so strongly about.

Downstairs again in the study, she started to read more from the book by Olaudah Equiano. She turned to the second chapter and learned, to her surprise, that Olaudah's father owned many slaves himself. Before Olaudah was captured, he had a happy childhood, playing with his brothers and his sister. He was the youngest and his mother's favourite, so he was always with her.

At dinner, Richard Jones reminded them that there was a music club concert that evening.

'This morning, your uncle, Thomas, told me he would not be able to see you before the concert, as he has to attend a meeting of the Court Leet. But he will be there in time to play in the orchestra. I shall go home after dinner and then return to accompany you to the Town Hall. We will be playing music by Corelli and Clementi. Jane, my love, your uncle, Thomas, told me your mother and father saw Clementi play when he was living in Steepleton.'

'Yes. I remember how mama said she thought he was a strange young man. But I believe he has done well in London.'

Charlotte also remembered her mama telling her how much she disliked Peter Beckford, the owner of Steepleton, and how his family owned slaves in Jamaica.

Later, listening to the music, she realised she felt happy for the first time since she had heard about William and Thomas. She had some very dear friends, whom she had known all her life. Sophia and Elizabeth Carruthers and their brother Robert were sitting behind her, and Eleanor, Sarah and George Hayter were in the row behind them.

The mist was obscuring the moon as they started for home after the concert. Richard Jones guided them along the street, holding a lantern so they could avoid the muddy patches left from yesterday's rain. Inside, the fire was still alight in the sitting room. Hester came in and lit the lamps.

'I shall bring some tea in for you all presently and Betty have made some of your favourite biscuits, Miss Jane.'

Charlotte sat by the fire, warming her hands. Nothing had changed. Life would go on as before. But she had so much to look forward to. Jane would soon marry Richard Jones and perhaps start a family of her own. And she smiled to herself, thinking that Anna Maria would almost certainly continue to fall in love with a succession of unsuitable young men.

You leave Charlotte, in the midst of her family, her life before her, and hope there will be happier times ahead. You wonder when you will see her next. At the bottom of the chest, you can feel something soft, wrapped in muslin…

Chapter 5
The Blue Silk Shawl

Monday, 4 June 1804 – East Street, Wareham, Dorset

Inside, are a neatly folded blue silk shawl with fringed ends and a white muslin cap edged with lace and trimmed with a blue satin ribbon, which has faded in places.

As fears of a Napoleonic invasion have once again intensified, mass enlistment has been resumed and a new barracks built in the town. In the event of invasion, the government has ordered that houses, crops and bridges should be destroyed and the entire area evacuated. In spite of this, life in the town continues largely as before.

Richard Jones is now training to be an attorney with Thomas Baskett and his partner, Thomas Bartlett. Five years ago, the surgeon, Robert Carruthers, died, and since then, his son, Robert, has run the practice alone. But a month ago, he was joined by another young surgeon, Henry Everingham. Three years after returning from India, Dr Andrew Bell became rector of St Mary's, Swanage. The following year, during one of her visits to Lewis and Ann, Charlotte met Dr Bell and was able to speak with him about William and Thomas. He also told her that he had met Benjamin Jesty and started to use his method to inoculate the people of Swanage.

Deborah Dugdale stopped teaching when she married John Cole four years ago, and Charlotte has been putting on plays and concerts at the school. She and her friends, George, Eleanor and Sarah Hayter, continue to support the anti-slavery movement. On a visit to Bath, they were delighted to be able to travel to meet Hannah More, at her house in Cowslip Green, Somerset.

Four years ago, Jane married Richard Jones and, to the delight of her sisters, they decided to remain in the family house on East Street. They now have two little girls, Mary, who is three today, and Jane, who is fifteen months. Molly

Brine enjoys having children in the nursery once more, and is now assisted by former kitchen maid, Edith. Their old gardener, Henry, has at last retired. He suggested that they should take on his nephew, Alfie, as new assistant gardener. The family have found Alfie is more reliable than Jamie, who still tends to forget what he has been asked to do. Robert and Charles are both still at school in Sherborne and arrived back yesterday for the summer.

It is a fine June day and you find Charlotte in the garden, Brune at her heels.

Charlotte could see Jamie working in the vegetable garden and hurried over to speak to him.

'We shall need some strawberries for dinner today, Jamie.'

Jamie stopped digging and leant on his spade. 'Alfie, he be pickin' them presently, Miss Charlotte.'

'We shall be eating in the garden, so the table and chairs need to be set out under the apple tree. There will be seven of us, and the little girls.'

Jamie nodded and continued his digging. Charlotte went back to the house and into the kitchen.

'Mr and Mrs Cockram are unable to come today, Betty. Mr Cockram is unwell. So, there will just be the family for dinner. Alfie is picking the strawberries.'

'Thank you, Miss Charlotte. I have cooked a good ham and a nice salmon to have cold and we be making an apple pie. And some special jelly for little Miss Mary.'

Charlotte was worried about her uncle, Lewis. He had been far from well recently. Aunt Ann had sent a message saying he had a fever again and was unable to travel.

Amelia, the new kitchen maid, stood at the sink, peeling apples for the pie. She stopped what she was doing and turned to Charlotte, looking agitated.

'Oh, madam, my brother, Jamie, he do say the French soldiers be coming here in a balloon. And my cousin, Tommy, he have heard they be marching to London through a tunnel.'

'Do not worry, Amelia. There are no reports of either of those things happening.'

'I do worry, madam. And my cousin, Robbie, he have joined the army and my aunt, Hannah, be afraid for him.'

Amelia belonged to a very large family from Stoborough, over the south bridge, and Charlotte found it difficult to know who was who. Betty raised her eyebrows in despair. 'Now then, Amelia, you peel they apples, so I can get on and make the pie.'

Charlotte herself, was concerned about the threat of invasion, but tried not to convey her fears to the servants, who seemed to believe every false rumour going around. There was great excitement in the town last year when a blue and gold balloon flew overhead. From the garden, they could see there were four people in the basket, which was certainly not big enough to carry an invading army.

She decided to go up to the nursery to see her little nieces. They were both happy little girls and always raised her spirits. They were to go down to the drawing room before dinner, so that little Mary could be given her birthday presents.

Mary was sitting on the floor, with her doll, Jemimah. It had belonged to Jane when she was a little girl and Charlotte could remember how her sister had refused to let her play with it. Charlotte herself had been given a doll called Pippy for her second birthday. Pippy went everywhere with her, until she went to school and was now carefully put away in a drawer by her bed, together with William's talisman and his journal.

Anna Maria was sitting at the table with her sewing as usual. She seemed at last to have come to terms with remaining unmarried. When Robert Carruthers arrived back in Wareham to join his father, she had been convinced his visits to the house had been because of her. But he took far more interest in Charlotte, who found him quite unattractive, with a round, rather red face and a strange, high laugh. She would always find something important to do in the kitchen or the nursery, to avoid having to sit with him to make polite conversation. Today, she had been invited to a supper party by his twin sisters, Sophia and Elizabeth, who also had a birthday today. She, together with Eleanor and Sarah Hayter, had been friends with them ever since they were all at school together.

Molly came in from the night nursery, holding little Jane by the hand. At fifteen months old, she was still unsteady on her feet at times. Charlotte bent down and the little girl staggered towards her and fell into her arms.

'I did change her clout and she be wearing a clean frock, Miss Charlotte, so she be ready for the party.'

'Thank you, Molly.'

'And Miss Mary be wearing her new frock.' The little girl scrambled to her feet, holding Jemimah.

Charlotte knew that Anna Maria had been sewing her niece's present for some time and had also made an outfit for her doll.

'What a lucky girl you are, Mary.' Charlotte gave her a hug. 'Now we can all go downstairs. I do believe your mama and papa are waiting in the drawing room, and there might be some more presents for you.'

Molly picked up little Jane and took Mary by the hand. Downstairs, Jane and Richard were sitting on the sofa in the drawing room, the presents on a table in front of them.

Mary ran up to her mother. 'Look, mama, Mimah has a new frock and a new bonnet.'

'Have you said thank you to your aunt, Anna Maria?'

'Yes, mama.'

When she had visited Bath with Eleanor Hayter last month, Charlotte had bought her niece some more animals for her farmyard. Sarah, who was sitting quietly in the corner by the fireplace, had given her *Mother Goose's Melody*, a book of nursery rhymes. Jane and Richard gave her some more furniture for the doll's house up in the day nursery. Mary jumped up and down in excitement.

Jane got up from the sofa. 'Now, I do believe dinner will be ready out in the garden soon. Molly, could you take Miss Mary's presents upstairs.'

'Yes, madam.' She smiled at Mary. 'You be a lucky little girl.'

Mary picked up her doll. 'Mama, Mimah wants dinner too.'

Charlotte looked out of the window. She could see Jamie and Alfie putting the chairs round the table and Hester and Amelia carrying dishes down the garden. She began to think about what she would be wearing to Sophia and Elizabeth's party that evening. Her new blue and white muslin dress would be perfect. And perhaps her blue silk shawl, and her bonnet with the blue ribbon. Sarah would be eager to arrange her hair. She wondered whether there would be dancing and if so, how she would be able to avoid the attentions of Robert Carruthers.

Once Robert and Charles returned from visiting friends in the town, they all went down to the bottom of the garden and sat around the table. Charlotte took some salmon and looked round the table at her family. Sarah was occupied in helping little Jane, sitting in her highchair, to eat her dinner. Brune sat under the table, waiting for the rejected scraps of food the little girl would throw on to the grass. Her brothers were eager to pile up their plates and start eating and to continue an argument they had obviously begun before they sat down. Little Mary squealed with delight when Hester brought her special jelly from the kitchen. She picked up her spoon and started to feed her doll. Richard was laughing at something Jane said to him. Anna Maria sat in silence as usual, pushing her food around her plate.

Once they had finished eating, Jane took Richard's arm and walked up the garden towards the house. Molly came to take the little girls back to the nursery and Hester started to clear the dishes. Charlotte's friends would be arriving in about an hour. George Hayter was to escort them all to the party. She felt a mixture of excitement and anxiety, although she knew, once she arrived, her doubts would vanish and she would enjoy meeting all the friends who would be there.

'Come, Sarah, you can help me arrange my hair and change my dress.'

'I wish I could come with you, Charlotte.'

'You will be able to go to parties with your own friends when you are older.'

'I do not believe the girls at school will invite me. My only real friend is Matilda Barker. Mary Filliter does not speak to me, and the Haines triplets are always laughing behind their hands when I go by.'

Charlotte knew that her sister had always found it difficult to join in the general chatter at school but tried to make light of it. 'I am sure they are not laughing at you, Sarah. Now, come, help me with my dress.'

Soon, she could hear her friends arriving and she went downstairs to meet them. George bowed his head to her in greeting.

'I shall be proud to escort three such lovely ladies through the town. My sisters have been trying to decide what to wear since before dinner.'

'Now, George, you know that is not true.' Eleanor turned away from her brother. 'Charlotte, your dress is charming. Is it new?'

'Anna Maria made it for me and I was anxious it would not be ready in time for today.'

It was not far to the Carruthers' house. They were greeted at the door by Robert Carruthers. 'My dear Miss Baskett. What a delight! And Miss Eleanor and Miss Sarah. You are all welcome. My sisters are in the drawing room.'

Charlotte could see that the furniture had been removed from the centre of the floor and the carpet rolled back, which meant there would indeed be dancing that evening. Sophia was in animated conversation with a young man whom

Charlotte did not recognise. Eleanor whispered in her ear. 'That is Robert's friend, Francis White. Elizabeth thinks he has proposed marriage to her. He has been visiting frequently lately.'

Charlotte could see that Sophia looked very flushed and a little confused. George clapped his hands.

'How good it is to see you all here to celebrate the birthdays of my dear sisters. As head of the family, I am very happy to announce that Sophia will shortly be marrying my good friend, Mr Francis White. My dear fellow, you are most welcome as a future member of our family. I just wish my dear father and mother could be here with us to see this happy day.'

As Robert carried on with his speech, Charlotte found her attention wandering and she looked around the room at the other guests. The party included Sophia and Elizabeth's sister, Mary, and their brothers, George and Walter, standing by the window.

Then she noticed that another young man had just come in. She had never seen him before. Could he be Robert Carruther's new assistant? Or perhaps he was a friend of George Hayter. He was wearing spectacles, which made him look thoughtful and solemn. His hair was dark and cut short. His cravat was neatly tied and his shirt did not have any frills, unlike that of Robert Carruthers. He wore a dark blue coat over grey breeches. As she looked at him, he turned towards her and saw she was watching him. To her embarrassment, she could feel herself blushing, which she never normally did.

Beside her, Elizabeth Carruthers sighed. 'I wonder if my brother will ever stop talking. He likes the sound of his own voice far too much.'

Charlotte laughed. 'Let us hope he cannot find anything more to say soon. Tell me, Elizabeth, who is the gentleman standing by himself by the door?'

'My dear, he is Robert's new assistant, Mr Henry Everingham. I shall introduce you, as soon as I am able. I do believe my brother is coming to the end of his speech!'

'Now, my friends, I am pleased to tell you that my sister, Mary, and my brother, Walter, have agreed to play fortepiano and fiddle for dancing. We shall then proceed to the dining room where you will find a fine spread for your supper.'

Elizabeth took Charlotte's arm and took her to where Mr Everingham was standing. 'Allow me to introduce you to my very dear friend, Miss Charlotte

Baskett. Her late father was a surgeon in the town before Mr Carruthers set up his practice here.'

'Delighted to meet you, Miss Baskett.'

Before they could say anything else, Robert announced that the first dance would be the Cotillion. Charlotte could see him approaching them and turned away.

'Miss Baskett, may I have the pleasure of this dance with you?'

Henry Everingham looked at Charlotte and smiled. 'Robert, I must apologise. Miss Baskett has just accepted my invitation.'

Elizabeth smiled. 'Perhaps you could ask Eleanor Hayter to dance, Robert. I see Sophia and Francis are already waiting.'

Mary and Walter started to play the introduction and Henry Everingham took Charlotte's hand and led her into the centre of the room. George Hayter and Elizabeth made the fourth couple.

Charlotte started to laugh. 'How did you know I did not want to dance with Robert, Mr Everingham?'

'I could see by your horrified expression. And although he is a good surgeon – and my colleague – I can see he is not the most presentable man in the room!'

As the dance proceeded, it was necessary to change couples and Charlotte found herself opposite Robert Carruthers. When she was once again dancing with Henry Everingham, she could see he could hardly suppress his laughter.

The next dance was a Quadrille, in which she partnered George Hayter, but after that, she could not avoid Robert Carruthers without appearing to be uncivil. But she always found herself watching Henry Everingham and saw he always seemed to be looking at her.

There was a pause after the third dance and Eleanor came and sat down beside her.

'I do believe, my dear Charlotte, that you have made a conquest!'

'I have no idea what you mean, Eleanor.'

'Our friend, Henry Everingham, cannot take his eyes from you. And do not pretend you have not noticed!'

Once again, Charlotte could feel a blush coming to her cheeks. She always considered herself sensible. She could see how domestic life had changed her sister, Jane, and had decided she much preferred her life as it was now. If she had a husband and family, she would not be able to continue to be involved in the school or go visiting with her friends or continue to support the campaign to abolish slavery. But she had to admit to herself that the feeling she was starting to have for Henry Everingham was something she had never experienced before. She had no interest in becoming involved with any of her friends' brothers or any of the other young men in the town and had convinced herself she would never fall in love.

There was more dancing before supper, and Henry Everingham partnered her most of the time. He asked to accompany her to the supper table and they sat together. Charlotte was aware that Eleanor was smiling and nodding to her from the other side of the table. By the end of supper, she had learned that Henry had studied to be a surgeon in Edinburgh and then returned to his home county of Surrey. He had heard that Robert Carruthers required an assistant from her uncle Thomas's friend, Robert Farquharson, who lived in nearby Camberley. He was lodging with her uncle, Thomas, and was anxious to become involved in the affairs of the town.

She had told him how she had written plays for the students at the school to perform. And how she helped her uncle, Thomas, with the musical society. And she told him about her brothers, William and Thomas, and how upset she was when they died. And how William had always taken care of her, especially after their father had died. And how, because of him, she had become interested in the question of slavery. And that she had William's ammonite, his talisman, which had been given to him by their father, in the drawer by her bed, together with his Indian journal.

When it was time to go home, Henry took Charlotte's blue silk scarf from one of the servants and carefully put it around her shoulders.

'It will be quite cold outside, now the sun has set.'

'I believe it is still a fine, starry night.'

All the guests left together. Robert Carruthers stood at the door. 'My dear friends, thank you all for coming to help us celebrate my sisters' birthdays and Sophia's engagement. Now, I insist on lending you a lantern to light your way. The moon is waning and the streets will already be dark.'

Francis White took a lantern and strode out in front. George Hayter turned to Henry Everingham.

'I should be most grateful if you could escort Miss Baskett, my dear fellow. I can then take my sisters straight home.'

Eleanor smiled at Charlotte. 'That is an excellent idea, George. I am quite ready for my bed.'

When they came to the crossroads in the centre of the town, George and his sisters turned to the right, along West Street. Charlotte took Henry's arm and they turned left into East Street.

After the chatter and laughter with their friends, Charlotte suddenly felt shy and could think of nothing to say. They continued along the road in silence. When they arrived at the house, they stood facing each other.

'Miss Baskett, I should like to say how much I have enjoyed this evening. And, in particular, your company.'

'And I too, Mr Everingham. I have to visit my uncle tomorrow, to discuss the next concert for the music society. Perhaps I shall see you there?'

'I shall look forward to it very much. Goodnight, Miss Baskett.'

He took Charlotte's hand, and with a brief bow, turned and walked back along the street.

Jane came out of the drawing room to greet her as she went inside.

'I hope you enjoyed the party, Charlotte. You look happy and somewhat flushed!'

'Sophia Carruthers is engaged to be married to Francis White, a friend of Robert Carruthers. And there was dancing and wine with the supper.'

'And perhaps a young man with whom to dance?'

'I tried to avoid Robert, and I danced with George Hayter. And Robert's new assistant, Henry Everingham.'

'You are blushing, Charlotte. I do believe at last you have found a suitable young man.'

'He comes from Surrey and knows Uncle Thomas's friend, Robert Farquharson. We had a very interesting conversation, Jane.

'I shall be interested to hear more in the morning. It is late and we need to be in our beds.'

Upstairs, Charlotte undressed as quietly as possible so that she would not wake Sarah. As she took off her silk scarf, she remembered how Henry had put it around her shoulders so carefully. Once she was in bed, she lay awake, wondering how it was possible for the world to turn up-side-down so abruptly. She knew her life would never be the same again. All she could think about, as she tried to sleep, was her conversation with Henry Everingham. He probably knew more about her after a few hours than her own sisters did. She felt she had known him all her life. And she remembered how he had taken her hand to dance, how he had smiled at her, how his hair curled slightly at the nape of his neck.

You find yourself feeling delighted that Charlotte appears to be falling in love. You look once again into the chest and at first think it is empty. Then you see, at the very bottom, a small embroidered bag...

Chapter 6
The Silver Locket

Sunday, 12 October 1806 – East Street, Wareham, Dorset

The bag is made of faded blue silk, embroidered with white flowers and green leaves. You loosen the drawer string and inside, you find a simple silver locket on a fine chain. You open the clasp and see inside a lock of dark, curly hair. Down at the bottom of the bag is a plain gold ring, with the initials "H & C" engraved on the inside.

Although the war with France continues on land, the imminent danger of invasion, following Nelson's victory at Trafalgar, has passed. Everyone in the town was shocked when, earlier this month, the passage boat travelling from Poole to Wareham sank in rough weather. The three crew members and thirteen of the passengers drowned. Two of those were cousins of the kitchen maid at East Street, Amelia Randall. Mr Edward Everett, of Wareham, one of only two men on board, was able to swim ashore, dragging Mrs White, of Church Knowle, with him. Seven bodies were recovered and buried three days later.

Life in East Street continues largely as before. Robert and Charles have both left school. Charles will go up to Oxford next week, but Robert has not yet decided what he wants to do. Richard Jones has finished his apprenticeship and is now qualified as an attorney. He continues to work with Thomas Baskett and Thomas Bartlett. Henry Everingham became a frequent visitor to the house after the party for Sophia and Elizabeth Carruthers. He eventually proposed to Charlotte, who had no hesitation in accepting. Henry has decided to set up in practice by himself and he and Charlotte will be moving into a house in West Street, after their wedding tomorrow.

It is a fine, but chilly, Sunday morning and the family have already been to church. You find Charlotte and Sarah in the bedroom they have always shared.

'I will find it very strange, Charlotte, to wake up and find you are no longer beside me.' Charlotte could see there were tears in her sister's eyes.

'You will enjoy having the room all to yourself, Sarah. And we shall see each other very frequently. I shall visit you all nearly every day.'

'And I wish you were not taking Brune with you, Charlotte. He belongs here.'

'You know he has always been my dog. I believe Jane and Richard are planning to get a new puppy for the family soon. You will enjoy looking after him, I'm sure.'

Sarah nodded. 'It will be something to keep me occupied, I suppose.'

'And I am sure the little girls will love him.'

Charlotte had already packed most of her clothes into her trunk and, on top, carefully placed her mother's books – her journal and picture book, her dictionary, the gardening and cookery books and the one about shells. She would leave her mother's looking glass for Sarah. She opened the drawer beside her bed and took out her doll Pippy, the book by Olaudah Equiano, William's journal and his talisman, ready to take them to the new house. For the wedding tomorrow, she had decided to wear the blue and white muslin dress she was wearing when she first met Henry. Mary and little Jane would accompany her, and Anna Maria had made them white dresses with blue sashes.

Charlotte took a deep breath and looked around the room. She would sleep in it for the last time tonight. She felt a mixture of excitement and trepidation. A new chapter in her life was beginning.

'Sarah, can you go downstairs and tell Jamie to bring my trunk down into the hall, please? Henry will be arriving soon to take it to West Street. I need to go to the kitchen to see Betty about the special dinner for tomorrow.'

Sarah picked up her book from her bedside table and went downstairs. Charlotte worried about her sister sometimes. She loved helping in the nursery, but still had very few friends of her own apart from Matilda Barker. Downstairs, in the kitchen, Hester was busy making pastry and Amelia was stirring a pot on the stove. The plum cake for the wedding meal was on the table. Jane was already there, speaking to Betty.

'And when we return from the church, the food should be set out on the table.'

'Yes, madam. Amelia will help me to ice the cake this morning.'

Amelia was keeping her head turned away, still stirring the pot. Charlotte went over to her and saw there were tears in her eyes.

'Mr Everingham tells me your cousin, Nancy, has settled down in our new house and is cooking some splendid meals for him already.'

'Thank you, Miss Charlotte. She have told me she is happy there. It be helping her to get over the drowning of our cousins.'

The door to the garden opened and Jamie stumbled in, carrying some carrots and onions.

'Has Miss Sarah seen you, Jamie?'

'Yes, Miss Charlotte. She have told me to bring your trunk down. I be going to ask Alfie to help.'

Betty took the vegetables from him. 'Wipe your boots, Jamie. And when you have done, we need more potatoes.'

As Jamie shuffled out into the hall, the doorbell rang and Hester went to answer it. Charlotte felt a little shock of pleasure as she heard Henry's voice.

'Thank you, Hester.'

'Miss Charlotte be in the kitchen, sir.'

Charlotte went into the hall to greet him. Henry smiled and took both her hands in his.

'I trust everything is ready for our big day tomorrow, my Mouse?'

Henry had decided to call her his Mouse when she told him about William. Charlotte thought she would never want anyone else to use his affectionate name for her, but was actually delighted.

'Jane seems to have it all under control. I have lost count of how many dishes she and Betty are planning. Yesterday, I heard them speaking of buttered chicken, a fillet of beef, turbot, cheesecakes, apple pie and I forget what else. Then there is the wine.'

'It sounds as if we are feeding the whole town.'

'We have heard that my uncle, Lewis, is well enough to travel, and he and Aunt Ann will be arriving in time for dinner today. He was my father's special friend, so he will be able to tell you about him. I was only nine when he died, so he never spoke to me about his medical practice.'

'I shall be most pleased to meet him at last.'

They watched as Jamie and Alfie came down the stairs, struggling to carry Charlotte's trunk.

'My carriage is outside, Jamie, so the trunk can be put straight into it.'

'Yes, sir. It be very lumpy, sir.'

'I shall be back as soon as I have taken your trunk home. I hope not to be called out again. I have already visited Mary Hodder this morning. Her baby is due next month and she has been in pain. It is not easy for her, as they already have four little boys, who are very lively.'

'Henry, can you tell Nancy to come here in the morning to help Betty in the kitchen. And perhaps the new kitchen maid, Jenny, could come too.'

'Of course, my love.'

Once Henry had left, Charlotte went into the drawing room, where Sarah was sitting quietly, reading her book.

'I was able to get the next volume of *The Mysteries of Udolpho* yesterday at the booksellers, Charlotte. I have been waiting for a week to find out what happens to Emily.'

'I believe Eleanor has been reading it. She tells me she has enjoyed it.'

'Matilda will be reading the volumes after me, so will be able to talk about it when you have left us, Charlotte.'

'Sarah, I want you to promise me that you will not mope around the house. You can come to visit me and I shall always be pleased to see you – and Matilda. And the little ones always enjoy going for walks with you. And you will soon have the new puppy.'

Sarah looked down at her book and said nothing. Charlotte could hear her uncle, Thomas's voice in the hall. When she went out to greet him, she saw that her brother, Robert, had come in with him. They were obviously in the middle of a conversation.

'Charlotte, Robert has been telling me that he has agreed to be apprenticed to the apothecary in Blandford, where your father trained before coming here.'

Robert shook his uncle's hand. 'And my generous uncle has agreed to pay the apprenticeship fee. My dear uncle, I cannot thank you enough.'

'Your grandfather made provision in his will for your education, so it is he, you should thank. He would have been very pleased to know you are making good use of the money. As you know, it has also enabled Charles to study at Oxford. When does the new term start, Charlotte?'

'He will be leaving later this week, after the wedding. Uncle Lewis and Aunt Ann will be here in time for dinner. And Henry's father and two of his sisters are coming from Surrey. They will all be staying the night at the Black Bear. I cannot believe so many people will be here, just for me.'

'It is a special day, my dear, the first wedding in the family since your sister married Richard.'

When Henry returned, it was a relief to take a walk round the garden. Henry pushed his spectacles further up his nose and smiled affectionately at her. Charlotte took his arm.

'I shall enjoy working in the garden of the new house, Henry.'

'Nancy says she knows of a young man who is looking for work as a gardener. He belongs to the Old Meeting House and lives in Stoborough, next door to her parents.'

'I would like to grow our own vegetables and herbs, so I shall need help. My mother designed this garden. I used to help her sometimes. And see, Henry, I planted an acorn ten years ago from the tree my mother planted and it has grown quite tall already. I have asked Uncle Lewis to bring another acorn from her tree for me to plant in our new garden.'

They turned to see Robert walking towards them. 'Jane has sent me to say Uncle Lewis and Aunt Ann have arrived.'

'I can't wait for you to meet them, Henry. They have not been here for several years now, as Uncle Lewis is not in the best of health.'

Charlotte was quite shocked to see how her uncle had aged since she was last at Newton Manor, three years ago, and her aunt was quite stooped. She embraced them both warmly and they went into the drawing room.

'I am so pleased to see you both.'

'My dear Charlotte. Nothing would keep us away. John sends his apologies, but he cannot leave the farm. And you must be Henry. You have made my niece very happy, young man.'

'I have heard so much about you, sir. I am eager to hear more about Charlotte's father. I understand you were at school together.'

'Indeed, we were. Come, sit by me.'

Charlotte looked at them both fondly.

'I shall leave you to talk, while I go to the kitchen and ask Hester to bring in some tea. You must be tired after your journey.'

When she returned, Lewis and Henry were still deep in conversation.

'Charlotte, I have been telling Henry about how your father used the method of inoculation from cowpox, and how he and I went to meet Benjamin Jesty while he was still living in Somerset.'

'I know Dr Jenner published a paper about the inoculations he had been performing using the same method, sir. He called it vaccination. The name is derived from the Latin for cow, of course. I have been vaccinating my own patients with cowpox since I set up by myself. Robert Carruthers was reluctant to use the method. It was one of the reasons I decided to leave his practice.'

'You will be pleased to know that Dr Bell has become a great champion of Mr Jesty. Last year he arranged for Mr Jesty to go to London with his eldest son. They were introduced to members of the Vaccine Pock Institution, and they were so impressed with him that they arranged for his portrait to be painted while he was there. You will be amused to know that Mr Jesty refused to change his attire to suit the London fashion. I believe he is quite a stubborn man.'

When Hester brought in the tea, they were joined by Jane, Anna Maria and Sarah. Charlotte was pleased to see that Sarah seemed more cheerful and was actually smiling as she listened to the chatter around her. Anna Maria, of course, sat in a corner and said nothing. Charlotte suspected she was a little in love with Henry. She kept looking over towards him, then looking away when she saw that Charlotte had noticed. She was thirty-three and Charlotte had lost count of how many young men she had fallen in love with, but had always been disappointed.

When she had finished her tea, her aunt, Ann, rose from her chair.

'My dear Jane, I cannot wait to meet your little ones.'

'Of course, Aunt Ann. Come up to the nursery. They will be delighted to see you.'

Thomas and Lewis went into the study, and Anna Maria and Sarah joined Jane and Ann in the nursery. Charlotte and Henry found themselves alone once more.

'You must feel rather overwhelmed by all my family.'

'No more than I am overwhelmed by my own, my Mouse.'

In the summer, Henry had taken her to Mitcham, in Surrey, to meet his family. She had become confused when he introduced her to his numerous brothers and sisters, and thought she would never be able to remember all their names.

'I cannot remember which of your sisters will be coming to the wedding, Henry?'

'Mary Ann and Caroline. They are both younger than me and I have always been close to them.'

'We have always welcomed people into our own family. I am so looking forward to being welcomed into yours.'

'Which you certainly will be. But most of all, I look forward to starting our life together, my own Mouse.'

The doorbell sounded. When Hester went to answer it, Charlotte could hear a voice she did not recognise. She went out into the hall. A young boy was standing there, his cap in his hand, looking embarrassed.

'Where be Mr Everingham, madam? I were told he were here.'

Henry joined them. 'I am here. What is the matter, Charlie? Charlotte, this is Mrs Hodder's boy.'

'Me pa, he have told me to come, sir. He do say the baby is nearly here, sir.'

'I shall come with you. Charlotte, I shall be back as soon as I can. Mrs Hodder's baby is arriving much too early. Please give my apologies to everyone. I fear you will find out that being late for my dinner will not be unusual!'

'Of course, you must go. And I am looking forward to being involved with your work as much as I can.'

Shortly after Henry had left, his father and sisters arrived and Hester showed them into the drawing room. Charlotte rose to greet her future father-in-law.

'Mr Everingham, I am delighted to see you. You have arrived in good time for dinner. But you have only just missed Henry.'

'My dear, we saw Henry leaving as we arrived, so he has explained why he is not here to greet us.'

'I have already asked our maid, Hester, to bring tea in for you as soon as you arrived. I hope you had a good journey.'

'We stayed at Winchester last night, before travelling here. We have left our coach and horses at The Black Bear.'

Caroline embraced Charlotte. 'My dear, this is such a happy occasion. When Henry visited us shortly after he met you, he told us that he knew he had found his future wife, did he not, Mary Ann?'

'Indeed, he did, Charlotte. And he said that you were not only beautiful, but that you were also very thoughtful and kind.'

Charlotte could think of nothing to say and could feel herself blushing. She was pleased when her own sisters joined them and she was able to introduce them to their visitors. She suddenly felt rather overwhelmed. She sat down and listened to the chatter going on all around her. All she really wanted was to be alone with Henry. More introductions were needed, when her uncles, Thomas and Lewis, and her brothers, Robert and Charles, all came in from the study, and Richard returned home shortly afterwards.

'I must apologise for being late. I had an appointment with George Filliter's daughters. They are selling two of the properties their father left them in his will.'

Jane smiled at him in greeting. 'I met Mary Filliter last week and she told me that her father had advised them to sell their properties and invest the money.'

When Hester came in to say that dinner was ready, Henry had not yet returned. Charlotte knew he would return as soon as he could.

'Henry is attending a difficult birth, Jane. He asked me to give you all his apologies. We should start without him.'

'I have asked Betty to make all the dishes cold today and so they could be prepared in advance. His meal will not spoil.'

Just as they were all seating themselves at the table, Henry returned, looking tired and worried and took his place next to Charlotte and took her hand.

'Mrs Hodder has had a very small baby boy. They have called him Gabriel. I fear he will not live long.'

'I am sorry to hear that, Henry. I know she was happy to be welcoming another little one into her family. I shall visit her next week.'

'My own dear Mouse. That is why I love you. And that is why I have something to give you after dinner.'

'What is it?'

Henry laughed. 'It is a surprise. You will know soon enough.'

Before Charlotte could say anything else, her uncle, Thomas, rose to his feet.

'As Charlotte's uncle, may I welcome you all on this happy occasion. I know my brother, Samuel, would have been delighted to welcome Henry into our family, as would Lewis's sister. I have already given one of my nieces away, when Jane married Richard, and we have now welcomed their two lovely little girls into the nursery. I look forward to seeing you all tomorrow. Now, enjoy your dinner.'

He sat down to a general murmur of approval. Charlotte was relieved that they could at last start eating. It seemed a long time since breakfast. After they had finished and tea was served in the drawing room, no one seemed to notice that Charlotte and Henry did not join them. Henry took Charlotte's hand and led her out into the garden. They sat down on the seat under the oak tree. Henry took a small bag from his pocket.

'I should like you to wear this tomorrow.'

Charlotte pulled open the string of the bag. Inside was a silver locket on a chain.

'It is beautiful, Henry.'

'Open it, my Mouse.'

Curled up inside was a lock of dark hair.

'You will always have something of me next to you when you are wearing it.'

'And I will always wear it, not just tomorrow.'

Henry fastened the chain around Charlotte's neck.

Through an open window, they could hear the sound of laughter and chatter coming from the drawing room. For the time being, they were content to be in their own little bubble. They could see Hester lighting the lamps. Jane was passing round the teacups. Lewis stood up and came to the window and closed it. Ann joined him and they stood looking out over the darkening garden. Eventually, Charlotte stood up.

'It is starting to get cold and since this party is for us, I suppose we should join them. There will be all the time in the world to be just by ourselves.'

She took Henry's arm and they walked up the garden to join their families.

You know the story of the family will continue, but there are no more objects in the chest. You carefully put everything back, fasten the clasp and push it back into the corner of the attic.

Epilogue

I have now found out what happened to the main surviving characters after the end of the novel, from the parish records, wills and censuses.

Samuel's brother, Thomas Baskett, died in 1821 at the age of 79. In his will, written in 1792, he left an annuity for his wife's sister, Jane Weedon, and money to his friends James and Robert Farquharson and to Thomas Bartlett, who were to be his executors. The rest of his estate was divided between his brothers, William and John, and for the support of Samuel's children. In a codicil dated 1808, he appointed Henry Everingham and the widow of James Farquharson as executors.

Mary's brother, Lewis Cockram, died in 1812 and left all his estate to his wife, Ann, and after her death, to his son, John. In 1819, after the death of his mother in 1816, John eventually married, but I could find no record of his having had children. He died in 1830.

Charlotte and Henry had three children, two girls, Mary and Sarah, and a boy, Henry. Charlotte died in 1837 and in the 1841 census, Henry is living with his son, Henry, aged 24, a solicitor, his daughter, Sarah, aged 30 and Charlotte's sister, Sarah Baskett, together with three servants. Henry was mayor of Wareham three times, in 1824, 1831 and 1841. By the 1851 census, Henry was living with his daughter, Sarah, who never married. His son, Henry, had moved to Harlow in Essex and was living with two servants. By 1861, he was married to Georgina, with a son, also called Henry.

Charlotte and Henry's other daughter, Mary, married Stephen Bennett, a brewer and farmer in Wareham and they had three surviving children, a daughter, Charlotte Brinsden, and two sons, Stephen and Henry, both of whom, in the 1861 census, were pupils at Sherborne School, which is why I decided that Samuel and his brothers had also gone to Sherborne. Stephen Bennett also became mayor of Wareham several times.

I can find no records for Jane and Richard Jones, after the birth of their second daughter, in 1803, and no record for Anna Maria, although a Maria Baskett died in early ¹306.

Samuel and Mary's youngest daughter, Sarah, never married and, after living with Henry Everingham and his family, she died in 1850. A death notice in the Sherborne Mercury said, she was "deeply lamented by her family and friends and died after a painful and lingering illness born with Christian resignation". In her will, she divided her estate between members of her family and left her wearing apparel, trinkets and ornaments to Charlotte's daughters, Sarah and Mary.

Samuel and Mary's son, Robert, married Dorothea King Good and had three daughters, Mary Good, Anna Maria and Harriett, and two sons, Charles Henry and Thomas. In Pigot's Directory for Blandford Forum in 1831, he is listed as a chemist, in Market Place. In the 1841 census, he is living in Spettisbury, near Blandford, Dorset, with his wife and his three daughters.

Samuel and Mary's youngest son, Charles, married Harriett Dancy, but they appeared not to have had children. He was Mayor of Wareham in 1836 and 1842.